W9-BMM-966

NORMAL

NORMAL

GRAEME CAMERON

Oak Brook Public Library
600 Oak Brook Road
Oak Brook, IL 60523

MIRA

If you purchased this book without a cover you should be aware
that this book is stolen property. It was reported as "unsold and
destroyed" to the publisher, and neither the author nor the
publisher has received any payment for this "stripped book."

ISBN-13: 978-0-7783-1850-7

Recycling programs
for this product may
not exist in your area.

Normal

Copyright © 2015 by Graeme Cameron

All rights reserved. Except for use in any review, the reproduction or utilization of this work
in whole or in part in any form by any electronic, mechanical or other means, now known or
hereinafter invented, including xerography, photocopying and recording, or in any information
storage or retrieval system, is forbidden without the written permission of the publisher,
MIRA Books, 225 Duncan Mill Road, Don Mills, Ontario M3B 3K9, Canada.

This is a work of fiction. Names, characters, places and incidents are either the product of the
author's imagination or are used fictitiously, and any resemblance to actual persons, living or
dead, business establishments, events or locales is entirely coincidental.

® and TM are trademarks of Harlequin Enterprises Limited or its corporate affiliates.
Trademarks indicated with ® are registered in the United States Patent and Trademark Office,
the Canadian Intellectual Property Office and in other countries.

For questions and comments about the quality of this book, please contact us
at CustomerService@Harlequin.com.

www.MIRABooks.com

Printed in U.S.A.

First printing: April 2015
10 9 8 7 6 5 4 3 2 1

For Oscar, Lewis, Sophie, Eve and Tracie

and

To Jamie Mason, for everything.

NORMAL

CHAPTER
ONE

I'd learned some interesting things about Sarah. She was eighteen years old and had finished school back in July with grade-A passes in biology, chemistry, physics and English. Her certificate stood in a plain silver frame on a corner table in the living room, alongside her acceptance letter from Oxford University. She was expected to attend St John's College in the coming September to commence her degree in experimental psychology. She was currently taking a year out, doing voluntary work for the Dogs Trust.

In her spare time, Sarah enjoyed drawing celebrity caricatures, playing with the Wensum volleyball team and collecting teddy bears. She was also an avid reader of fantasy novels and was currently bookmarking chapter 2, part 8 of Clive Barker's *Weaveworld*. She'd been seeing a boy named Paul, though she considered him a giant wanker. He refused to separate from "almighty slut" Hannah, who was evidently endowed with a well-developed bosom and a high gag threshold. This caused Sarah considerable consternation, but she could not confide in her mother because "she wouldn't understand" and would "just freak out again like last time." She instead turned to her friend Erica, who was a year or two older and thus possessed of worldliness and abundant wisdom. Erica's advice, apparently in line with her general problem-solving ethos, was to "cut off his dick and feed it to him." Sarah didn't talk to her mother about Erica, either.

All four walls of Sarah's bedroom were painted a delicate shade of lilac, through which traces of old, patterned wallpaper were still visible. She had a single bed with a plain white buttoned cotton cover. She also had a habit of leaving clothes and wet towels on the floor. Her stuffed animals commanded every available inch of shelf and dresser space. The collection consisted of plush bears manufactured in the traditional method, and all had tags intact. It was too vast to waste time counting. But there were sixty-seven.

That morning, Sarah had spent just under half an hour in the bath and just over five minutes cleaning her teeth. She had no fillings or cavities, but the enamel on her upper front teeth was wearing thin from overbrushing. She also applied toothpaste to the index and middle finger of her left hand in a vain attempt at stain removal. There were no ashtrays in the house, and her cigarettes and lighter were hidden inside a balled-up pair of tights in the middle drawer of her dresser.

The following day was Sarah's birthday. Many cards had already arrived and stood in a uniform row on the living-room mantelpiece. Someone had tidied in there early in the morning, but there was already an empty mug and a *heat* magazine on the coffee table. Sarah had a habit of leaving the TV on, whether she was watching it or not.

I'd discovered, too, that she plucked her bikini line. Most of her clothes were green. She dreamed of visiting Australia. She had a license but no car. The last DVD she watched was *Buffy The Vampire Slayer*—the feature film, not the more popular television series—and coincidentally, or rather perhaps not, Buffy was also the name of her cat.

Oh, and I knew three more things. I knew that her last hot meal was lasagna, her cause of death was a ruptured aorta and her tongue tasted of sugar and spice.

O   O   O

Fortunately, the kitchen floor was laid with terracotta tiles, and I easily located the cleaning cupboard, which held a mop and bucket, bleach, cloths, a roll of black bin liners and numerous antibacterial sprays. I hadn't planned on doing this here, since I had a thousand and one other things to do and not enough time to do them, so my accidental severing of the artery was inconvenient, to say the least. Happily, I'd reacted quickly to deflect most of the blood and keep it off the walls.

I'd used a fourteen-inch hacksaw to remove the limbs, halving each one for portability. The arms and lower legs fitted easily inside a bin bag with the head and the hair lost in the struggle to escape. Using a separate bag for the buttocks and thighs, I'd placed these parts by the back door, away from the puddle of blood. The torso was unusually heavy despite Sarah's small frame, and required a heavy-duty rubble sack to prevent tearing and seepage. Thoughtfully, I'd brought one with me.

The cleaning operation was relatively easy. My clothes went

into a carrier bag, and I washed my face over the sink. Warm water followed by Dettol spray was adequate for removing the spatter from the cupboard doors and for disinfecting the worktops and the dining table once I'd swiped most of the blood onto the floor. Mopping the floor took three buckets of diluted bleach, which went down the drain in the back-yard. The waste disposal in the sink dealt with stray slivers of flesh; the basin was stainless steel and simply needed a cur-sory wipe afterward.

The only concern was a couple of small nicks in the break-fast table, courtesy of my clumsiness with the carving knife. One or two spots of blood had worked their way into the wood, but these were barely visible and since the table was far from new, it was unlikely they'd be noticed by chance. Altogether, you'd never have known I was there.

In fact, the only thing out of place, once I'd moved the bin bags to the yard and returned each of Mum's implements to its rightful home, was me. Fortunately, Sarah's father was about my size, and I'd already dug out a pair of fawn slacks and an old olive fleece from the back of his wardrobe. The fleece was frayed at the elbows and smelled a little musty, but more importantly it was dry and unstained.

Satisfied, I slipped into my jacket and shoes, stepped out-side and closed the door gently behind me.

In keeping with modern town-planning philosophy, the Abbotts' house was separated from those to either side by the width of the garden path. In a token effort at providing some privacy from the neighbors, each garden had been bordered on both sides with high, oppressive panel fencing, secured at the bottom of the plot to a common brick wall. This wall was a good six inches taller than I was and, mindful of the difficulty in bundling Sarah over unseen, I elected to fetch the van and come back for her.

I took a lengthy run-up and hauled myself over, dropping down onto a carpet of twigs and soft brown leaves. The tree line was a matter of feet from the edge of the plot, at the foot of a steep incline. It was from here that I'd seen the upstairs window mist over and heard the bath running, watched Sarah in silhouette pulling off her clothes, waited until she closed the door and her ears were full of the roar of running water before I let myself in.

It was an altogether different scene now, as I picked my way back between the rows of pines toward the road. All that had made the dawn so perfect was gone—the dusting of snow on the rooftops, the faint crackling of twigs under muntjac hooves, the rustling of leaves disturbed by inquisitive foxes. In their place, the clatter of diesel engines and the grating thrum of cement mixers, the white noise of breakfast radio and the tap-tap-tap of trowel on brick. It had started soon after my arrival and, whilst the development would be blissfully quiet and neighborly once complete, for now the inescapable din of suburban sprawl rendered it a living hell. Although, on the other hand, it had at least allowed me the luxury of not having to tiptoe.

Thinking about it, there was something else missing, too—something I couldn't quite put my finger on. Some weighty comfort I was accustomed to feeling against my leg as I walked, and which just wasn't there anymore.

It wasn't until I reached the van that I realized I'd locked the bastard keys in it.

○ ○ ○

I was loath to break a window, but the Transit was fitted with reinforced double deadlocks, and I specified the optional full-perimeter alarm system when ordering. Consequently, just as anyone else would have trouble breaking in, so did I. Having weighed up this option, considering my various time constraints against that of taking a cab home for the spare key, it didn't take me long to find a brick. I was back in business, albeit at the mercy of the heater.

I'd left Sarah just behind the side gate, and I backed right up onto the two-car driveway to minimize my exposure. I took a moment to double-check the small toilet window at the back of the house; I'd chipped some of the paint away, and there were obvious indentations in the wood, but it was shut, and the glass was intact. Judging by the number of boxes and blankets piled up inside, and the concentration of long-abandoned cobwebs, the damage wouldn't be discovered this side of summer. Good.

I was happy to find that Sarah hadn't leaked out of any of the bags, and it took seconds to load the lighter ones into the van. But as I turned to collect the rubble sack, I happened to glance toward the doorstep, and my heart dropped. The face staring inquisitively back at me was a familiar one; I'd studied it briefly, in a tiny photograph from one of those instant booths you find in malls, fallen from Sarah's diary as I lay on her bed. But it was unmistakable.

Erica's hesitation was such that I could almost hear the whirring of her brain as she stood there, finger poised over the doorbell, eyebrows cocked, mouth agape. I knew all too well where her train of thought was carrying her, and so diverted it with a smile and a friendly wave.

"Hello, there," I called. "Don't panic, I'm not a burglar."

Her expression turned instantly to one of apology. "Oh, no, no, I wasn't thinking that." She laughed, letting a few ringlets fall down to hide her eyes.

"Age Concern," I explained. "Just collecting some old bags." Ha ha. "I mean bags of old clothes. Are you looking for the young lady?"

She was walking toward me now. Dark curls bouncing, woollen scarf swaying to the rhythm of her hips. Breasts struggling to work the top button of her jacket loose with each confident stride. The blood began to race through my veins, the noise of the mechanical diggers and pneumatic drills fading to a low hum. "Yeah, do you know where she is? She's not answering the door." Close enough now that I could hear the rub of the denim between her thighs. I could take this one of two ways, probably avoid a scene by way of swift, decisive action, but as so often happens in the face of outstanding natural beauty, my honesty beat me to the punch.

"Yes," I said. "She's in the garden."

CHAPTER
TWO

My insurance company impressed me. First, they managed to answer the phone without dumping me in a queue and torturing me with a scratchy looped recording of "Greensleeves," or whatever it is they play nowadays. Second, the operator, who spoke with an Indian accent but insisted his name was Bruce Jackson, was sympathetic to the plight of the freezing man and directed me to the local branch of Auto Windscreens, who not only had my window in stock but also fitted it while I waited. They even gave me a cup of tea, although I have to say that's a loose description. Tea should not be served in a plastic cup from a sticky push-button machine, and should *never* contain coffee whitener. But since I wasn't offered an alternative, and it was at least warm, I feigned gratitude and drank it.

————

Repairs completed and schedule abandoned, I stopped off at B&Q for a pack of saw blades and some lye, and somehow also left with a cordless electric sander. Might come in handy. Next I popped into CarpetRight and was able to pick up half a dozen large offcuts, which matched almost perfectly the sample I carry in my glovebox. You can never have too much carpet, believe me.

Hypnotized by the siren call of beef on the breeze, I then drove over to the adjacent McDonald's where a pretty blonde girl with four gold stars but no name provided me with what she claimed was a cheeseburger, but which upon closer inspection revealed itself to be a cheap imitation of one. Eating it was only marginally more fulfilling than getting stuck in the pitifully narrow drive-thru lane. This was a disappointment, since Miss Gold Stars looked as though she had the potential to make *great* burgers.

The snow had returned by the time I was back on the road. It came down in a dense flurry, blanketing the ground in minutes and forming a bright, focus-bothering tunnel as I drove.

The road through the forest was unusually quiet, even accounting for the weather; I was making my own tracks and hadn't passed another vehicle since leaving town. At times like this, unlikely as it seems, it's perfectly possible to feel at one with nature from inside a heated van.

Two miles after the trees moved in to hug the road, I pulled onto the unmade Forestry Commission trail that follows the main railway line. It's used in fair weather by dog walkers and cyclists and is inaccessible to motor vehicles, thanks to a steel pole secured to its trestles by a chain and padlock. Fortunately, I have a key.

I locked the gate behind me and, swallowing my regret at disturbing the virgin snow, guided the van along the rutted track for the half mile that would take me out of sight of the main road.

———

This is what winters were like when I was a child. The snow shin-deep on the ground. Soft, delicate flakes falling around me in their thousands, settling in my hair and gently tickling my face. The air so crisp and still as to dull the cold. Breath rising in front of my eyes, floating up toward a pure, white sky. The soft crunching underfoot with each deliberate step. The blissful, unbreakable silence.

Back then, winters were long and filled with all kinds of mystery. There were the treacherous road trips with my father to far-flung outposts in rented cars. The old stables along the driveway became an arctic shipwreck; discarded junk on high shelves was pirate treasure. And then there was the birch wood beyond the garden, where the ground stayed dry enough to sit and read under a canopy of blankets, and where the shouts and screams from the house could never reach.

Today, though, I had little time to reflect. I'd parked the van where the track meets a swathe of open heathland cut through the forest. From here the ground slopes away toward the railway line, beyond which is a steep drop into a wooded marsh, which lies alongside the river. Where I was standing, the ground falls sharply into a tree-lined crater, about a hundred yards across; at the bottom is a shallow pond fed by a tributary of the river, which winds its way through the marsh and under the railway. Down here the line is supported by a brick tunnel, built when the railway was laid in the 1840s to allow the passage of boats into what was then a working flint pit. Repeatedly pinned and reinforced over the years in a valiant yet inevitably vain struggle against gravity and decay, it shudders and wails with the passing of every train.

Reaching this place requires care even in ideal conditions. In deep snow, carrying a dead weight, it's a pain in the arse. I had to make two trips, leaving the heavy rubble sack beneath the bridge and returning for the smaller bags and shovel. This time of year, unfortunately, calls for something of a compromise. There's plenty of good ground out here, firm enough not to be turned over by the occasional trampling; after all, what's accessible to me is accessible to you, too. However, in these temperatures it's impossible to dig a hole in it. Any ground soft enough to dig in the depths of winter will be all but impassable in the summer, and therefore, almost inevitably remote and overgrown and generally no place to be carrying luggage.

The error giving rise to the term "shallow grave" is a classic one made time and again by panicked first-timers. It's common for them to underestimate the time and effort involved in digging up a forest floor; the net result of this is, generally, a very small hole. In order to adequately cover the body, they are forced to build up a sizeable mound of earth from the surrounding area. Since this looks just like a shallow grave, they will then attempt to disguise it with a layer of bracken and moss. And of course, at the first sign of a stiff breeze, the toes are poking out.

Today, I'd be going five feet deep. This could take all winter.

CHAPTER
THREE

In death, my father finally smiled. He was still warm when I left him the first time, his skin still soft, cheeks flushed. The blood pooled in the sawdust under his neck, tiny woodchips floating, dancing with one another, drawn together into little snowflake patterns that mimicked the ones still melting into my coat.

I knelt over him, searching his eyes for a flicker of life. The first and only time this strong, proud man would look up at me—his last chance to look at me at all—and yet still unable to truly *look* at me.

In those few moments, I saw the full range of his emotions pass across his face. The pain of betrayal. The regret of self-inflicted failure. Perplexity at the fascinations of a small boy. Frustration at the demands for attention. Disappointment, anger and loathing. Fear.

———

After breakfast, I returned and sat beside him, shivering for hours on end, watching the blood congeal and his face wax over. Around midday, the snow on the roof became top-heavy and slid to the ground, startling me. Every now and then a curious vulpine nose snuffled along the gap beneath the door. Otherwise, I had only the silence and the cold for company.

By nightfall he was cool to the touch, his fingers curled into rigid claws, and my hunger got the better of me.

I stumbled back through the garden to the warmth of the house, praying all the way that I'd find my dinner in the oven, my mother there to make sure I ate my vegetables before she tucked me into bed with the promise that tomorrow, everything would be just fine. But I'd seen the look in her eyes when she'd kissed me goodbye that morning, a life and sparkle that I'd never seen there before. Deep down, as I'd watched her grab her bags and sail out of the house, leaving me alone with my porridge, I'd known this exit was different from all the others. This one felt final.

I did the only thing I knew how. I gorged myself on shoo-fly pie and waited for someone to find me. Funny thing is, they never really did.

○ ○ ○

Preheat the oven to 260 degrees centigrade.

Juice six oranges; zest two of the rinds and roughly chop the rest. Take two medium-size fillets from the bird of your choosing and make an incision in each. Insert equal measures of the chopped rind and place the whole ensemble in a baking tray with half an inch of water. Bake in the oven until the skin is golden brown and lightly crisped, then turn it down to 150. It's going to take about an hour.

While that's cooking, take your zest and the freshly squeezed juice and pop them in a pan along with two-thirds of a cup of sugar. Place the mixture over a medium-to-high heat and reduce it until you're left with about a quarter of the volume. Throw in a tablespoon of bitters, and set the pan aside.

Boil two cups of chicken stock in a separate pan, then add the orange mixture and simmer it for ten more minutes.

When the meat is done, drain the fat from the baking tray and place the tray on the stove. Pour a cup of Grand Marnier into the tray and cook off the alcohol. Make sure you've got a wooden spoon to hand as you will need to scrape the bottom of the tray almost continuously. Next, pour a cup of the orange sauce you made earlier into the tray and cook it for a minute or so.

Finally, remove the orange rinds from the steaks and combine the orange sauce with the remaining juices from the baking tray. Serve with a simple accompaniment of new potatoes and runner beans, *et voilà*. *Sarà l'orange*.

I built my garage large enough to comfortably accommodate a full-size van and three cars. An automatic climate-control system maintains a constant temperature of sixty degrees Fahrenheit and minimizes humidity. Twin reinforced canopy doors are operated by remote control, which utilizes a double rolling-code system to ensure maximum peace of mind. I have three transmitters; I keep one on my keychain, and the spares are in a locked box in one of the kitchen cupboards, along with a collection of souvenir door keys amassed over time. The key to the box is on my keychain. Note to self.

The stairs leading down to the basement are accessed via a cupboard, or more specifically the false back thereof, which is lined with lipped shelves containing half-empty paint cans and other objects disinclined to topple when disturbed, and which opens at the flick of a concealed catch into the void between the outer and false inner walls to the rear of the garage. The steps are covered with a heavy-duty nylon cut-pile carpet, mulberry in color with a crisp multipoint stipple-effect pattern, perfect for camouflaging a vast range of dark stains. It's certificated to all European flammability and antistatic standards for office applications, and is Scotchgard-protected to prevent ingraining. There isn't an awful lot you can't drag across a carpet like that.

Twenty-two feet down at the foot of the stairs is a door; galvanized steel featuring twin-cylinder mortise locks with drill-resistant casings and a seventeen-bolt backup. The internal bracings are separated by layers of sound-deadening thermal insulation, and the door is finished with attractive natural beech panels.

Beyond this door is what I described to my builder as a games room. Forty-five feet by thirty and of concrete construction, it's lit by an octet of spotlights, one pair at each corner of the ceiling, and furnished with an integrated antenna loop connected to a cellular repeater for reliable mobile phone reception. The walls are plastered and painted a delicate eggshell-blue. The floor is covered with three-inch-thick rubber matting. The builder, sadly, was confused by my explanation and now resides four feet above the ceiling, under eight feet of earth.

In the center of the room is a twenty-by-twenty security cage, built from ten-gauge steel wire with a two-and-a-half-inch diamond mesh and one-and-a-quarter-inch channel frame. The cage has a five-by-seven door with twin cylinder locks and a reinforced titanium padlock.

Inside the cage is an iron-framed single bed, anchored to the floor with seven-inch bolts. It has a pocket sprung mattress, white cotton sheets and a cozy lambswool blanket. At each corner of the bed, bolted to the floor through the rubber mat, is a steel ring, six inches in diameter. In the far corner of the cage are a toilet and sink with mains plumbing.

And finally, on this day at least, there was one other item in the cage. It was located in the middle of the floor, rolled into a tight ball. It was sensitive to light, to the sound of slamming doors and to the smell of home cooking. Covered in layers of brown wool and dark blue denim, it started as I entered the cage and stared at me silently through wide, hateful eyes. It was tired, disoriented and hungry. And its name was Erica Shaw.

CHAPTER
FOUR

The self-confident bounce was long gone. Erica didn't move as I balanced the dinner tray in one hand and removed the padlock with the other. The sound of the key in the door, however, had her bolt upright and scrabbling backward across the rubber floor until her back thumped hard against the far side of the cage. She pulled her knees to her chin and glared up at me, wide eyes blazing with venom and fear, the tight, glowing curls of her hair now a matted, lifeless mess that covered her face and clung to the tears as they streamed across her cheeks. Silently, she trembled.

"Erica," I said softly. "It's dinnertime." I placed the tray carefully on the edge of the bed. A wooden tray, decorated with piglets and ducklings, with a built-in knee cushion filled with tiny beans. A plastic plate, dishwasher friendly, with a daisy-chain print around the rim. A matching tumbler filled with ice-cold Highland Spring. Still, not sparkling. Plastic knife and fork.

She neither moved nor spoke; just stared, knees shudder-ing, shoulders heaving with each shallow breath.

I joined her on the floor, sat facing her. "Come on, you need to eat something besides cereal. You're looking thin." No response. "It's tasty. Try a bit, see if you like it?" Noth-ing. "Erica, listen to me. I'm not going to let you starve to death here."

I could sense a change in her then, though she gave no vis-ible sign. I felt her desire to answer me back, to demand to know exactly what she *would* be dying of. But she still said nothing.

"Okay." I sighed. "I'll leave you alone. Do your best." I pulled myself back up, turned to leave the cage. "Oh, and the sheets on that bed are brand-new." I swung the door shut, turned the key on both bolts, reached down by my feet for the padlock. "You don't have to keep sleeping on the floor."

And then I took a full serving of orange sauce and green beans square in the face.

"I'm not eating fucking meat, you psycho freak!" Erica screamed, grabbing handfuls of steel mesh as the offending fillet plopped to the floor. The plate rolled the length of the cage and clattered against the toilet. Potatoes bounced in all directions. Sauce ran from my hair. I kicked myself.

"Good shot," I conceded, "but honestly, you're not in a position to pick and choose."

"No, you're right," she spat, gripping the mesh, her knuck-les white, eyes flashing like those of a cornered tiger. "Which reminds me, how long are you going to keep me in this fuck-ing dungeon?"

A reasonable question, and one to which I wished I knew

the answer. The simple fact is that time, tendency and tourism are fickle bedfellows, and one can rarely predict when they might deign to coincide. Probably best not to tell her that, though, so I tried to look halfway confident as I asked, "How long's a piece of string?"

She pushed herself from the door, backed away with a half skip. "Well," she said, smiling, "you're hardly going to keep me here for the next eighty years, and you already said I'm not allowed to starve to death, so either you're holding me to ransom or you're just going to kill me. Either way, I guess you'll want to get it over with fairly soon."

I returned her mocking grin. "Well," I said, "I'm certainly not intending to sell you." Her spark retreated. "And I'm sorry to keep you waiting, but I simply haven't had the opportunity to do anything with you yet. At some point, I'll take you out, and we'll play some games, and if you're lucky, maybe you'll get to go home. But if you're too weak to run, you won't stand a chance, and if you starve, it won't be any fun for either of us."

Silence revisited her forthwith. The defiance, the loathing, even the fear vanished from her eyes, leaving only great dark pools of sorrow.

"So, you'll get what you're given, and it'll be good for you, and you'll eat it, so perhaps you'd like to salvage what you can while I go and find you a mop."

Fucking vegetarians.

○ ○ ○

I didn't really know what I needed, but I figured I'd make a run for the supermarket on the near side of town. February's snow was gone, but the onset of spring had been lazy and as darkness fell, the temperature dropped below freezing, the remains of a misty evening turning the roads to ice.

Had the gritters laid any grit, this would have been an easy five-minute drive. As it was, however, I faced an invigorating struggle against the renegade forces of physics. With friction an early casualty, the van slithered maniacally about the rink, seemingly intent on meeting its fate belly-up in a frozen trench. The rush hour had barely ended, but I didn't pass a single car; no one else was stupid enough to take on the elements out here. I couldn't help thinking that were I to come to grief, spring would arrive before help did. I liked it.

After twenty-three minutes of sheer exhilarating uncertainty, I reached the motorway. Coated with a layer of brine, and bustling with weary souls packed into grubby tin cans, it brought me crashing back down to the dreariness of everyday life. I felt like a tuna.

————————

Quietly wondering whether vegetarians ate tuna, I followed the usual shopping routine. In the magazine section, I browsed gawky uniformed schoolgirls with braces on their teeth. A petite brunette in a pinstriped suit leafed through the local paper, the familiar headline barely raising an eyebrow. Missing Girls Almost Certainly Abducted. The greeting card aisle was brimming with fat-bottomed mothers ignoring their bored, fidgeting offspring in favor of tired punchlines and nauseating sentiment. Women's Clothing: deserted but for the fragile, gray-haired fitting room attendant, fixing the floor with the sorrowful gaze of the undervalued, desperate to believe that there might—nay, *must* be more to life.

In Fruit & Veg I selected a peach. Small, rosy and perfectly rounded, she set my mouth watering the moment she caught my eye. Her burly, bruised companion, however, swiftly killed my appetite. Or rather, his uniform did.

There were no sweet cupcakes to be found in the bakery aisle, just an abundance of greasy doughnuts. In fact, I was struck by how few of those loading up on golden syrup cakes and Danish pastries looked like they could really be trusted with them. Unlike the redhead in the pet-food aisle with the wide hips and the skinny arms, none of these creatures could claim to be big-boned. Considering all implications, I moved on.

Pasta and Sauces: a towering blonde with a hook nose and bandy legs which, under cursory inspection, seemed too thin to support the weight of her body or offer any stability in the face of prevailing winds. She walked in a disjointed manner, which made it difficult to judge between prosthetic and anorexic; either way, I prefer a little meat with my spaghetti.

Things began to look up in the frozen food section: another redhead, younger and narrower this time and more auburn than ginger, in tight jeans that showed off the delicious curve of her slender thighs and rounded hips. I leaned past her to peer into the chiller, barely brushing her ponytail with my cheek. Tea tree and mint and an underlying hint of vanilla. All at once invigorating and relaxing. "Excuse me," I said, gently laying an apologetic hand on her arm as I reached around to grab a tub of coconut Carte D'Or. She glanced at me and offered a polite smile, made no attempt to move away. Not wishing to push my luck, however, I returned the smile and backed off. I lingered over the frozen vegetables, waited for her to close the chiller and pass by before following at a half-aisle distance, carefully matching my pace to hers.

She was pushing a trolley-for-one, but this was clearly a weekly shop; meal-wise she had the makings of seven single servings and was now selecting an eight-pot pack of *fromage frais*. She clearly let her hair down one night a week.

She'd already covered most of the store: baked beans, tuna, sweetcorn, tinned cat food, Fairy Liquid, pasta and rice and couscous and a couple of cook-in sauces. The items seemed largely to follow a pattern. Perhaps these were things vegetarians ate.

Her allure all but overshadowed by the sudden wisdom she'd bestowed upon me, and knowing now what needed to be done, I released the redhead from the clutches of my intent and set off on a vital quest to reclaim the moral high ground and secure my reputation as an impeccable host.

I made it as far as the fish counter.

———————

It's a rare and fortunate man who can pinpoint precisely the moment his life began to unravel. Most can only guess, grasping at distant memories of wealth and security and happiness and wondering just where the hell it all went while they scrape their attempts at independence off the bottom of the oven. Yesterday it was a detached cottage with creeping ivy, a pretty and talented wife who was never too tired and kids who tidied their rooms and kept their elbows off the table. A retriever. A study. A Volvo. Today, a rented one-bed cesspit with grease stains on the ceiling. A portable TV. A Metro. Fleas. The decline, though outwardly long and tortuous, passes in the blink of an eye.

For these people there is no time stamp; their fall from grace occurred over months and years, but still they search the depths of their souls for a date and time in the vain belief that a single moment revisited might serve to reverse their fortunes. Often, they search for the rest of their lives.

I, on the other hand, am one of the lucky ones. I know exactly when it all started to go wrong for me. It was April 5 at 19:23:17, and it started with a pair of eyes.

———————

Most of the eyes I see stare right through me. Some linger on the pavement, desperate to avoid meeting other eyes. Others gaze into the middle distance, vacant and expressionless, betraying a desire to be somewhere, anywhere other than here and now. Some eyes flicker and glaze over and roll back and just stare at nothing at all. But most eyes stare through me as if I'm simply not here.

These eyes, though, these eyes were different. They met my own, bored through them, stared right *into* me. They carried a charge of some intangible recognition, a magnetic déjà vu trailing its spidery fingers down my spine, throwing sparks of invitation and longing tinged with fear and denial, rendering me at once both intoxicated and drained. My train of thought derailed; my empty head floated free of my shoulders, legs threatening to buckle under the weight of my directionless body. I don't know how long this electrifying gaze held my own, nor how these eyes came to be mere inches from mine, but sometime later, they blinked and released me from their spell.

My head snapped back into sharp focus. The rancid stench of cockles and mussels headed straight for the back of my throat, giving me the insufferable task of appearing not to gag. Arched eyebrows and a flickering smile told me I'd failed and, for the first time since childhood, I felt the onset of a blush. Frankly, I didn't know where to look—but I settled on her chest, where I found comfort and understanding in four neatly printed words.

Her name, apparently, was Caroline. And she was Here To Help.

CHAPTER
FIVE

At night, through a motorway spray, it's impossible to see the faces of those who pass by in the next lane. Scores, hundreds even, of nameless, faceless drones, nothing more than hazards to be avoided, reminders to check your stopping distance. Even when unfettered and unobscured, in the supermarket or in a busy shopping street on a weekday afternoon, they serve only to delay your progress, bumbling around in front of you when they should surely all be at work. In short, strangers seem altogether less than human. They're just something that gets in the way.

Anyone who's stood on a crowded corner wondering where so many people are in such a hurry to go has, then, unwittingly uncovered the perplexing irony of human existence. As you stand in idle surveyance, taking a break from the million and one stresses coursing continuously through your mind, it occurs to you that the withered old lady holding up that increasingly irate bus queue has a life not far removed from your own. She has a family who don't call her often enough, a home she can't afford to maintain, a pet she feeds before feeding herself. She has a birth certificate and a shoe size. She sees the same sky, the same pavement, the same faceless drones that you see. If you tickle her, she'll laugh. Sometimes she's happy; sometimes she's sad. Mostly, she's resigned. She has thoughts and feelings, hopes and fears. Eighty-eight years of vivid memories.

Her name is Ivy, and she's been a widow for almost a decade. Right now she has somewhere to go. You don't know where that is; only she does. Later, when Ivy gets home, she's going to feed her cat a tin of store-brand chunks-in-jelly before she unpacks the shopping. The cat, a long-haired tabby named Foggy, will then watch her collapse to the kitchen floor with a breathless gasp, clawing at the center of her chest. In exactly a week, Gemma, Ivy's granddaughter, makes a rare and unannounced visit to show off her ultrasound photos. There's no answer at the door; the lights are on, the curtains closed, and the cat screeching to be let out. Through the frosted glass she can make out an untidy pile of letters and bills on the doormat. Naturally concerned, she fetches a spare key from the car and lets herself in. The cat bolts.

For eighty-eight years, the world revolved around Ivy. That which she could see and touch was real to her, everything else a mere figment. Departing visitors, setting off back to their own lives, were swiftly dispatched from her conscious thoughts, taking with them all tangible evidence of their existence. She would lock her doors to the outside world and settle down with a cup of tea, but for Foggy entirely alone in her world. And yet conversely, whilst the conversation in that departing car might revolve around Ivy for a handful of miles, the reality of *her* existence would soon be forgotten in favor of the more immediate stresses and strains pervading the lives of Peter and Janet. Out of sight, out of mind.

Every human being occupies a space at the dead center of his or her own universe. When Ivy's universe imploded, when she made the transition from leading lady to cat food, the myriad separate worlds occupied by her family and friends were fleetingly altered. Gemma's world was naturally rocked the most; the sight that greeted her that morning changed her flippant outlook on life permanently. At Ivy's funeral, thirty-two universes were briefly united in mourning, both for Ivy and for Gemma's unborn baby.

Right now universes are being created, thrown together and destroyed the world over. Seven billion souls, each preoccupied with their own unique reality, each with a head full of memories, plans, learned knowledge and accumulated trivia; birthdays, telephone numbers, bus routes, passwords. Each one with somewhere to go, something they need to get done. They all have birth certificates and shoe sizes. Every single one has a story.

––––––––––

I wondered what this girl's story was—not Caroline, though her face was still beaconing through my brain like the terrain warning on a stricken aircraft, but rather the one sitting alone at the bar, fidgeting with her mobile phone and trying to buy a drink. She was hard to read from this angle, being, as she was, so remarkably unremarkable. Average height. Average face. Average bust. Mousy, nondescript hair of average length. Ten-a-penny jeans and a plain black shirt. Even the barman didn't notice her.

I sat in the corner with a glass of house red and a week-old *Telegraph*, ostensibly ogling the revealingly attired blonde at the next table. The center of almost universal male attention in the bar, her smirk cruised from admirer to admirer as she feigned interest in her companions' conversation. Having no desire to distinguish myself, I allowed her to see me looking.

By eleven-thirty, Annie Average was one of a mere handful of stragglers left clinging to the bar, stubbornly ignoring all requests to drink up and leave. Seemingly tired of continuously checking her inbox, she had taken to scrutinizing the small print on the back of a train ticket she'd pulled from her purse. Neither her expression nor her posture had altered throughout the evening, save for a gentle swaying that started around ten. Finally, she stood and wrapped herself in the ankle-length black woolen coat she'd been warming all night with her average-size bottom. I drained the last few dregs from my wineglass; I'd dispatched a whole bottle of the wretched stuff, though most of it went in among the shrubbery on the windowsill, conveniently located just beside my left knee. As such, I affected a vacant gaze and a John Wayne swagger as I headed for the door.

Stood up and fed up, Annie did exactly as I'd expected and headed for the railway station. She set a moderate pace, allowing me to match my footsteps to her smaller strides without tripping over my own feet. We joined the flow of drunken teenagers migrating to the clubs across the river, a steady bustle despite the bitter cold. Once over the bridge, we would meet head-on the tide of out-of-towners pouring into clubland from the railway station. And since this dimly lit center of jostling confusion headed down the side street in which I'd parked the van, I was anticipating a swift conclusion to an easy hunt. At least until her phone rang.

———

Her "hello" carried a tone of mock disapproval that belied her grave demeanor, and she met the offered excuses with expressions of humor and sympathy. She clearly wasn't one for confrontation. I hung back as she slowed to an idle stroll on the bridge, running her free hand along the icy railings and cracking frozen puddles with the toe of her boot. An occasional husky laugh drifted back to me above the passing stream of profane taunts and leering catcalls. Her lovelorn dawdling pleased me somewhat, since I was both optimistic that her improved mood would make my job easier and anxious that she should be finished on the phone when it did so.

In the event it didn't matter. Lost in flirtation, Annie found the stone stairs leading to the towpath beside the river. One dreamy step at a time, she giggled her way down into the darkness beneath the bridge. I watched her from above as she paced in a circle, distractedly kicking small stones into the water, head tilted over to hold the phone in the crook of her neck, hands thrust snugly in her pockets. At length, I watched her drift ever farther from the bridge. And when she was all but out of sight, I followed.

In the shadows beside the water, the air was heavy and still. The towpath is bordered by a high stone wall, at the top of which is the busy station approach. Most of the traffic noise wafts overhead, making the path a relative sea of calm. The bridges along this stretch of the river are too low for a sail mast but passable by small pleasure cruisers which, at night, occupy every available inch of mooring space. The sounds here are of water lapping against fiberglass, fiberglass rubbing against wood. The only light is that which drifts across from the carvery on the far bank, or down from the streetlights on the road above.

The path was deserted but for Annie and me; the lights of the restaurant faded behind us, the riverbank widened and the horse-chestnuts thickened, and all was impeccably dark and serene. Beyond the far shore, the cathedral spire rose proudly above a blackened tree line, a glowing beacon of humanity against a soulless gray-orange sky.

Annie finally stopped wandering to rest against a life-buoy station; the orange float was long gone, an easy and attractive target for small-minded vandals. I melted into the trees, listening silently to a conversation winding down: can't-waits and won't-be-longs, okay-I-promises and hold-that-thoughts. I wondered what Caroline was doing just then. I heard Annie say her goodbyes, waited while she wallowed in the misty-eyed afterglow. I watched her dawning realization of having strayed farther than she'd intended; she spun around and around, taking in the darkness, the silence, her solitude. Her unremarkable eyes flashed disorientation and frustration, and weariness at the prospect of the long walk back.

And then, movement. In the shrubbery not twenty feet away, a dark form, hunched, creeping. Annie sensed it, too; she snapped her head around, peering into the blackness behind her. The dark shape turned statue. I could all but smell the adrenaline coursing through it as it crouched, barely breathing until, after what surely felt like hours, Annie released a long breath of her own and turned back to the path. I remained rigid, upright; I let her pass me, glancing nervously behind her as the figure moved almost silently through the brush. It was among the trees now, virtually on top of me as Annie quickened her pace, and then in a blink it was out on the path and running.

She certainly heard it then. She turned, eyes wide, to face it as it bore down on her, let out a half gasp as it knocked her off her feet. Before I could react, she was in the undergrowth, cursing and spitting, coat ripped open. Her assailant hunched over her, alternately swatting away her flailing limbs and working on her belt.

Incensed, I broke free of my incredulous trance and the cover of the trees and, snatching up a fallen branch from the ground, stepped into the open mere feet from the struggle. A clearing of my throat was enough to gain the predator's attention. He looked up at me sharply and froze, mouth agape, eyebrows hitched up almost to his hairline. A kid, no more than twenty-one, dressed from head to toe in black synthetic fibers, his blazing orange eyebrows a fair giveaway as to the identifying feature hidden beneath his beanie hat. Annie had stopped struggling and stared up at me, her eyes undecided between panic and relief. The kid, small but solidly built, had straddled her, pinning her wrists to the frozen earth with his spidery hands, her ankles with his own. Eyes fixed on the hefty limb I held before me, he didn't move a muscle.

"Leave," I said. "Now."

The kid, to his credit, didn't need telling twice; he was off, vanishing into the darkness from whence he came minus his wallet and one of his shoes.

"You okay?"

"Oh, my God." Annie lay there, coat spread, shirt hitched up, belt unbuckled. "How stupid am I?"

"Not your fault," I lied, tossing the branch back among the trees. "Are you hurt?"

She shook her head, reached up to take my outstretched hand. "No, I'm a mess, though." I helped her to her feet, and she straightened out her clothes, fastened her belt, shook out her hair. "I don't even know what I'm doing here," she mused. "Christ, if you hadn't come along—"

"Yeah, I did, though, so don't think about it." I gave her space to gather the few contents of her bag from where they'd exploded across the path. "Do you want me to take you to the police?" I offered. "I'm just parked up at the train station."

"God, I don't know whether I can go through all that tonight." She slung her bag over her shoulder, gave her pockets one last check. "I do need to find a train, though, so if you're walking that way…" She finally looked up at me, puppy eyes at the ready. She seemed remarkably untraumatized.

"You're sure you're okay?"

"I'm sure," she said. "I just want to get home."

I conceded. She turned off her phone and dropped it into her bag, and I spitefully kicked the kid's shoe into the river as we set off briskly back toward the lights and the noise. "So," I asked her, "what's your name?"

"Annie," she said.

What were the odds on that?

CHAPTER
SIX

Annie made a hell of a mess.

I'd convinced her that the last train had probably gone and that even if it hadn't, I was going her way and could get her home sooner and in greater comfort. On the basis that I'd saved her from an unpleasant mauling and was therefore to be trusted, she happily accepted a ride.

To be quite honest, when she invited me in for tea, I fully intended to just drink it and leave. In spite of my earlier intentions, I found Annie's company pleasant and her conversation lively and interesting—sufficiently so to distract me from looking out for deserted lanes and vacant lots along the route. I also felt an unexpected pang of protectiveness, and by the time we reached the coast, my only urge was to see her home safely.

However, one cup of tea became several, and Annie matched every one I drank with a tumbler of vodka. As we talked, it quickly became apparent that this was no one-off, that the dismissive actions of the man in her life drove her most nights into the arms of a bottle.

His name was Jeremy and by two in the morning, when I finally removed the last of the stains from the carpet, I'd grown to dislike him intensely. He seemed to me grossly egotistical and of low moral standing.

"He wouldn't tell me where he lived," Annie recounted as she filled her glass for the third time, halfway with vodka and topped with a splash of cranberry juice. "Said he had nosy neighbors and they were friendly with his ex-wife, and that she'd make life difficult for him if she knew he was seeing anyone. I know, I didn't buy it, either. So I followed him one night." She took a long gulp of her drink, one that took her three attempts to swallow. "I did that thing, you know, 'follow that taxi!,' and I followed him right to his front door. I was expecting to see… Well, I don't know *what* I was expecting to see, but it was just this crappy little two-up-two-down, nothing like as posh as he said it was."

Contrary to the impression her flowery telephone manner had given me, she wasn't painting an endearing picture of Jeremy. She told me that he'd lied about his home, his job, his background. Christ, she wasn't even sure Jeremy was his real name. "He stands me up all the bloody time," she continued. "Usually when I complain, he tells me he was stuck in the office finishing a report or his Jag wouldn't start, which is bullshit because he hasn't even got a car—he gets buses everywhere because they're free because he's a bloody bus driver, not a *regional transport coordinator*, which is what he said he was. And the stupid thing is, I've never let on that I know that because *I* don't want to look like a psycho. Why, I don't know. It's only been six weeks, and half the time I actually resent the fact that I even bother." Gulp. "But hey, it keeps me on my toes, right? And to be honest, when he's not being a lying toerag, he's quite a nice guy. And I'm grateful for the distraction—I mean come on, my life is just so...so..."

"Average?" I suggested.

She nodded and emptied her glass. "That's right," she said. "Annie fucking Average."

As much as I admired the simplicity of her explanation, she was clearly deluding herself. We both knew that she put up with it because she was drunk.

———

By 1:47, it was all over for Annie. She'd pulled a spicy beef pizza from the oven and promptly dropped it facedown on her cream sofa. Recoiling in horror, she'd then knocked the open cranberry juice carton from the coffee table.

Overcome with exasperation, she rushed to the kitchen sink and, without first removing the dirty dishes, liberally threw up.

So it was, then, that I came quite literally to undress Annie and tuck her into bed. She was asleep before she hit the pillow.

———

I liked Annie a lot for some reason, and so on my way back through the city, acting on information copied from her address book, I stopped by to pay the weasel Jeremy a visit. She was right; the house was crappy—paint peeling from the doors and window frames, guttering cracked and loose, garden overrun with weeds and nettles.

Getting in was easy; the kitchen extension at the back had

a flat roof, above which a boxroom window had been left open—presumably on the assumption that the fresh air would combat the condensation running down the walls. Helpfully, I closed it.

Jeremy's bedroom was at the front of the house. The thin curtains were no match for the streetlight right outside the window, which made the ceiling and the flock wallpaper glow fluorescent orange. The dresser, a mahogany-look junk-shop special, was strewn with hair gels and torn envelopes and half-empty coffee cups, some of which showed signs of life. In the opposite corner, the matching wardrobe sagged under the weight of bulging black sacks and sports bags, piled so high that the shirts didn't hang straight and the doors wouldn't close.

The bed, on the other hand, looked new. A full six feet wide, with an antique-brass-effect frame in an overdone neo-Gothic style. The bedspread was patterned counter-contextually with meaningless stylized Chinese characters and, I was less than surprised to note, concealed two distinct forms in repose.

I chose to let Jeremy sleep, not out of consideration but simply because I hadn't thought to ask what he looked like. This would not normally have been an issue, since the majority of couples are distinguishable by clear, simple and universal gender-specific identifiers. Put simply, the clue is in the cock. This couple, however, quite obviously had two.

———————

Judging by the collection of photographs on the mantelpiece downstairs, Jeremy's predilection was clearly not a recent discovery. The hairstyles on display dated right back to a New Romantic flick and were unerring in their attachment to one hirsute, muscular torso or another. This was a man who knew his own mind.

In the void beneath the stairs, opposite the mantelpiece and the tasteless log-effect gas fire it so shamefully highlighted, was a computer. The desk it sat on was strewn with scraps of paper carrying scribbled tidbits of personal information: email addresses, first names, hometowns, occupations, pets and vital statistics. Aliases like "Hunnybunny" and "Lucy-luvsit." Some had telephone numbers. A handful noted dates and times, names of pubs and restaurants. One, sadly, said "Burger King."

Tacked to the small triangle of wall above the desk were a dozen photographs printed on copy paper. A dozen women sat at a dozen corner tables, alone, staring into their drinks and fingering their mobile phones.

I was glad I'd taken the time to stop by. That Jeremy should devote his leisure time to stalking straight girls seemed like a new twist on something I'd encountered a hundred times before and couldn't be bothered to try to understand. In any case, his motivation was none of my business, but that he might have a photographic record of the recent movements of every desperate, lonely woman in the county most certainly was. God alone knew how many of them I might be in.

Affirmative, proportionate action was therefore the order of the night, and so by the time Jeremy awoke in the morning, his hard drive and memory cards were blank, his printer was out of ink and the only photograph above his desk was of himself, naked and asleep, with a pair of pinking shears artfully arranged about his under-endowment.

O   O   O

To those of us startled into forgetting what we went shopping for, and perhaps hoping, subliminally or otherwise, for a second attempt at a first impression, the 24-hour supermarket must surely rank alongside tea bags and ambiguous social-network privacy tools as one of modern mankind's most useful inventions.

In the early hours there are no screaming children to contend with, no half-hour queues at the checkout. There are hundreds of empty parking spaces, and you can always find a trolley.

For the most part, the only activity you're likely to encounter is the gaggle of fellow insomniacs charged with the unenviable task of restocking the shelves. These people are paid a reasonable wage and are therefore usually polite and unobstructive. They've always got what you're looking for, and it's always fresh.

Unfortunately, however, the fish counter was closed, and the acute sense of disappointment this brought about came as something of a shock. I was distracted and listless as I pushed my express trolley from aisle to aisle, supplementing my earlier haul of melted coconut ice cream and two defrosted salmon by randomly tipping in anything and everything purporting to be free of meat. Carrots, olives and limes. Carnaroli rice and a can of lima beans. All sense of direction and purpose again fled to the outer reaches of my mind, beaten away by the horde of metal roll cages obstructing every aisle. A blanket of frustration fell over me then, obscuring my vision and blocking my ears. The back of my neck bristled with the distinct sense that I was being watched, and I felt an overwhelming desire to be somewhere else.

I left the trolley and wandered to the entertainment aisle, where bored husbands congregate to inspect cheap laptops and watch football. It was blissfully empty, quiet but for the bank of televisions, each one tuned to a different channel, muttering to me as I passed:...*according to Inca lore, once rail operators pledge to iron lace while damp, a real icon like Elvis Presley is likely to command the council to loan Eric an electric wheelchair. Detective Chief Inspector Lowry made the following statement. "Whilst we will never give up hope of finding Sarah and Erica alive, we have to face the reality that with every passing week, our chances of doing so continue to fade. I am, therefore, again appealing to anyone in the local community who thinks they may have any information, no matter how trivial you might think it is, to pick up the phone and call us, either directly to my team here in the incident room, or anonymously via Crimestoppers. Somebody out there knows something, and only with your help can we hope to bring Sarah and Erica home, or to track down the person or persons responsible for their disappearance."*

This wasn't any better.

———

At night, the checkouts are deserted. In the absence of queueing customers, there is no sense in paying the staff to chew gum and stare into space. I was alone as I loaded the conveyor; the echo of cage doors, dropped boxes and idle chatter was disembodied and distant. I nudged the trolley to the end of the belt, folded my arms and turned around to rest against the counter, idly reading the covers of the leaflets on the stand opposite. Car insurance. Home insurance. Pet, travel and life insurance. Broadband internet and pay-as-you-go mobile phones. Banking and credit cards. I thought back to a time when supermarkets simply sold groceries; when a loaf of bread was a loaf of bread, and beans really did mean Heinz. A time when, on a Friday afternoon, I'd obediently follow my mother through a fluorescent maze of checkered tiles and bright white freezers in the hope of being rewarded with a Crunchie bar and a—

"Hi. Are you all right with your packing?"

There was something in the voice, something so barely there that the question of what it was kept me from turning even after the effect had passed.

"Hey!" Masked now by a broad smile, a teasing melody: "Hello! Wake up! I'm over here!"

I could feel those eyes playing on the back of my neck and spiking my hair before I turned clumsily to face them.

Blue and green and aquamarine, like pools of sunlit gasoline. The kind of eyes that make men like me walk into doors and spill our tea.

The base of my spine wound itself into a twitching, tingling knot. "Hello," I croaked. "Yes, thank you, I'm well versed in the art of packing my bags."

Caroline pursed her lips, narrowed her startling eyes at me. Studied me for a split second with the intensity of a prowling panther before her face softened to a bemused smile. "Nope," she said. "I don't think I'm going to ask."

"Sorry, long night. Very tired." Dry, oilless fingers were making hard work of separating the slippery plastic bags. I could feel the frustration welling again inside me as I grasped and fumbled vainly at the neck of each in turn.

"I know, me, too." She gathered up the fine cascade of dirty-blond hair from her shoulders and threw it into a careless ponytail, held in place with a simple black band from around her wrist. As she did so, her name badge rode up under her chin. "Rachel," it said. "Here to help." She caught me looking, and a fragment of a smile told me she knew I'd been reading "Caroline" in taillights all night.

I hoped, then, as she set about swiping my pitiful collection of rabbit food through the scanner, that she'd blindly pass each item in front of her without pausing to read the labels; that she had no interest in judging me by my shopping list. Sadly, though, I had her full attention. "Tell you what," she remarked. "It's a nice change to meet a herbivore who hasn't got that pale, scrawny thing going on."

I smiled, absurdly willing myself to believe it a greater compliment than it really was. Maddeningly, the food was coming thick and fast and I still had nothing to put it in. "Actually, I think I do need some help here."

"Here…" She slid gracefully from her chair and reached over the counter, her plain white blouse tightening across a modest bust, sleeves riding up to reveal the faint specter of symmetrical scars adorning the underside of each wrist. Her approach to the separation and opening of carrier bags was swift and effective, though I unfortunately failed to note her precise method before she melted back into her seat, distracted as I was by the lithe twist of her hips.

"You can't learn by watching," she said, presumably just to let me know that she could read my fucking mind, though which part of it I wasn't quite sure. "You're not a conscientious objector, are you?" she noted, eyebrows raised behind an up-held fillet of cod. "Clearly, you can't get enough white meat."

"No," I agreed. "I lapse just about every other day."

"Ah, well, we all need at least one vice. Nobody's perfect."

My eyes fell to the loose, flowing cuffs of her blouse as she passed tuna steaks and potato bakes from hand to hand. "I don't know," I replied. "Maybe the perfection is in the flaws."

Her hands trembled then, barely perceptibly and for the merest sliver of a moment as she overrode the impulse to tug at her sleeves. She reddened half a shade, and her eyes drilled into mine, luring them away from the door to her self-consciousness. "Meaning?" she pressed, with a challenging smile.

"Well," I said, "look at it this way. Some collectors are only interested in things that are like new, factory fresh, mint in the box. If something looks like it's had a life before they got their hands on it, it loses its value. But then, other people believe that an object's worth more if it's been used for whatever it was designed for, so a stamp should have been stuck to an envelope and posted to somewhere a long way away, and a comic book is meant to be read and enjoyed, not sealed in a protective case and never opened, and an old racing car should be scuffed and grimy and—" with no particular emphasis "—scarred. And it's the same with people. How much time do you think you'd want to spend with Barbie and Ken? Anodyne, by definition, is not entertaining."

She gave a tight nod and handed me my plums. "So," she said, slapping her totalizer and twisting the display for me to survey the damage, "what exactly is it that *you* collect? I mean, apart from frozen fish."

I shan't repeat what I said. Suffice it to say the ensuing silence was awkward enough that I might as well have just told her the truth.

———————

It was on the dot of 6:00 a.m. that I wearily slammed the door of the Transit, remote-locked the garage and hauled my half-dozen bags of flora and fish into the house. The melodic, almost hypnotic sound of Caroline/Rachel's voice still rang in my ears, our conversation looping over and over in my head. I knew nothing of her, and yet somehow I knew everything I needed to know. I knew the conversation wasn't over.

An unprecedented calm enveloped me as I made space in the pantry freezer, between the joints of topside beef and the waitress from the Hungry Horse.

CHAPTER
SEVEN

I cooked a late breakfast of smoked salmon and scrambled eggs, picturing Caroline-or-possibly-Rachel passing me each ingredient and implement as I needed it. I presented the result to Erica with a steaming cup of fresh coffee. She threw it at me.

Having chained her to the floor and cleaned up the mess, I brought her a sealed box of Rice Krispies and an unopened carton of milk. She threw those at me, too. Since no contents were spilled, however, I chose to leave them where they fell. I laid a plastic bowl and spoon beside them on the mat and left her to it.

I gave her an hour to sort herself out, then returned to the garage to fetch the hooker from the van. Naturally, she'd remained where I'd left her, slung hammock-like from the roof; secured with four-inch nylon webbing and suspended, spreadeagled, five feet from the floor, there was little chance of her wriggling free. What did surprise me, though, was that she'd managed to fall asleep. She didn't even stir as I blindfolded her, and it wasn't until I'd released her extremities and stood her upright that she began to flail and scratch like a cat in a bath. Needless to say, she no longer wanted to go anywhere quiet with me, and I literally had to throw her down the stairs.

———

Erica regarded her new cellmate with a mixture of elation and disdain. Whilst a problem shared is a problem halved, she clearly wasn't overjoyed at the prospect of sharing hers with a bleeding, screeching harridan.

The hooker had told me that her name was Kerry. Then again, she'd told me that she was clean in every respect, where both her profession and her trackmarks suggested otherwise.

I'd picked her up a mile from Jeremy's house on a foolish and immediately regrettable impulse fueled by raw adrenaline and the sheer bloody-minded need to catch something, so to speak. She'd directed me to a remote riverside picnic area on the south side of the city, and had been only too eager to jump into the back of the van, the false promise of mattresses and pillows offering a welcome relief from the repeated prod of a gear lever in the sternum.

Until that point, this, in a nutshell, was the reason I never interfere with ladies of the night: it's just too damn easy. It's a game for impotents and bed-wetters. These women queue up to get in the car with you, for Christ's sake. They actually *expect* you to take them somewhere dark. That they exercise free will in putting themselves in harm's way only makes obligingly slaughtering them all the more cowardly.

And as if that wasn't reason enough to rue my lack of self-control, Kerry was about to give me a couple more to think about.

———————

In her first few minutes in the cage, Kerry, despite the removal of her blindfold, seemed unaware of Erica's presence. She flung herself at the door, screaming unintelligibly as she clawed at the mesh. As she ran simultaneously out of breath and fingernails, she began wailing that her children were home alone and that the electricity meter was empty. I suggested that had Kerry considered her parental responsibilities the night before, rather than offering to fellate me in a car park, their collective predicament might have been avoided.

Erica, on the other hand, was strangely subdued. She sat cross-legged on the bed watching this leather-skirted animal, knees skinned and blood dripping from its fingertips, howling and spitting at its captor just inches away on the other side of the door. "You bastard," she said, simply.

Kerry whirled around then, threw herself off balance. She scrabbled on all fours to the corner of the cage and curled herself into a tight ball, fixing Erica with a petrified stare.

"What are you, starting a fucking zoo?" Erica's face was a picture of self-righteous indignation as she jabbed an angry thumb toward the sobbing, fetal prostitute. "You can't be fucking serious, surely?"

Not fully understanding the question, I chose not to answer.

At 6:00 p.m. I returned to the basement with two plates of tuna and pasta bake. The hooker appeared not to have moved from her corner; she merely continued to tremble and heave.

Erica had returned to the bed, where she lay silently gazing at the cage roof as I laid her dinner on the floor beside her.

"I'm not eating that," she said.

This did not surprise me. "What's the matter now, you don't eat fish?"

"Of course I eat fish. I'm just not eating anything you've made."

"Great, so now it's no meat and nothing cooked, is that it?"

"Who said anything about meat?"

"You did, yesterday."

"No." She sighed. "What I meant was, I'm not eating any meat *you've* given me. And, yeah, I do prefer my dinner cooked. I just don't want it cooked by you. I know your sort."

Charming, debonair, handsome? Probably not what she meant. "Have you got any idea of the effort I went to last night to make sure you were catered for? And now what, you want me to hire you a chef? What do you think this is, the Savoy?"

"You could always just let me starve," she said. "And yes, I can clearly see the kind of effort you went to last night, and I'm far from fucking impressed." Her eyes never left the ceiling.

Erica hadn't thrown her pasta bake at me, but by the following morning she hadn't eaten it, either. To all appearances, she hadn't moved from the bed.

Kerry was a different picture. She'd managed to piss herself three feet from the toilet, and had clearly stood in the resultant puddle. She was still pacing back and forth, leaving dirty wet footprints, when I got there. It took the threat of severed fingers to persuade her to mop.

In the evening, with Erica having eaten nothing more substantial than Rice Krispies since her arrival, I took the microwave oven from my kitchen and delivered it to her downstairs. Since I'd used the thing only twice in the three years I'd owned it, this seemed the simplest option if I wasn't to be stuck with a weak and starving Erica.

I found them huddled together this time; Erica draped protectively over the hooker, shushing and stroking her hair as she lay curled on the mat, shuddering from head to toe. Kerry's babbling was only barely coherent and preoccupied with her need for some "stuff." Her domestic situation seemed all but forgotten.

Not wishing to interrupt such a tender moment, I left them a pair of microwave mushroom stroganoffs and went to run a bath.

By Monday evening, there were clear signs of disharmony. The junkie still had not stopped wailing, and had taken to writhing on the rubber floor like a snake with an ache. The perspiration poured from her, and she wiped it across the mat with her arms and legs, leaving an impression that could only be described as a sweat angel.

Erica had taken to pacing now, teeth clenched, arms wrapped tightly around herself as she circled the cage. She turned to face me as I entered, the hatred in her eyes replaced with a look of haunted despair. "You need to get her out of here," she pleaded. "She's sick, and she needs a doctor, and this noise is doing my fucking head in." She jabbed an accusatory finger then; as a gesture from Erica this was not unremarkable, though its direction of travel raised at least one of my eyebrows. She aimed it not at me, but at the wriggling whore on the floor.

I could see her point. I only had to see Kerry for minutes at a time, and she was already getting on *my* nerves. It was, however, only a temporary annoyance. "She'll be out of here by the weekend," I promised.

"The weekend?" Erica regarded me somewhat incredulously. "Are you taking the piss? Do you think I have any idea what fucking day it is today? I don't know whether I've been here a day, a week or a fucking month. I don't even know how long *she's* been here. What the fuck does *the weekend* mean?"

Ah, what the hell. "Well, today is fucking Monday and it's just gone ten past six in the fucking evening. That fucking irritating creature will be out of your fucking hair by ten o'clock on Saturday fucking morning. Provided you tone down your fucking language, which is starting to wear a little bit fucking thin."

Predictably, she told me to go fuck myself.

———————

I'd purposely built the basement under the garage rather than the house so that I wouldn't feel compelled to run down and check it out during every ad break. I like to keep a little distance between rest and recreation. I did, however, find the developing situation strangely fascinating, and so on Tuesday I nipped into town and purchased a closed-circuit television camera.

Erica had reverted to gently rocking the shivering hooker when I set about installing the camera above the basement door. "Why are you doing that?" she asked as I wobbled atop my stepladder, up to my elbows in power cord and co-ax.

"So I can keep an eye on you and make sure you're all right," I explained.

"Oh, right, like you care." She scowled. "What, you're not violating our human rights enough so you've got to watch us on the toilet now, as well, right?"

It actually hadn't crossed my mind. "Erica, I have no interest in watching either one of you on the toilet. And if I did, I'd get a much better view if I just stood in there with you so, all things considered, I wouldn't concern myself too much with that if I were you."

"Where's Kerry going at the weekend?"

"That's none of your business. If Kerry wants to know, Kerry can ask me when she's stopped dribbling like a baby."

"What are you going to do to her?"

"Look…" The four screws I was holding between my in-turned lips fell out, plink-plinking down each step of the ladder and scattering across the floor. "Shit, now look what you've done."

"How did I do that? I'm over here, locked in this fucking cage."

I allowed my diminishing patience to show across my face. "Erica, is there anything else I can do for you?"

She seemed to take the hint. She looked around her for a moment or two, deep in thought, before her eyes settled on the quivering wreck in her arms. "Yes," she finally replied. "We could really do with some soap."

———

It took me until just past one in the morning to install the cable, which had necessitated among other things the drilling and filling of two walls and a ceiling. By the time I'd figured out how to feed the signal into the television, it was almost two o'clock and, unsurprisingly, both subjects were asleep. Erica had not yet lowered herself to sharing the bed, and was tucked up most cozily. She had, however, managed to throw Kerry a blanket.

I tuned in over breakfast on Wednesday to find them both awake. I got the distinct impression from Erica's demeanor that the hooker's cold turkey had been first to rise. There was no conversation, no sound at all but for a soft, breathy whimper. After three minutes of inactivity Erica rolled off the bed and approached the toilet, whereupon she turned around and glared up into the camera. She gave it a dismissive wave, pointed at the bowl and stagily covered her eyes before taking a step back and hooking her thumbs over the top of her knickers. I flicked over to the BBC breakfast program and ate my toast.

———

By Wednesday evening, the cuddling and the rocking were history. After refusing a dinner of mushroom tagliatelle, Erica returned to bed to stare silently at the ceiling, while the junkie threw up and paced around the cage, clawing at her own arms with her broken nails. This made for uninspiring viewing, and I soon turned my attention to the sudoku in the newspaper. My glances at the screen became increasingly infrequent, and by ten o'clock I was reaching for the remote, rueing the time and money wasted on such a poor source of entertainment. And right then, swallowing a yawn with my finger poised over the off button, I witnessed a moment that, somehow, I sensed would come back to haunt me.

Unmoving, unblinking, she spoke so calmly and softly that mere seconds earlier, for better or worse, I would have heard only the rustling of my newspaper. "Bitch," she said, "if you don't sit down and shut up in the next five seconds, I will come over there and I will fucking kill you."

Erica had begun to unravel.

O   O   O

On Thursday at 06:23, Erica graciously prepared her cellmate a bowl of cereal, using the fresh milk I'd provided. Kerry was lethargic and unresponsive, and at 06:46 had to be spoon-fed.

At 09:42, Kerry collapsed into a bout of uncontrollable shuddering accompanied by loud, breathless sobs. Erica wasted no time in slapping her violently across the face and demanding that she pull herself together.

At 13:39, the event was repeated, though this time one slap became two and set off a period of intense wailing. After twelve minutes, the hooker was silenced with a swift kick to the abdomen.

At 13:59, Erica sat on the edge of the bed with her head in her hands and silently wept for seven minutes, before letting herself down with, "Kerry, I'm sorry, I didn't mean to hurt you." Which just made Kerry cry harder.

At 18:02, after an uneventful afternoon, I entered the basement and was greeted with the now-standard scene: Erica horizontal and staring, Kerry bunched up in a twitchy little ball. Neither spoke a word to me.

———————

Thursday evening passed without further incident, and both Erica and Kerry were sound asleep by ten. With the dawn on Friday, however, came a perplexing turn of events. The hysterical hooker failed to wake up.

In her place come 6:00 a.m. was a quiet, still, steely-eyed bird of prey. She sat on her haunches against the side of the cage, silently watching Erica as she murmured and stirred, rolled slowly out of bed and headed straight for the toilet. I buttered my toast.

Erica regarded Kerry through sleepy eyes and paused only for a split second before shrugging to herself and snatching up the cereal packet. "Where's your bowl?" she yawned.

"I've already eaten."

The flat, aggressive tone made her pause longer this time. Finally, she moved to Kerry's side, knelt down beside her, leaned in just a little too close. "Are you feeling okay?" she asked with what at least sounded like genuine concern. "You look a little bit…odd."

Kerry wasn't waiting for a slap this time. In the blink of an eye, she curled the fingers of her right hand and lashed out with her jagged, splintered nails, carving three savage gashes across the width of Erica's cheek. "Get out of my face, bitch," she snarled as she rose to her feet.

Erica fell back, the box slipping from her hand, Rice Krispies spraying out across the floor. "Jesus!" she gasped, kicking out at the rubber matting, propelling herself backward until she could reach to pull herself up on the metal bed frame. "What the fuck was that?"

"You're a selfish, patronizing bully, and I'm sick of the fucking sight of you." Kerry was circling now, her eyes burning into Erica's like red-hot needles.

"Oh, that's rich." Erica pressed her hand to the side of her face; blood trickled between her fingers and dripped onto her bare toes. "You're lucky you're still breathing, girl."

"Oh, yeah?" Hackles truly up now, eyes wide, cheeks flushed. Here we go. "I'll fucking—" She was on Erica in an instant, knocking her off balance and coming down heavily on top of her. Erica, flailing, grabbed a handful of hair; she jerked Kerry's face back and pulled it down violently against her own forehead. Claws and teeth flashed.

I was there inside a minute. "Enough!" I shouted, throwing open the cage door and pulling Erica by the scruff of her neck from atop the now-prone hooker. And then, without hesitation, I took her by the arm and hauled her from the cage.

———

Erica made no attempt to struggle as I led her in her underwear across the frost-slick gravel of the driveway. She stepped obediently inside the house, looked to me for directions, followed me silently up the stairs to the bathroom.

She sat still on the side of the bath while I soaked a wad of cotton wool in TCP. She made no sound, beside a sharp intake of breath as I pressed it to her cheek. She was patient while I mopped the blood and applied a gauze, secured it in place with a cotton swab and an Elastoplast. And after a fleeting, longing glance at the gleaming bathtub, she followed me willingly back to the basement. She even carried the etorphine.

———————

Kerry caught Erica's defiant stare as I reunited them in the cage. She stopped pacing.

"Of course, you know you're a day early, right?" Erica handed me the miniature bottle and accompanying syringe and took to her perch on the edge of the bed.

Kerry edged away toward the far corner of the cell, her impending fate slowly dawning across her bloodied face. "Oh, you have got to be kidding me." She laughed, strangely.

I didn't have to say a word. Erica tossed her hair, crossed her knees and smiled at the doomed whore. "Looks like it's your lucky day, Kerry," she taunted. "I think you're going to go and play a little game." She fixed me with a look then, one so commanding that it stopped me in my tracks. "And you," she said, "when you're done with her you can go and buy me some clean fucking knickers. I'm filthy."

CHAPTER
EIGHT

I wasn't expecting a knock at the door so early in the morning. And if I had been, I certainly wouldn't have expected a pair of thirtysomething strangers in polyester suits. I don't get too many visitors.

She stood a step behind him; both had their hands folded behind their backs. Their suits were identical—navy, double-breasted, showing signs of bobbling—though his didn't feature a pencil skirt. Hers reached just below the knee, affording a view of sporty calves clad in sheer black nylon running directly into sensible lace-up shoes that swallowed her ankles. Her face was dusky and exotic-looking, her hair jet-black and tidied into a businesslike knot. Turkish? Iranian, maybe.

Her colleague stood within inches of the doorstep, implausibly large feet firmly together, all five-o'clock shadow and a dutiful half smile.

I almost had them pegged as Jehovah's Witnesses until I spotted the big Ford on the drive, poverty blue with a whip antenna and cable-tied wheel trims. And then I was confirming my name to a black leather wallet, flipped open right in front of my nose and snatched away too fast to allow me to focus. Not that I really needed to.

"I'm Detective Inspector Fairey, CID."

Shit. No, really—shit. Shit shit shit. Don't flinch. Whatever you do, don't narrow your eyes. Keep your hands still. Look him in the eye. Smile. Not like that—smile nicely.

"This is Detective Sergeant Green." He shot her a nondescript glance; her expression didn't change. Her name didn't sound very Turkish, either. I smiled at her, anyway. "We'd like to ask you a few questions, if you don't mind."

As a matter of fact, I do mind. "Of course." *That's enough, stop smiling now. It's not reaching your eyes.* "What can I help you with?"

He took one of his ridiculous clown feet and placed it firmly inside the door. "Okay if we come in?"

You already fucking did. "I guess so." I stood stock-still in the doorway. "This isn't going to take long, is it? I'm kind of in the middle of something."

It was his turn with the false smile. "I'm sure it'll only take a minute." He nodded. And just stood there. Staring. Nodding. I wondered how long he'd stand there, head bobbing up and down like a plastic dog on a parcel shelf, smile turning to a grimace, waiting politely for me to step aside. A minute? Two? Five maybe? Place your bets now.

Actually, no, I haven't got time for that. I told him okay and waved him into the hall; he held me in a defiant stare as he passed. The one called Green bowed her head and followed silently. I left the door open.

"Nice house," Fairey remarked as he scanned the blank

walls of the entrance hall. Obviously highly skilled in the art of small talk.

I led him through to the kitchen and pointed to a chair at the breakfast table. Green fared a little better; I pulled one out for her. "So, Mr. Fairey—sit down, make yourself comfortable. What is it exactly that you'd like to ask me?"

"I'll stand," he said bluntly. He considered me for a moment; a lingering leer I found vaguely suggestive. I hoped he was merely waiting for me to offer him a cup of tea, though whatever he wanted, he'd have a long wait. And then, finally, he spoke. "We're here," he said, "because we're investigating the disappearance of Kerry Farrow."

The ceiling fell down. Crockery jumped from the racks, shattering across the floor. The boards undulated beneath my feet, pitching me off balance. Blood pounded through my temples, spots of white light dancing around my eyes to the staccato beat in my head. I felt my palms moisten and my pupils dilate. Every hair on my body stood on end. The windows rattled. The door flew off its hinges. I reached out to steady myself but my fingers just grasped at thin air, the same air that was whistling out of me like I'd taken a kick to the stomach.

This is the other reason I stay away from hookers: there's always some knitworn do-right from the Prostitutes' Collective taking down numbers. Decades without a glitch, and then I'm undone by a needless whim in a moment of weakness. It's an age-old story, and one of those things that always happens to someone else. Fuck me, I'm an idiot.

Gun. I can get to the gun, no problem. In the time it takes this Fairey to cross the kitchen, I'll have torn open the cupboard and swiped aside the oven cleaner and the bin bags and he'll be staring down a twelve-gauge barrel, eyes widening, trying to shake his head, trying to form the word *no* with his cotton-wool tongue and his cracked lips while his mind clouds with terror and despair and thoughts of his plump wife and gurgling babies and everything he didn't tell them before he left for work today. And his accomplice will make it to her feet in time to take a faceful of blood and skull and brain, and she'll raise her hands to shield her eyes and let out a shriek of fear and surprise, and she'll trip on the chair as she runs for the door, and I'll stand on her neck as she sprawls on the floor, and she'll look up at me like a stunned rabbit, and her breathing will turn shallow and frantic and she'll whimper, "Please, no," and I'll think about the floor and what it'll cost to repair and I might let her get to her feet. I might haul her up and escort her out to the fields behind the house where the topsoil's loose and the stains won't show. I may even let her run for the car, see if her comfortable shoes offer any practical advantage. Or to hell with the floor, I can be in Belgrade by nightfall.

Okay, breathe. Slow down. Think it through. They're only a pair, and drones to boot. Whatever they suspect, they only suspect. There's no mob with machine guns abseiling from the roof. No one's kicking down doors or crashing through the windows. They've got nothing to go on. It's just a man with a cheap suit and fucking great feet asking a single, simple question. For Christ's sake, he hasn't even asked it yet. And if the question's that hard to answer, well, there's room for them both under the barn.

Keep calm. Keep smiling. Eye contact. No sudden movement. Maybe raise an eyebrow, as though listening intently. Which one? The right. No, the other one. All right, then, Ronald McFuckingdonald. I'm ready for you.

"And we think you're potentially an important witness," he said.

Oh?

○ ○ ○

"You own a white Ford Transit," he informed me, a statement with which I could only reasonably agree. "Showed up on cctv on Queen Street at 3:11 a.m. That's about two hundred yards and fifteen minutes from where Kerry was last seen," which certainly made me Idiot of the Week, but was far from a smoking gun. Fairey flipped a seven-by-five print from his jacket pocket: a six-month-old mugshot, Kerry sullen and bedraggled and black-eyed, eight inches of dark roots chasing the tail of a home peroxide. "The blond's gone," Fairey continued, "but the expression hasn't changed. Maybe you remember seeing her? Talking to someone, getting into a car?"

I took a moment to think, considering the farthest distance to which I could remove Kerry in the shortest possible time. Finally, I shook my head. "I wish I could help," I said. "I just don't recognize her at all," which was actually not all that far from the truth. Even after a week of cold turkey and cage fighting, she looked nothing like the harridan in the photograph.

"You're quite sure?" Green asked. Something in her eyes told me my acting was flawed. Before I could reassure her, however, Fairey shot her a look that told her he'd be asking the fucking questions, thank you very much, all but striking hers from the record.

"You Batman?" he said, returning the mugshot to his pocket and flipping out a notebook in its place.

"I'm sorry?" I replied.

"Insomniac?"

Green rolled her eyes. "Get to the point," I said, forcing her to hide a smirk.

Fairey smiled graciously. "What were you doing driving around the red-light district at three in the morning?"

Finally, a question I could answer truthfully. "I was on my way back from the seaside," I told him. "I spent the evening with…" With what? "A friend?" Accurate description or not, I'd said it aloud and it was in Fairey's book.

"Name?"

"Annie."

"Annie…?" He stopped scribbling, looked up at me expectantly.

"Yes," I replied.

"Surname?"

"Almost certainly."

"Address?" He laughed.

I recited it as well as I could remember.

"I take it you only recently met?"

"Yes, that night," I confessed. "We…you know. Just talked."

Green's hand fell away from her mouth, and she stared at me in undisguised bemusement. Like her, I had no idea why I'd said that.

Whatever, Fairey seemed unconcerned. "I understand," he said with a dismissive wave. "Listen, how about we take a quick look at that Transit, and then we'll let you get on with your day?"

I liked the sound of the latter, at least.

The van was empty but for the load straps and a large, plain cardboard box. On the top of the box was a folded woolen blanket. "Box of blankets," I said.

"May I?" Green preemptively ignored her superior's silent admonition and stepped up onto the load bed.

"Be my guest." I smiled, mentally locating the garden fork hung on the wall three feet behind me.

"Thank you," she said, rubber soles squeaking against the steel floor as she strolled over to the box, squared her jaw and carefully lifted one corner of the blanket. Finding another beneath it, she lifted the second blanket to reveal a third. "Box of blankets." She nodded.

"What's under *those* blankets?" Fairey asked, indicating what was quite plainly a sheet-draped car occupying the opposite side of the garage.

I heard Green nudge the box with her foot as I turned. "My car," I said, sounding rather unnecessarily uncooperative even to myself.

"Looks like an Interceptor," he decided, unperturbed.

"Good guess," I conceded.

"Mind if I look?"

I don't know why he bothered asking; he was already across the garage and peeling back the covers before I could utter, "Knock yourself out."

Green hopped down from the back of the van. "We'll be here all bloody day now," she remarked, nevertheless casting an appraising eye over the Jensen's scruffy gray flank as she swept past. Quite rightly, she was unimpressed.

I followed her to the threshold, where she gazed out beyond the house to the barn midway across the field. "Nice place you've got," she noted. "What's in the barn?"

"Flatbed trailer, workbench, assorted lumps of wood, a fiberglass speedboat without an engine," I informed her. "Tours are free if you want one." Maybe not Belgrade. Maybe somewhere warm, like Las Palmas or Santo Domingo.

She stared a moment longer, then shook her head. "I'll take your word for it," she said, reaching into her jacket pocket and pulling out a pack of Juicy Fruit. "If he's off the clock, so am I."

Fairey had found the bonnet unlatched and was staring aghast at the jumble of disconnected wiring within. "Oh, bloody hell," he said.

Green and I made a show of checking our watches. Clearly, we both wished I were alone.

———————

"If you do happen to think of anything that might help us—"

"I'll be sure you're the first to know." I shook Fairey's hand as I walked him out of the garage; his grip was decidedly limp and more than a little clammy.

He nodded. "And get that engine fixed."

I gave him a weary salute as he and Green walked back to

their car. Waited until Fairey had one leg inside before calling after him. "Actually, there is one thing," I said.

Green slumped into her seat and slammed the door behind her. Fairey, after a brief hesitation, withdrew his leg and strolled back into my personal space, leaning in close, offering his confidence. "Sure," he replied. "What is it?"

"Save me a walk and shut the gate on your way out, would you?" I gave him my brightest smile. "Helps keep the undesirables out."

Fairey laughed. "No worries, bud," he said, and returned to his muddy Mondeo.

Under the fourth blanket, Kerry was none the wiser.

CHAPTER
NINE

She awoke to the creak of lush green pines swaying gently against a beautiful, clear blue sky. She lay on her back in the grass, surrounded by bluebells and lingering frost, eyelids fluttering against the morning sun, wet hair splayed out like the shadow of a halo. She looked almost serene as she took in the ice water dripping from the trees, the soft cooing of wood pigeons. She watched her breath rising into the crisp, cold air with a dreamy fascination. And when her eyes settled on me, standing patiently over her with a welcoming smile, the recognition seemed anything but startling. She simply smiled back and took a long, luxurious stretch, looking for all the world like the contented lover she might once have been, woken from a sensual dream to the thrill of a blossoming romance, her loneliness, for now at least, behind her.

"Where are we?" she murmured, shivering a little. She rubbed her bare knees together and tucked her hands into the opposite sleeves of her coat.

I flicked the dregs of tea from my cup and screwed it back onto the thermos, tossed it into the van and locked the door.

Kerry's expression grew quizzical and she craned her neck to peer off into the depths of the wood. "Did you kill me?" she asked.

"No," I replied.

"I don't understand. Where are we?"

"We're in the forest, in a place called Emily's Wood."

"Okay." She nodded. "Why is it called that?"

"I don't know." Never occurred to me to find out.

She narrowed her eyes thoughtfully, lips poised for further questioning, but something had already distracted her; a far-off noise, rasping and mechanical. It rose to a crescendo, dropped off, peaked again; a distant, eerie echo stalking through the trees. It faded to unmask a different sound, fainter still, not unlike that of the breeze in the branches and yet somehow flat and unnatural. Pushing herself up onto her elbows, listening intently, she asked, "What is that?"

I stood, took in the distant murmur. "It's traffic," I said.

Realization dawned across her face. She sat bolt upright, eyes darting around her from tree to tree and to the dark places in between. She surveyed the narrow strip of grass on which she sat; twenty yards wide and arrow-straight for an eighth of a mile, the forest crowding in on all sides to consume it. "Oh, Jesus Christ," she gasped.

On any other day, I might have made one of those corny B-movie remarks upon an understandable case of mistaken identity, but today, for some reason, my heart wasn't in it.

Kerry leaped to her feet, whirled around on the spot, panic

flashing. "What the fuck!" she shrieked. "Oh, my God, what the fuck?"

"You've come here to die," I said.

She hitched a breath and staggered in a vague half circle, shaking her head as if to deny me.

"Probably."

Streaming tears, she spun around to face me, lost her footing, fell back down on her tender rump. "What?" she cried.

"All depends on you," I continued. "We're going to play a game together. That sound you can hear is the sound of the main road. If you can work out which direction it's coming from, and make it there with a two-minute head start before I catch you, then I'll let you go, and you can hitch a ride home, or walk, or I'll give you a lift if you want." On my way to the airport. "Whichever you prefer."

"A game…" She stared up at me for several moments, seemingly trying to take in what I'd offered. "And you'll let me go," she repeated.

"Yes, if you win. Don't get too excited, it hasn't happened yet. And the catch," I continued, snatching up the catch from the ground behind me so that she could see it, "is this hundred-pound competition hunting bow." Kerry froze; even her tears stood still as she stared at the weapon. "I'm only going to use one arrow. It's aluminum, fifty-five grain, flies at around two hundred and twenty-five miles an hour, so I'd suggest you don't stop for a cigarette. The ground's prickly, and it's going to hurt your feet, but you're going to have to run through the pain, because I guarantee the arrow will hurt more. If you don't stop moving, two minutes will get you a long way, and if you head in the right direction, there's

a good chance that you'll make it to the road. Straightforward enough?"

She nodded slowly, eyes fixed on the bow. "This—" she
sniffed "—is a fucking joke, right?"

A tight shake of the head told her that it wasn't. "That's
the game," I said.

"That's not a game, it's a fucking…" Bloodsport? Whatever,
she couldn't find the word, but her unwavering, unblinking
stare signaled that, whether or not she realized it yet, we had
ourselves a deal. "What if I don't want to play?" she ventured,
though we both knew the question was rhetorical.

———————

Sound travels through the forest in a strange and magical
way. A squeaking trailer at two miles and a squawking crow
at thirty feet can often sound very much alike. As such, Kerry
didn't have a clue which way to run. The moment I started
counting, she simply bolted straight for what looked like the
clearest path through the trees.

As promised, I held station for the full two minutes. She'd
taken off like her tail was on fire, and she'd been out of sight
within twenty seconds, but I could still hear her crashing
through the undergrowth as I shouldered the bow and as-
sumed the hunt.

The direction she'd chosen was not the easiest. The gen-
erously spaced pines this side of our starting point range no
more than two hundred feet before they give way to tightly
packed elm, their branches low and intertwining, trunks en-

veloped in thigh-high nettles and prickly gorse. No place for the bare-legged.

Initially, tracking Kerry was an uncomplicated affair. There was a clear path of least resistance which, in a state of blind panic, a fleeing quarry could be relied upon to follow. And as the underbrush thickens, so the passage of animals becomes quite conspicuous. There were numerous flattened paths through the gorse, but in only one were the thistles still visibly unfolding. If a deer had bounded through here, it had been hot on the hooker's heels.

I paused momentarily to take in the sweet, fresh aroma of damp bracken; the air was thick and cosseting, like a cold woolen blanket. The swishing and crackling of Kerry's flight had trailed off, leaving nothing but silence. The distant motorway roar was inaudible here.

I pressed on, and at fifty paces I passed a half-dozen strands of dark brown hair, snagged on a splintered outcrop.

At seventy five the first drops of blood appeared on the thorns.

At a hundred, I snatched up a torn strip of black fleece, complete with washing instructions, claimed from the lining of her jacket.

And at a hundred and ten, amid the thistles and the dew and the dappled sunlight, I discovered the most heartening thing of all: the sudden, complete, dead end of the trail. Kerry was playing the game, and she was playing smarter than I'd expected.

———

Logic suggested I turn around and retrace my steps. Instinct, however, dictated otherwise. I used my arrow to part the nettles in front of me and, sure enough, she was bluffing. She'd taken a running dive and, not six feet in, had sprawled headlong into the weeds before regaining her feet and scything ahead. I had to admit, the girl had guts.

She was fast, too. I reached the far side of the thicket at full pelt, and she was nowhere in sight. The trees spread out and grew taller, the ground between them carpeted in dead leaves and fallen branches. The canopy was thicker, the light patchy; I had, however, a two-hundred-yard line of sight through a hundred and eighty degrees and not a creature was stirring. I stopped dead, crouched down close to the ground to listen. The silence was heavy, unnatural. Deceitful. She was there all right; I could taste her blood, sweat and tears in the air. She was rigid, holding her breath, skin pressed tight against bark. The deer, the squirrels, the crows could all smell her fear, and they mocked her silently, knowing as well as she did that sooner or later, she'd have to breathe. And it was deathly cold out here.

I scanned the shadows. "Give yourself a chance, Kerry," I called. "It's hard to keep still in this cold when you're only half-dressed. You've got strong legs, I'll give you that, but as soon as they start to shiver, you'll give yourself away. You're weak-willed, your stamina's all physical. Use it while you can—it's still fifty-fifty that you'll outrun me." I stopped still, cocked my head theatrically at an imagined sound. "Oh, wait." I smiled. "Too late. I've seen you."

The lie had the desired effect. Amid a raucous crackling of twigs, she obligingly bolted from the shadow of a twisted elm not fifty feet in front of me. Head down, bloodied arms pumping, she exploded across the forest floor like a wounded bear, charging directly across my path before I'd so much as unslung the bow. She was headed for a spray of daylight, a glittering oasis some five hundred feet distant. I made a break for the same target, my diagonal path through the wood more of a gentle loping slalom than the obstacle course facing my quarry. She hurdled fallen branches, stumbled through patches of nettle and fern, skittered over loose bracken and leaf mulch. Even at thirty feet and in spite of the resounding racket, I could hear the rasping, heaving panic in her breath. Bearing down on her, the bow on my back a mere accessory now, I made the last ten feet airborne, arm thrust out superheroically before me, hand brushing the back of her neck, fingers closing around streaming hair.

And then she was out of the trees. The sunlight hit her like a bullet, knocked her straight to the ground. Her flailing limbs slapped against concrete, mimicking the sickly sound of dropped oranges, and she lay there, screwing her eyes tight against the glare as I sprawled in long, damp grass just inside the tree line, a dozen strands of wet brown hair clutched in my fist. The traffic noise drew nearer by the second; the rumble of heavy axles, the swoosh of displaced salt water. And then the deep, grumbling roar of a big diesel engine, closer and louder, drowning the air, the earth trembling under its weight. Kerry yelped and sprung to her feet, eyes wide, disoriented, flinging herself to the safety of the verge as the truck thundered past—twenty-five yards away, beyond the copse into which she stumbled.

She stood motionless, staring off toward the road. A steady stream of cars hustled by, their reflected sunlight shimmering through dripping thaw and rising mist. She turned to me across the narrow farm track, her jubilant face crossed with hesitation, as though seeking my permission to turn and run. Her eyes widened, the corners of her mouth drawing back into a grimace as she stared down the shaft of my arrow. I held her in the sight as she stumbled back, turned to run in a whirlwind of elbows and hair, all wintry soft-focus and adrenaline-rush slow motion. I thought of Lindsay Wagner, briefly. And then I fired.

CHAPTER
TEN

My biggest flaw, I think, is the attachment I have to my comfort zone. Sure, I like to challenge myself from time to time, but the unknown is something I consider best avoided.

It was with trepidation, then, that after a long afternoon on the road I found myself in something called a "New Look," uncomfortably unsure of what I was looking for and, indeed, at. I was surrounded by low chrome rails, hung in a seemingly random manner with numerous headache-colored garments. The racks were overfilled, making it virtually impossible to examine their contents; those items hung on the ends of each rail, which apparently were representative of the stock in general, appeared entirely inappropriate for the season.

The staff was no help—two girls of around school-leaving age, preoccupied with inspecting their nails. They were big on teamwork where the customers were concerned; it took one of them to ring up each sale, and the other to fold and bag the merchandise. A single trained chimpanzee would perhaps have been more cost-effective. Needless to say, neither saw fit to offer me assistance, and I was left alone in my bewilderment.

The problem with being lost, of course, is that it naturally makes one *look* lost. As a consequence, I imagined every eye in the shop to be trained on me, deriding my helplessness, thanking their lucky stars that they didn't have one like me at home. Or maybe just questioning my motives for loitering in a women's clothes shop. The frustration and self-consciousness gnawing at my spine signaled a crushing defeat and so, with an affected expression of disappointment, I hastily tur—

"What do you think? How does this look?"

Oh, no.

———

Stay calm. Appear unfazed. Drop shoulders. Smile. For Christ's sake, say something. "I'd say you were about three months early with it, but I like it, it suits you." A town of twenty thousand people, and I have to get caught browsing ladies' underwear by this one.

"It suits me?" Caroline, or possibly Rachel, threw me a smirk and turned to the full-length mirror screwed to the wall. "What does that mean?"

It meant that her arse looked fantastic in it, and I wanted to bite her perfectly toned ankles as they peeked out below the hemline, but "I mean it looks like it was made especially for you."

"Should I take that as a compliment, or are you saying I look like a gypsy?"

"Well, I *meant* it as a compliment." As if it wasn't written all over my face.

"Well, thank you, then, that's settled." She turned to offer me a warm smile. Those eyes held mine for a fleeting moment.

"I probably wouldn't buy it, though," I added. "It's too pale. It'll get dirty easily. And it's cotton so you'll have to hand-wash it every time."

She regarded me with something halfway between suspicion and amusement. "That's a fair point," she agreed. "But if my bum looks good in it, I don't care." She skipped back toward the fitting room with a wide grin. "Wait right there," she instructed.

I complied without thinking. Loitering at the fitting room door colors a man patient and loyal, and attracts far less attention than perhaps it ought.

Caroline-until-further-notice reappeared within a minute, the intended new skirt draped over her arm. "Okay," she said, "why are you still standing there empty-handed?" She looked as though she could hear the cogs grinding in my head. "Hmm, let me guess. It's your wife's birthday, and she's seen a sexy little set she likes, but you weren't listening when she described it."

I laughed at her accusatorially raised eyebrow. "I'm not married," I assured her.

"Girlfriend?"

"No."

"Boyfriend?"

"No."

"You like dressing up?"

"Um…"

"Mind my own business?"

"Yes, my niece," I blathered.

"Ahhh…" She allowed herself a brief, satisfied nod of approval, just long enough for her to tie up the loose ends. "Wait, you're buying underwear for your niece?" She cocked her head at me, eyes narrowed in scrutiny. I opened my mouth to respond but she cut me dead. "No, you don't have to answer that. Really. None of my business. I shouldn't—"

"No, it's fine." I smiled. The lie was unusually slow in formulating. "I mean, I *am* buying underwear for my niece, but that's only half the story. I'm actually buying *everything* for her. She's…got no clothes." I wasn't helping myself here. The returned expression was one of bemused concern. I laughed as confidently as I could under the circumstances. "I wish we could start this conversation again," I said.

"Yes, let's."

It came to me. I took a deep breath, swallowed my frustration. "She's down on business and she's staying at my house. When she arrived last night she put her suitcase down in the station, and someone walked off with it."

"Oh, no."

"Yes. So she's had to go into work wearing the clothes she traveled down in, and because she's in meetings all through the weekend and into next week, she's not going to get a chance to pick anything up, so I said I'd help her out." The plot holes were apparent even before I'd finished speaking.

The spark, however, had returned to Caroline's eyes. "Well," she said brightly, "that's very noble and a huge relief. I thought I was going to have to start backing slowly away from you."

"Of course, I don't have the slightest idea of what I'm doing. I can confidently tell you that your skirt looks good when you're wearing it, but on a hanger? I couldn't even tell you it *was* a skirt."

Caroline held up her free hand, signaling that enough was enough. "Okay, stop." She laughed. "I can spot a hint, but I don't often take them. If you want me to help you, just ask."

I couldn't have hoped for a finer recovery, and I didn't need a second invitation. I cooed in exaggerated helplessness. "Will you help me, please?"

"On one condition," she warned.

"Anything."

"When we're done, you buy me a cup of tea and some cake. My time most certainly doesn't come for free."

Despite the butterflies, I managed an honest smile. "Sold."

———————

It took Caroline two minutes shy of two hours to model virtually everything in the shop and a further fifteen minutes to locate the approved outfits in a size twelve. She made a vain, token effort to explain how, with an extra four inches in height to offset her less-pronounced curves, she could require a smaller dress size. Since I was growing increasingly hungry, and the exercise showed no sign of condensing itself into a neat Roy Orbison-backed montage, I only pretended to understand. I did, however, gain a new concept of the price of a good time. As pleasantly as I'd been surprised at my ability to relax and enjoy Caroline's spoof mail-order poses, set to the sound of her own infectious giggle, I was painfully aware that I was now four hundred pounds the worse for wear. Erica was becoming quite an investment.

My discontent was weak, however, and vanished altogether as Caroline's Danish pastry flaked all over her jumper. "Balls," she muttered, the tangled, wiry wool foiling her attempts to swipe the crumbs away. "That's not gone well. God, I'm so ladylike..."

I stifled a grin. "You know, the sole purpose of that cake is to be enjoyed by you, and you can't enjoy it properly if you're worried about making a mess. Savor it, make more crumbs. Get some in your hair."

She laughed, shook her hands free of worry. "That's funny. You'd be amazed at what I manage to get in my hair sometimes." She sipped her tea and winced. "Don't think too hard about that," she said. "It came out wrong."

I nodded in sympathy. "I took it as it was intended," I assured her. She thanked me graciously.

Outside, the sky darkened abruptly. The rows of dim spotlights set into the ceiling cast a warm but unnatural glow across Caroline's face. The shadows of mugs and menu stands lengthened across the checked tablecloth. A sudden gust of wind snapped at the coattails of shoppers passing by the window. One by one they turned up their collars as the first drops of rain struck the pavement.

"So, here's a question." I gulped down the remainder of my tea. It was hotter than I expected. Caroline recoiled on my behalf. "How is it that you're single and working on a supermarket checkout?" I held my breath, silently willing her not to contradict me.

"Who said I was single?" She laughed. I resisted the urge to stare into my own mug. "Although, actually, you're right, I am," she conceded. My sigh of relief was unintentionally audible and, I knew, glaringly obvious. Happily, she overlooked it. "And more to the point," she said, "what's wrong with working in a supermarket?"

"Oh, nothing at all." Furious mental backpedaling. Christ, this was difficult. "It just…" *Turn it into a compliment while you've still got the chance.* "You seem intelligent and free-spirited, and I find that hard to equate with something so repetitive and enclosed."

"Ah," she agreed, "but that's just the thing. I could get a job doing something I care passionately about, but once your interests become responsibilities, it's kind of hard to keep enjoying them. I want to *choose* to pursue them, not be forced into it. And what I do takes up such a tiny percentage of my concentration that I can spend the whole eight hours thinking about whatever I want to think about and not be too mentally exhausted to do what I want to do when I get home. And when I'm not busy, I can just close my eyes and go lie on a beach in the Bahamas, and get paid for the privilege. Not many people can say that."

"Holiday reps, perhaps," I suggested. "And lifeguards."

"Yeah, and I don't particularly aspire to be either. I burn too easily."

"So what *do* you aspire to?"

"Just to be happy," she said. "Corny, but true."

Outside, the heavens opened. A rumble of thunder heralded the arrival of a downpour. Fat drops of rain pounded the windows, hit the ground hard enough to bounce right up from the pavement.

"There's nothing corny about it," I said. "I'm sure we all aspire to that."

"In different ways." She blew gently into her tea, took a thoughtful sip.

"And what's your way?" I glanced at the thick sleeves of her jumper, stretched down almost to the tops of her fingers as they curled protectively around her mug. "What makes you happy?"

The trace of smile left her lips then; her gaze turned inward for what seemed like minutes. "As soon as I figure that out," she said finally, "I'll let you know."

I turned to look out into the storm-ravaged street. Shoppers clamped scarves and hats to themselves as they scurried for cover. Umbrellas turned inside out. A shop board skittered a few feet across the pavement before collapsing into an inch-deep river of rainwater. Leaflets and plastic bags swooped like deranged kites, clinging to awnings and rubbish bins and the occasional windswept child. Thunder cracked ominously overhead. "Jesus," I said. "You know, whether you like it or not, you're certainly safer in here with me than you are out there."

"I think you're right." She laughed. "After all, my mother never said anything about strange men and coffee shops."

And then I lost my breath. With a wet *slap*, the front page of the *Evening News* pasted itself to the window mere inches from Caroline's face. She frowned as Kerry Farrow glared at her through the glass, a mess of tangled hair and glazed eyes beneath the bold, simple headline: Fears Grow For Missing Vice Girl.

"Of course," Caroline said, "she'd never forgive me if I got into a car with you."

I attempted a smile. She took another bite of Danish.

○   ○   ○

"I don't know, I'm starting to wonder if we're not just living in some sort of Bermuda Triangle." Caroline swiped the mist from her window with a sleeved hand. "I mean, I've got this friend at work. Conscientious as you like, always there, always on time. Never had a day off sick, never turns her phone off in case someone *else* calls in sick... She leaves work on Friday, waves bye bye to everyone, 'See you Monday' and all that, happy as can be because she's got the whole weekend off for the first time this year, and then come Monday morning, she's just not there. Gone. Vanished. And I mean *vanished*, as in without a trace."

I know what you're thinking, but I had nothing to do with it. I flicked the wipers onto full speed, edged a car-length or two closer to the lights. "She never told anyone where she might be going?" I suggested.

"Nope. Not a word. If she'd told anyone, I'm pretty sure she would have told me—she got on better with me than she did anyone else. But no, the first I heard of it was 'Rachel, can you get in here as soon as you can? Caroline's gone AWOL and the fish needs laying out...'"

Aha! "Rachel." I nodded, hopefully silently to myself.

"Uh-huh?"

Shit. "Mmm?"

"What?"

"Sorry, no, I didn't..." This was awkward and might take some getting used to, but at least I'd be subliminally seeing the right name everywhere from now on.

"No, go on," she insisted.

"No, nothing. Really."

"No, you can't do that. You have to tell me now. It's the law."

"Call a policeman."

"I will."

"Fine."

"Fine." She laughed.

I studied her as she gazed out over the traffic, gently tapping her fingers in her lap to a song on the radio. She blushed a little, but seemed perfectly at ease; no self-conscious scratching of her ears, no humming along to break the silence.

"Still," she said. "That's just the way it goes for some people, isn't it? Here today, a mystery tomorrow." She offered me a pensive frown. "And then forgotten by the middle of next week." I nodded in silent, sad agreement. "Whereas you—" she smiled, brightening as suddenly as she had darkened "—you're different, you're already a mystery. I bet I won't have forgotten *you* by then."

I laughed, though inside I truly hoped she was wrong.

CHAPTER
ELEVEN

"What have you done with her?"

"Who?"

Erica backed away from me slowly as I unlocked the cage. "You know who. That tart you took out yesterday. Where is she?"

"What do you care? You've spent the whole week begging me to get rid of her."

"Oh, my God." She turned and braced herself against the sink. "I meant get her away from *me*, not take her round the back and fucking kill her."

"Well, unfortunately, it's not you who makes the decisions around here." I locked myself in with her, dropped fresh milk and a new box of cereal at the foot of her bed. "What did you think I was going to do, drop her off in rehab?"

She whirled around to face me, her cheeks suddenly pale and drawn, her mouth curled into a sad grimace. Her dark eyes fluttered back sticky tears. "Why?" she murmured.

I felt something stirring, not in my trousers as I would have expected but deeper, somewhere down in the pit of my stomach. I felt my fingers twitching at my sides, my arms fighting their own urge to reach out to her. "Erica," I said firmly, "don't cry for her. She left her children at home so she could go out and suck off strangers for smack." She stood rooted to the spot, covered her face with her hands as she began to sob. I changed tack, gave up hiding my frustration. "All right," I said, "she's had a miserable, tortured life, and now she's in a far better place, and I'm sure someone's looking after her kids. Is that preferable? For fuck's sake, Erica, get over it."

"I'm not crying for her!" she wailed, hands gone, the sadness in her eyes joined by just a trace of the familiar venom. "Are you completely fucking stupid? I'm too busy being locked in this fucking cell waiting to die to be worried about that horrible whore!" I sat down quietly on the edge of the bed as she let herself go. She spun around, tugged at her hair, jabbed at her thighs with her fists and let out a screech that I feared might shatter the lightbulbs. And then finally, she breathed a heavy sigh and shook it all right out of her head. "I'm crying for myself," she whispered.

———

I've never once had the inclination to open the cage door and just stand aside. I've faced it all in this room: tears, seduction, attempted hanging. They come, they brandish their feminine wiles and eventually, inevitably, they go. But it's never of their own accord. They all insist that they want to be free, to taste the fresh air and to gaze up at the clear blue sky. They coo, they demand, they beg me to open the door and to let them run. And yet without fail, when the door is finally opened, they beg me to let them stay because in their hearts, they know that they're safe in the cage. There are no ghosts in here.

"Trust me," Erica said, sniffing, "if you opened that door right now, I'd take my chance."

I didn't know how much I'd said aloud. It didn't matter. "I know you would, Erica," I said softly. "And right now—" for some reason I couldn't even begin to understand "—that's exactly why I'm not going to open it."

———————

For the first time in over a week, I slept right through the night. I dreamed of flight, of soaring over jagged peaks and rolling hills, landscapes filled with colors I'd never seen and cannot describe. By morning, when I was woken gently by the patter of rain on the windows, I was refreshed and blissfully relaxed. I hummed a made-up tune while I fetched my tea and toast and flicked on the television. It was almost unnerving.

Erica was up before me and was leafing through a *Cosmopolitan* I'd left her. Not having sought her preference before buying it, I was unsurprised to note her bored expression. I resolved to rectify it at my earliest convenience; in the meantime, though, she had a more pressing engagement.

She tossed the magazine to the floor as I let myself in. The expected complaint, however, didn't come; she simply smiled politely and said, "Good morning."

If her mood was alarmingly bright, her appearance was

quite the opposite. Dark rings under bloodshot eyes, hair tangled and limp, clothes creased and torn and dark with dirt. Cotton wool dressing, stripped of its fabric plaster, held to her face with dried blood. Her pillows and sheets stained black with grime and sweat. A stale, oppressive odor in the air. "Good morning to you, too," I said.

"No new roommate for me today?"

"No, no such luck." She spoofed a huff of disappointment. "Don't be disheartened, though, I've got some good news for you."

"Great. I could do with some of that. Don't tell me...you died in your sleep?"

"No, that's obviously not it," I assured her. "No, the good news is that you're coming out with me."

Her face fell. "Coming with you where?"

"Outside."

"I don't fucking think so. In fact, I don't think I'm going anywhere with you unless you drag me."

"Well—" I laughed "—that's obviously not a problem, but there's really no need. I've run you a bath, that's all, but if you don't want it, I'll happily get in there myself."

Erica simply stared, mouth agape, eyebrows furrowed, clearly struggling to comprehend what I'd just said. I hoped she was making better sense of it than I was. "What happens when I get out of the bath?"

"You dry yourself with a towel, get dressed and come back to your room, and then maybe tell me what you'd prefer to read," I said.

"And what about you? If you're expecting to sit on the toilet and perv over me..."

"We've been through this. Are you coming or not? I don't want to let it get cold."

She shook her head in perplexed amusement and slid hesitantly off the bed. As unconvinced as she plainly was, she threw on her jumper and followed.

———

"Stick your clothes in here." I held open a bin bag through the crack in the bathroom door, behind which I'd allowed Erica the privacy to undress.

"Are you going to wash them?" She dropped in her tattered pants.

"No, I'm going to burn them."

"I like this jumper."

"It'll only fall apart if I put it in the machine."

"Well, can you at least try?" She thrust it into the bag, along with her blackened bra. "It's not like I've got anything else to wear."

I snatched away the bag and held out an unopened pack of briefs.

"Oh, my God, is it Christmas already?" She snatched the knickers from me. "And if so, can I have a heater in my room?"

"Bra." I passed it through.

"This is the wrong size."

"No, it isn't."

"I fucking knew you'd been peeking. Anything else, or can I get in the bath now?"

One by one, I slid each of the half-dozen shopping bags

into the bathroom. "These are all a bit summery," I said, "but they were the best I could do."

She was silent for a moment; I could only sense her, as still as stone. Finally, softly, her voice cracking, she asked, "How long have I got?"

"Take as long as you need," I said.

"That's not what I meant."

"I know." I listened to the gentle sniffs and sobs drifting around the door frame. My hand reached out to push the door open, my feet itching to step inside; I quietly cursed them, stood firm in spite of them. "Erica," I said flatly, "all of the windows and doors up here are locked. The window in there has a rockery below it and two miles of open country beyond that, so it's simply not worth the effort."

"I know," she whispered.

"You've got everything I could think of in there—shampoo, conditioner, there's some nice coconut soap. You've got scrubs, moisturizers, a new toothbrush because you've somehow ruined the last one I gave you, and there are some little bottles of bath oil in there, too, if you like that sort of thing. That leg wax thing, I don't know if it's any good or not, but it's the best thing I could find without a blade in it. Oh, and there's a hairbrush in one of those bags. I forgot to hook it out. Okay?"

"Okay."

"If you want to have a shower afterward, make sure you pull the curtain round. And when you're done, come down and we'll find you some lunch. Enjoy."

"You're a sick bastard," she muttered as I gently closed the door.

CHAPTER
TWELVE

I was coating strips of rump in a honey and mustard glaze when I heard the crunching of tires on gravel. I wiped my fingers on an old tea towel and was at the front door in time to see Detective Inspector John Fairey swing his Extra Value Feet out of his dirty blue Ford. He stared at me in scornful amusement as he slammed his door, rounded the car and waited for his sidekick, Green, to get her sensible shoes into gear. She struggled free of her seat belt and followed two steps behind him as he marched toward the house. He quite clearly thought that I'd step aside and let him in; since it was pissing down, however, I stopped him with an unwelcoming glare just beyond the threshold of the wooden porch. He stood there expectantly, but he was getting nothing but wet until he showed some proper decorum.

I raised both eyebrows, tilted my gaze toward his breast pocket. He took the bait and raised his badge. I saw his badge and raised him a smile. He folded his wallet.

"Back so soon, Inspector?" I chirped. "What can I do for you today that I couldn't do yesterday?"

"Well, you can start by giving me a satisfactory explanation for what I've got in my pocket," he said.

I was ready for him this time. My eyes held steady. My face retained its color. The sky hung steadfastly in its designated place. "If you've got a rash," I informed him, "I can assure you it didn't come from me."

Green choked on a chuckle beneath the umbrella she'd silently raised behind his back. Fairey soldiered bravely on.

"Come inside?" he said. "I'm getting very wet." His hair was already flat against his head, every furl of his long gray coat a raging river. He looked thoroughly miserable, unlike Green, who had taken to biting the back of her hand.

"Yeah, why not?" I could think of a hundred reasons why not, but I articulated none of them.

He shook himself down and stepped past me into the hall. Green followed, folding her grin into her umbrella and shaking it out behind her. "Morning." She smiled, with just a hint of apology.

"Good morning, Sergeant Green. You should have let me know you were coming. Lunch is nowhere near ready, I'm afraid. I'm marinating."

"Sounds painful," she deadpanned.

"Can I get you anything? Tea? Coffee? Gin?"

"Actually, I wouldn't mind a glass of wa—"

"This is a criminal murder investigation," Fairey boomed, somewhat extraneously, "not a fucking tea party."

"Fuck." I chuckled, before I could stop myself. "Somebody

got out of the wrong side of the bed this morning. Are you going to let him talk to you like that?"

Green signaled her agreement via an exasperated shrug. Fairey scowled back at me, eyes half-closed, plainly biting his tongue and attempting to count to ten. I turned away from him to address his diminutive colleague.

"I'm sorry," I said, grabbing a glass tumbler from the draining board and rinsing off the suds. "What is it you wanted to talk to me about?"

"Well," she began, "in case you weren't aware, we've found Ke—"

"I'll ask the questions," Fairey barked, stunning her into openmouthed silence.

"Look," I said, "you've obviously had a shitty morning, but honestly, storming into my house with all guns blazing and effing and blinding at Sergeant Green is only going to make things worse, because I'm just going to refuse to talk to you."

His leg was beginning to twitch. I wondered, as I handed Green her glass of water, what it would take to make him tapdance. "No, you look," he snarled. "We've found Kerry Fallow's body, and g—"

"Farrow," Green correc—

"That's what I fucking *said*!" he snapped. "Now you'd better start talking, my friend," he continued, tearing a crumpled sheet of paper from his coat pocket and thrusting it under my nose, "because you're not looking too clever right now."

"What's this?"

"That," he proclaimed, "is from a camera at the quarry, a mile and a half from where Kerry disappeared and fifty yards away from where we found what's left of her last night."

"Sixty thousand," I said.

Fairey's voice faltered, and he glared at me for a split second before spitting, "What?"

"Sixty thousand," I repeated. "The number of these vans sold by Ford in this country every year." Behind Fairey, Green issued a vindicated nod that told me I wasn't the first to set off along this route. "And that one—" I indicated the grainy surveillance photo in his hand "—is not mine. But you knew that, didn't you? Otherwise you'd be dragging it onto a low-loader and carting it off to be dismantled. If you want to go out to the garage and play Spot the Difference, you're more than welcome." Smile just the right side of smug. "But you're barking up the wrong tree. It's an entirely different van." Nor, in fact, had they found Kerry's body, but of course, I couldn't very well tell him that.

His toe was tapping now, his fists clenched at his sides. "Fucking hell," he seethed.

I swung open the key cupboard and aimed the garage door opener out through the window. "Door's open," I said. "Take your time."

"I've had enough of this. You're trying to make a fucking mug out of me."

"You don't need my help with that," I said.

He ignored my remark and launched straight into it. "I'm arresting you on suspicion of the murder of Kerry Fallow."

Green shook her head disconsolately to herself. "Farrow," she muttered.

"You don't have to say anything," he continued, "but it may harm your defense if you fail to mention when qu—"

"You're an idiot," I replied. "That's what I have to say. Sergeant, please tell Inspector Clouseau that—"

My words hadn't struck me as particularly harsh, but they hit a nerve in John Fairey. *"Right!"* he growled as he made a desperate, red-faced lunge for my throat.

Green let out a gasp of "What the f—" and grabbed clumsily at his coat, catching nothing but air. I leaned into him and allowed him the satisfaction of grasping the collar of my shirt, fighting the temptation to hook my fingers into his throat and gouge out his windpipe.

Fortunately for both of us, Green found her feet and, with a cry of "John, for Christ's sake!," seized her seething superior by the back of the neck and hauled him clear. "Go and check the van," she commanded, holding his arms tight against his sides, her warm face suddenly hard edged and ice cold.

Fairey didn't move when she loosened her grip; he just stared, his bared teeth betraying the red mist before his eyes.

"The false accusation is enough," I said. "Please don't compound the issue by assaulting me."

"That's enough," Green insisted, plainly seeing right through my impression of wounded indignation. "John. Go. Walk it off. Now."

Slowly, deliberately, he let his shoulders drop, his hips slouch. The fire in his eyes flickered and subsided, and he strolled on out of the house without another word.

"I'm so sorry," Green said. "Are you okay?"

"Why is that man so angry?" I frowned.

"Being called an idiot probably has something to do with it, but I'm not going to make excuses for him."

"No," I said, "quite right. Not your job. He is an idiot, though."

"He's not stupid," she said. "Just overeager. He acts before he's got all his facts straight sometimes."

"Quite," I agreed, "which is hardly any way to solve a crime, is it? I don't know if he's trying to spring some sort of trap by pretending to be inept and telling me everything he knows or doesn't know, but either way, someone needs to make sure he never plays poker. And then they need to remind him that a picture of a random van doesn't constitute evidence linking me to whatever it is you've found."

Green opened her mouth to reply before a frown startled across her face. "What?" she said.

"What?"

"What do you mean?"

"What do..." Did I say something wrong? "What?"

"What do you mean, *whatever it is we've found*?"

"You said you'd found the girl's body."

"Are you suggesting we haven't?"

"No, I'm suggesting it has nothing to do with me."

"Because it's not Kerry Farrow?"

I laughed. Someone had to. "Because I haven't murdered her and dumped her in a gravel pit," I said.

She paused, choosing her words. It came as a pleasant surprise when she didn't ask me where I *had* dumped her. "John's convinced you've got something on your conscience where this case is concerned," she said.

That made me laugh even harder. "Moral man, is he?"

"No, but he *is* goal-oriented, and he thinks you're as creepy as hell. He's dying to find something that'll stick to you, so if you've got anything you want to get off your chest…"

I glanced out the window to see Fairey screw his photo into a ball and throw it angrily at the side of my van. "And what about you?"

"Me? I'm moral beyond reproach. Also entirely convinced you're up to something. Little bit behind on the *what*."

"Well—" I laughed "—as soon as you figure out what it is, be sure to let me know. I've been convinced I was up to something for years."

She nodded her assurance and said, "What are you cooking?"

"Venison."

She pursed her lips and wrinkled her nose; a shiver danced over her shoulders. "Bambi."

"Didn't feel a thing," I said as I dropped a sliver into the glaze, although judging by the skepticism on her face, I suspected I knew less about slaughtering deer than she did. "Now, is there anything else I can do for you, or have you finished with your little good-cop-bad-cop routine?"

She watched me for a moment, thoughtfully chewing her lip as though searching for some snappy comeback with which to punctuate her exit rather than face a self-conscious walk of shame to the car. When it came, though, her response intrigued me. "Just as long as you know who's who," she said.

And then, with barely pause to consider what the hell kind of game I was being sucked into, I watched in silent, stunned horror as she turned and walked right into Erica.

CHAPTER
THIRTEEN

Beeeep. "Hi, it's me. It's Rachel. I, um… Ha ha. Okay, you caught me out. I was kind of hoping you'd be in and have something devastatingly important to tell me so I wouldn't have to pretend to have a reason for calling. I'm not very good at talking to machines. Um… Well, okay, I probably have got a reason for calling but now that I'm under all this pressure to sound like I'm not completely out of my mind… Okay, now I feel silly. Is there a button here I can press and just delete this and start again? I guess if you're hearing this, there isn't. Um… Okay, you know what? Just delete this message. I'll call later. This is…Dave, by the way. Wrong number. Bye."

Beeeep. "Hi there. Hi. It's, um…it's me. Rachel. Hope you don't mind me ringing you out of the blue like this, totally unexpected and everything, and…never having rung you before. Look, I was thinking about going to see a band tonight—no one you'll have heard of, just some friends of mine—and the thing is, I've got a spare seat in the car if you haven't already made plans, so give me a ring if you fancy coming along. Thanks. Bye."

———————

Beeeep. "Okay, stupid, stupid. What I meant was, I'd really like you to come with me. If you want to. And I haven't actually got a car, but…well, I was going to get a taxi. Anyway, call me if you want to. Actually, call me, anyway. If I'm just being a sad moron, you can at least let me down gently. And why am I thanking you? God, I'm so…blonde. Okay, I'll… talk to you later. Bye."

———————

Beeeep. "Hi, Sal, it's me. Guess you're not in. I was just going to cry in your ear about being a socially stunted old spinst…er… Shit, I pressed Redial, didn't I? You know, you should get a machine you can record a proper message on and then this wouldn't have happened, and I wouldn't look so dreadfully inept. Shame on you. Goodbye."

O O O

"Hi, this is Rachel. I'm either not in or I'm screening my calls, in which case I'm ignoring you because you're tedious. Just kidding. Not really. Leave a message, and I might call you back."

"Hi, Rachel. You clearly *are* out of your mind, but no, I

haven't made other plans and yes, I'd love to come with you tonight. Let me know what time. Bye."

I slotted the carving knife back into the block. The whir of the hairdryer wafted down from the upstairs landing; a relentless mechanical drone, yet somehow calming in its everyday femininity.

I turned the meat.

○ ○ ○

My mother left her mark. A single, lonely footprint; a parting comment in grass and mud. Size five. I preserved it diligently, the doormat wrapped in a clear plastic bag and rehomed on top of the fridge. Occasionally I'd take it out and study it, as though searching for clues to her direction of travel. It didn't help.

The fridge was all but empty when she left. By the second day, I'd finished off the cheese and onion quiche. By the third, I was all out of roquette salad, and still hungry. The freezer gave up legs of lamb, backs of bacon, strings and strings of sausages, all of it useless in the absence of instruction. By the end of the fourth day, I was hungry enough to start learning.

Cordon Bleu cookbooks spread out across the kitchen table like the blueprints to a giant Airfix kit. My bedtime reading was the oven manual. Jars of herbs and spices lined up along the worktop, each one smelled and tasted, labels read aloud and committed to memory.

The sixth day was Christmas Day. On that day, I feasted on succulent roast turkey with chestnut and cranberry stuffing, steamed carrots and leeks and Brussels sprouts with mashed potato. I followed it with a traditional Christmas pudding soaked in brandy.

On the seventh day, I rested.

○   ○   ○

As you know, Bob, the psychopath doesn't have access to the same set of emotions as the rest of us. Things that you or I might find horrific or obscene—murder, say, or rape, or mutilation—he responds to no differently than he might the birth of an infant or the changing of a tire. He has no conscience, no mercy, and no fear save for that of capture and incarceration, which he'll go to any lengths to avoid. We're dealing with a man incapable of feeling, a man entirely devoid of any sense of humanity.

"Who the hell writes this shit?" Indignant, I switched off the television and tossed the remote to the far corner of the sofa. I looked to the bookcase for inspiration. I noted that it held a number of books. Some were narrow, others wide. They varied in color. My heart wasn't in this.

I listened to the rhythm of the rain as it tapped softly at the window. I gazed at my reflection in the blank television screen. I glanced at the clock. An hour had passed. I wondered what I'd been thinking about. I hadn't *felt* sleepy.

"I'm all done."

I'd been aware of a certain silence; I could hear the ticking of the kitchen clock, the distant crackle of the rain on the gravel driveway. I'd stared up through my eyelids at the ceil-

ing, dreaming of being asleep, telling myself I should probably wake up. When I did, I wasn't sure I had. There before
me stood an angel, resplendent in white chiffon, the long,
loose curls of her hair catching the hallway light and throwing it out around her in a dazzling halo. She gazed down at
me with curious eyes, her soft skin glowing, a vision of perfection but for three jagged clawmarks, long and dark and
bruised. "You look beautiful," I whispered.

"Special occasion. Might as well dress up."

"Did you find everything you needed?"

"For now."

I looked down at my prone body, making a cursory count
of arms, legs, fingers and toes, running a mental check for
any new ache or pain. I seemed in good shape. "You missed
a trick," I said. "Could have stabbed me through the heart,
and I'd never have woken up."

Erica offered a faint smile. "For that to work, you'd have
to *have* a heart." I rose stiffly, circled the sofa to face her. She
stood her ground, utterly still, following me only with her
eyes. "I take it you got rid of her?" she said flatly.

"Yes," I replied. "She's gone."

She nodded slowly, turned away from me as she sniffed
back a tear. "She recognized me, didn't she?"

"I think so, yes."

"You think so. That's terrific. I'm glad you made certain
you had a good reason before you fucking—"

"Erica, I—"

"Who was she looking for?"

"What?"

"Who was she looking for? It wasn't me, obviously. Was it Sarah? Kerry? Someone else?"

"I don't think it matters who sh—"

"You think she recognized me, though?"

"Probably," I conceded, "but you're someone else's case, and you're not headline news anymore. Maybe she put two and two together, but it doesn't matter. Too late. She's gone. They won't find you here again."

"Don't bank on it," she muttered. "And by the way—" she whirled around to face me again, her cheeks suddenly flushed with anger "—I know you probably think I'm stupid, and I suppose the fact that I'm still standing here mostly proves it, but in future there's really no need to wave a kitchen knife at me to make me behave, like I might have just started running around screaming. I really thought you were going to bleed her out in front of me, and all that does is make me fucking nervous."

"I wouldn't do something like that."

"Oh, no, of course not. You wouldn't want to make a mess in here, would you? God forbid you should get a speck of dust anywhere, never mind a drop of blood. What is this place anyway, some kind of freaky experiment? I mean, have you even *used* that bath before? No, you're right, it's much better to take her out back and shoot her in the fucking barn."

"Have you finished?"

"You know there's such a thing as friendly bacteria, right?"

"Erica, I'm going to give you one chance to calm down."

"And then what? You're going to take me outside and shoot me t—"

I knocked Erica to the floor with an open-handed slap

across her wounded cheek. Felt a blush of shame as she gasped aloud, threw a hand up to her face and sat stunned, staring openmouthed at her buckled knees. She was silent for a moment, slowly regaining her composure before she took hold of the arm of the sofa, folded her legs under her and pulled herself to her feet. A fat drop of blood trickled between her fingers, rolled down across the back of her hand. She glared up at me, shock and revulsion blazing in her eyes. She took in a deep breath, let it out in a long, deliberate sigh.

And then she slapped me back.

"Don't you *ever* fucking hit me," she roared, pounding the heels of her hands into my chest as I reeled in surprise. I grabbed both wrists; she kicked out at me, painfully hammering my shins as I slammed her back against the wall. "Get your fucking hands—" She hissed, clawed and spat, feet lashing wildly as I lifted her clean off the ground. She wrapped her legs around my waist, heels pounding the small of my back, fingers bunched into talons, teeth snapping as they lunged for my face. I pressed into her, fighting for balance, flattening her wrists against the wall above her with one hand, the other clamped under her chin, pinning her firmly in place. She bucked and writhed and growled, repeatedly kicking me in the kidneys until, in a matter of moments, her energy started to wane and the struggle gradually subsided. "You gonna fuck me now?" she spat. "Gonna rape me now, big man? Come on, motherfucker, let's get it over with. Let's do it, come on."

"Calm down," I told her.

Finally, the talons became fingers. She let her legs hang loosely around me. Her eyes softened in resignation.

"Just calm down," I said. I released my grip on her throat and she sucked in great, whistling lungfuls of air.

"The next time you hit me, I'll fucking kill you," she panted.

That seemed like a fair challenge to me. "The next time I hit you," I said, "you'll have left it too late."

"I'm glad we understand each other." She smiled, her lips mere inches from my own. Her hair brushed my face as she blew it from her eyes. "I'm okay now, you can let me down if you're not going to rape me."

I breathed in waves of vanilla, almond and coconut, a hint of mint and a delicate undercurrent of fresh, clean sweat. My cheek stung, my heart raced and the pit of my belly was a tense, aching knot. My legs, though, were holding up fine. "I didn't lay a finger on her," I said.

"No," she replied softly. "I thought not. And she'll be back, won't she?"

"Oh, she'll be back." I nodded. "I absolutely guarantee that."

◯   ◯   ◯

Beeeep. "About eight. No need to dress up. See you then."

◯   ◯   ◯

"I wonder if they know I'm still alive. I mean, really *know.* You see all these poor fuckers on TV, banging on about how they're not giving up hope, and they know she's out there somewhere, and they won't stop looking until she's back safe and sound and please bring her home, she doesn't deserve it, she's never done anyone any harm and all that crap. But it's all bollocks, isn't it? They always end up finding out she was dead before they noticed she was gone. It's funny. I had this conversation with my mum. I bet she's gone over *that* one once or twice in her head. Bastards have probably already buried me. They're obsessed. They buried my nan, even though she told them time and time again she wanted to be scattered off the pier at Eastbourne. My sister's probably moved into my room already. She was gutted when she found out I'd got a job and wasn't going to piss off to uni. She kept telling Mum to kick me out and make me get a flat, but apparently I'm so good at cleaning and babysitting that I'm not allowed to get a life of my own. Which just sets me up perfectly to live in a cage and mop up after whiny little bitches. Wow, you know what? I never realized how little my life has changed. In fact, it's almost better, 'cause now I don't have to get up and go to work every day. I should actually be thanking you. I mean, you feed and clothe me, you keep a roof over my head, you bring me nice friends to play with…and all I have to do is get punched in the face every now and again, and you don't even do that as hard as my stepdad used to, so that's just like a fucking holiday. And here I was, daydreaming that you'd just throw me the key and walk under a combine harvester… How fucking ungrateful can you get?"

"There, how's that?" A curved aluminum rail, secured by three brackets bolted through the walls and ceiling of the cage to steel plates on the outside. Two-inch wooden rings supporting a pair of lavender cotton curtains which, when drawn, enclosed the toilet and sink and provided privacy from the wall-mounted camera.

"I'm not sure about the color."

"I'll bring you some crayons."

"And of course, you've only got to walk around the side there and you can still see me."

"As I've told you a dozen times—"

"Yeah, yeah, I know, you're not interested in watching me wee."

"Fine, then."

"Good."

"Anything else you need?"

"Girls' things."

"Girls' things? What are girls' things? Ugg boots? My Little Pony? An *actual* pony?"

"No, *girls' th*—"

"What the hell are girls' th—"

"Oh, for fuck's sake, I'm due on, okay? And I'm not spending another week with toilet roll stuffed down my pants, so I need Always Ultra, medium flow in the green packet. They're right next to where you got all that smelly stuff. Seriously, don't even argue, it's inhumane."

Fair, I suppose. "I'll try and remember. And if you've learned to say 'please' by the next time I see you, I'll try even harder."

"God, you're as bad as my d—" she started, but didn't finish. I trawled up a suitable retort from somewhere, but felt strangely awkward about delivering it. After a brief but uncomfortable pause, she rolled her eyes and dismissed me with an impertinent wave. And then, as I opened the outer door to leave, she called out to me. "Wait," she said, "I forgot something."

I turned to her from the doorway, cell keys at the ready, fighting a sudden, curious urge to deny her the opportunity to damn herself. "What is it?" I snapped.

She hugged herself, looked away to the floor. "Thank you," she murmured. "For the clothes. They're lovely."

Again, I didn't know quite what to say.

CHAPTER
FOURTEEN

"That's just wrong." Rachel laughed as we stood side by side in the car park of the Rampant Rabbit, puzzling over the thought process involved in so naming a public house. "It looks a bit…seedy. I'll bet you anything you like it's full of dirty old men in grubby macs. They'll all stop talking and turn round and stare at us when we walk in."

It was certainly quiet; only the flickering of lights and the passing of shadows behind the stained-glass windows betrayed any sign of life. "I'm sure they'll only be staring at one of us," I remarked.

"Probably." She giggled, nodding toward the fluffy pink bunny depicted on the sign above the door. "But which one?"

"Good point," I agreed. "Whose idea was this again?"

"I'm sure it must have been yours."

"Would it be ungentlemanly of me to remember things differently?"

"Only if you say it out loud."

Bite bullet. Swallow hard. "Did I mention that you look stunning in that dress?"

"In that case, I forgive you." She clicked her heels together, straightened her back, let out a deep breath. "Ready?"

"In a do-or-die sort of way."

She hooked my arm, and we led one another across the wet mud and gravel to the pub door. I'd never imagined that such a gesture could come so naturally; in those few seconds, the alienation melted away unnoticed, and I felt nothing but content. It wasn't until we reached the door, and Rachel took a step back to study me, that my head fuzzed over and my insides fell heavy and my anxiety's absence was made conspicuous by its return.

"By the way," she said, smiling wryly as she looked me up and down, "may I just say that you look devilishly handsome tonight?"

I couldn't say for certain, but I'm pretty sure I blushed. "Behave yourself," I warned her. "My ego's a real handful when it's inflated."

"Rubbish." She laughed as she ushered me inside. "You're a puppy and you know it."

I knew right away that I was in trouble. It took a weighty shove to free the solid oak door, its thick rubber seal giving an exasperated sigh as it released a sonic onslaught into the damp evening air. No one stopped and stared as Rachel, wide-eyed, took my hand and led me into a maelstrom of strobe lights and bare female flesh.

The heat was intense, the noise almost palpable—the crackle of shouted conversation against a rapped vocal, a sampled Hermann film score and a floor-thumping bass track. And around us, the young and the restless in the throes of their lazy twenty-first-century courtship. Cocky young men in designer shirts and baseball hats, hell-bent on unleashing their rampant hormones at anything more animated than a tissue. Tight gaggles of teenage girls displaying acres of artificially tanned skin, their tender, supple flesh squeezed into push-up bras and hip-hugging skirts of immodest length. They thronged around the bar, seizing the opportunity to press themselves blamelessly against one another, eagerly jostling to allow the safe passage of the drink-laden, each benevolent undulation of the crowd a brief but exciting chance to hump a stranger's leg. And they say romance is dead...

"The snot'll slobbery pucker off when the blanket's tarted," Rachel reassured me. "They bony peel to the udder ache cloud."

This could be a long night. I bowed to an awkward stoop, my ear an inch from her lips.

"I said this lot'll probably bugger off when the band gets started. They don't appeal to the underage crowd, the teenagers."

I could only hope she was right; I was in grave danger of showing myself up as we carved a path to the bar through a smorgasbord of overapplied lip gloss, trowelled-on foundation, crumbling concealer. My throat tightened against the fog of cheap perfume, the sickly stench of mandarin, gardenia and honeysuckle. I closed my eyes, focused on the soft warmth of Rachel's hand, the brushing of her arm against mine. I blocked out the profane chatter and the absurd bellowing laughter and the repetitive demands from the speakers above my head to "gimme some more" and for a fleeting moment, we were blissfully alone, sharing a peaceful stroll along some distant sun-drenched shore, away from prying eyes and groping hands and moronic sovereign-fingered binge drinkers. White sand between our toes, breeze barely feathering our hair, we watched the early-morning sunlight sparkle on the water, gazed up at an endless clear blue sky and swayed to the perfect lullaby of gentle waves rippling onto the beach. And then she turned to me, stretched up on tiptoes to whisper in my ear.

"I think *you'd* better try," she shouted. "I'm never going to get served—the staff are all teenage girls."

The noose tightened.

———

"Oh, my God, look at the state of that." Rachel planted her elbows on the table and buried her face in her hands, peering out between her fingers at the horror that stood before her. "Seriously, if you had that much going for you, you'd keep it under wraps, wouldn't you? Don't look."

I looked. I agreed. I nodded.

"I said don't look! She knows we're bloody talking about her now. She keeps looking over here."

"Go tell her not to look, then."

"Wait, she's coming over."

"No, she isn't."

"I think she wants to talk to you. Wait…she's got a rose

between her teeth and a family pack of Durex. She's going to take you home and suffocate you between her enormous sweaty bosoms. God, and you managed that with just one little look. Imagine what you could pick up if you put your mind to it!"

"I shudder to think what I could pick up in here."

"I know. I actually put paper down *and* hovered when I wen— You probably don't need to know this."

"No, you're absolutely right. I might have to make my excuses if I begin to suspect you've got functioning kidneys." Deep, wincesome gulp of wine. "On the other hand, I do want to know everything there is to know about you."

"Oh, believe me, you don't want to know *everything*." She deliberately crossed her arms over her chest, leaned forward to rest them on the table. "Most of it's incredibly boring. My dad always used to say, 'If you've got it, flaunt it—and if you haven't, get back in your box.' And staying in the box doesn't make for great stories. Ask your new girlfriend over there, I'm sure she'll agree."

I resisted the urge to look this time. "I don't understand," I said. "What is it that you think you haven't got?"

"*It.*" She shrugged. "Much worth flaunting."

"So this whole long-sleeved, ankle-length thing you've got going on…" Her eyes dulled and darted away to the crossed cuffs of her dress. My own eyes had clearly betrayed the root of the question. Mayday. "What I mean is, I only have to look at you to want to flaunt you myself. God knows *I* don't have much I can brag about." Not in public, anyway.

A whimsical smile returned to Rachel's face, and she looked up and laughed, that electric blue sparkle coursing through me, lighting up my nerve endings. "Well, I suppose that explains why we're both sitting here," she mused. "Because I've known you two days, and I'd kind of like you to flaunt me, too."

The silence between us, as I racked my brain for a suitable response, was blissful. Maddeningly, the band disagreed.

———————

Conversation thereafter was near impossible. The ear-blistering barrage of sleazy funk-rock was intrusion enough, but as the band settled into their performance, so the more drunkenly lithe among the crowd filled the makeshift dance floor. By the end of the first set, the rhythmic writhing of bare female flesh had brought my mind into sharp focus. I looked at Rachel, smiling inquisitively as she held my hand across the table. She offered me some pot. I declined. She shook her head and leaned in close. "I said it's so hot," she yelled. Relieved, I agreed.

I took stock. Saturday evening, nine forty-eight. Sitting at a sticky and unsteady table in a room full of Wonderbra cleavage and naked thighs, hand in hand with a spellbound stranger, a persistent ringing in my ear. The feeling was suddenly no longer a comfortable one. The fluttering in my stomach was gone, replaced by a gripping, itching anxiety. I felt my free hand begin to tremble, my right knee bouncing out of control beneath the table. Rachel was still talking, still laughing, her comments presumably punctuated by my own; they registered only as waves of distant sound. The intriguing tingle at the base of my spine gave way to a knot of tension, already unraveling, tendrils creeping slowly but surely up my back toward my brain.

"…fuck me while you drink my blood." Rachel rolled her eyes and laughed at her own lack of foresight. Mercifully, I knew what she meant.

My buxom admirer hovered at the periphery of my vision, chancing frequent furtive glances in my direction. At the opposite corner, the close, shouted conversation between a bottle-tanned peroxide blonde and her bling-soaked beau was growing increasingly animated by the second. Puffed chests and violent hand gestures signaled impending fireworks and, sure enough, within seconds she was on her feet and reaching for the nearest full glass.

I gave Rachel's knee a gentle squeeze and mouthed the words "be right back" through an approximation of a carefree smile. From earlier investigation, I knew that the corridor leading to the toilets led also, by way of a twist and a turn and a fire escape, to an alley at the corner of the car park. I passed the couple's table as the blonde dropped her empty glass into the lap of her cider-soaked friend, snatched up her bag and staggered through me with a token slurred "Sorry, mate." I smiled falsely at her back, submissively raised my hands and slipped out of sight into the corridor.

I rested the fire door on the latch and bolted from the alley. The blonde had paused, swaying in the glow from the windows, engaged in a struggle with the contents of her bag as I stalked briskly to the van. Happily, when she withdrew her hand it held a set of car keys, and she embarked upon a zigzag swagger across the gravel toward me, and variously toward other things. I opened up the rear of the van and retrieved the syringe wedged behind the top of the ply-lining, flicking off the rubber cap and coiling for the strike as she passed by without so much as a glance.

She knew I was there, though. Her neck stiffened. Her grip on the keys tightened. She staggered in a circle as her focus shifted. "Whathefuckayoulookenat?" she drawled. And then she fell over.

Reflexively, I clamped the syringe between my teeth and scooped her up out of the dirt, hauled her about-face and propelled her into the back of the van. She slid the length of the floor and connected solidly with the bulkhead. Flopped like a mop, all splayed arms and legs and hair. A nice choice of veins ready to receive a light dose of etorphine. Hard part done.

Except, that wasn't the hard part. The hard part was what came next. I squirted the excess out of the syringe and tucked it back in its place, and I unhooked the two load straps closest to the bulkhead, and I stared down at my feeble prey lying cock-eagled on the floor, and I felt all of the craving, all of the desperate, clawing need simply evaporate. Abruptly, everything in my head was Rachel, everything in my gut was regret and everything at my feet was a ridiculous, unfathomable error of judgment.

"Shit," I noted, shameful bile rising in my throat. "Great dating skills, dickhead."

I could still undo this. Maybe the knots in my belly, too, if I was quick. Just leave her where she fell and let her soggy boyfriend scrape her up when he was ready. I bent and took an ankle in each hand, dragged her back toward the doors. "I'm sorry," I informed her. "I'm not myself tonight. You're very sweet, and I know it's cold out but, you know…three's a crowd and all that."

And so is fourteen—the approximate number of noisy hoodlums who chose that precise moment to spill out into the car park for a smoke.

"Bollocks," I said, in summary.

○   ○   ○

"I'm sorry I wasn't a lot of fun tonight." I was more relaxed as I threaded the van between pitch-black rows of towering pines, watching the headlights cut a hazy path through the mist.

Rachel was certainly more relaxed; she'd matched me three for one on wine and was resting her head against the cold, damp window with closed eyes and a soft smile. "Don't be silly," she said, her voice lilting with tired contentment. "I had a good time. I'm just sorry the place was such a dive."

"It was only a dive until you walked in." Christ. *Come here often? What's a nice girl like you doing in a place like this? Your legs must be tired 'cause you've been running through my mind all ni—*

"Ugh!" She threw her head back into a fit of giggles that proved unavoidably infectious.

"Sorry, I have no idea who just said that." I laughed. "I'm either a terrible lounge lizard or Tony Bennett's crawled in the back while we weren't looking."

"If it's Tony, I hope he doesn't think he's staying at mine tonight."

"No, no strangers in parad—" Shit. My punchline was cut short by a hump in the road; the ensuing lurch brought about a heavy slap on the bulkhead behind us, followed a beat later by an almighty crack and a wet-sounding thump that I felt through the heels of my shoes.

Rachel bolted upright, shot me an anxious look. "What the fuck was that?" she muttered.

I didn't need to fake a concerned expression. "I'm not sure I want to know."

She removed her seat belt and clambered to her knees, pressing her ear against the thinly upholstered wall behind her seat as I looked out for a place to stop. Within yards the grass verge gave way to the mouth of a logging trail, and I pulled carefully off the road, swinging the back of the van in to face the trees. "Stay in here and lock the doors," I instructed her, hooking out a penlight from the glovebox. "I'll be right back."

"Wait." She gripped my arm, fixed me with a terrified stare. "What if… What if it *is* Tony Bennett?"

"Put on a happy face," I said. "He knows *the rules of the road.* If I find him stowing away back there *in the wee small hours of the morning,* he'll *touch the earth* with his face. It certainly won't be the start of *a beautiful frien*—never mind." I swung my door open and stepped out into the cold.

"Poor Tony. Oh, well, *easy come, easy go.*"

"Well played." I could have watched her laugh all night, but, "Lock the door." I slammed it shut, and was alone in the darkness. The fog had settled and thickened, an impenetrable wall circling not twenty feet away. The air was heavy, damp, silent but for the sharp echo of my footsteps; they followed me as I walked to the back of the van, squinting into the mist for any sign of movement, my ears alert to the cracking of twigs, the rustling of leaves. I stood for a moment, my back to the doors, willing the creatures of the night to betray their presence. But there was nothing. Satisfied that I was alone, I turned and unlatched the door.

The bad news was that two of my load hooks had snapped, and the load was no longer secure.

The good news: Tony was nowhere in sight, and the blonde was out like a light.

———————

"That was a lot of clunking around!" Rachel scooted over from unlocking my door. "Find any fare-dodging crooners back there?"

"Sadly, no. Just an upside-down toolbox."

"Shame. We could've had a *moonlight serenade*." She peered out at the gray blanket enveloping the van. "If there was any moonlight."

"I could sing, of course, but historically it hasn't been pretty."

She smiled and returned to her restful pose against the window. "In that case," she said, "let's go home. We can dance naked through the trees another time."

"I definitely want to do that." I smiled, making a mental note to clear my schedule as I steered the van back onto the road and left the blonde to sleep off the lesser of two evils behind a holly bush.

CHAPTER
FIFTEEN

Sunday dawned with the fairy-tale splendor of a child's painting; a ragged patchwork of red and pink and orange blazed across an endless blue-black sky dotted with shimmering stars and cotton-wool clouds. I watched the sun rise over the trees; listened to the distant call of a cuckoo as I sat in the garden with my tea, breathing the sweet scent of honeysuckle and remembering Rachel's good-night.

I'd stopped in front of her building, and she'd invited me inside. I'd fought my temptation and declined, albeit unable to hide my immediate regret. She'd smiled happily to herself as though I'd passed some unwritten test. She'd expressed her wish to see me again soon. And then she'd slid across the seat, squeezed my hand and kissed me softly on the cheek. The feeling of warmth was unprecedented and exhilarating, and I wanted it again, and again, and again and again and again, and was this what all those songs were talking about?

The sun burned away the clouds as it rose, painting the sky a glorious Wedgwood blue and warming my skin as I rolled the Jensen out of the garage and commenced battle with its new wiring loom, whistling while I worked and generally marveling at the beginnings of a perfectly beautiful day.

I should have guessed, then, that at eleven o'clock, Detective Sergeant Green would show up and ruin it.

"What a rare pleasure," I said with a welcoming smile as she stepped from the backseat of the BMW before it had come to a full stop. The cheap suit was gone, in its place a more reassuringly casual ensemble. Her top was tastefully cut, but willing to ride up an inch or two as she slammed the door behind her. Her jeans sat on shallow hips and ended several inches above her sneakers. Contrary to my earlier assessment, she had ankles. "We must stop meeting like this," I said. "Familiarity breeds contempt, or so they say."

"Hence DI Fairey's staying in the car," she said.

The privacy glass at the rear of the BMW rendered Fairey little more than a silhouette, but I could see enough to know that he was honoring me with a single-fingered salute as I peered in at him.

"I take it you've got a minute?" she added, redundantly.

"For you, always." I gritted my teeth. "Who have I murdered this time?"

She turned to the car and smiled thinly at the pair of tailored suits emerging from the front seats. "This is Detective Chief Inspector Lowry," she said, indicating the shorter of the two men. Fortysomething, hadn't shaved in a week, slight trace of a limp. Weathered face with what I guessed was a permanent expression of impatience. "And Detective Sergeant Diaz." Mid-thirties, well-groomed and filled his suit better. Walked with a slight bow to his legs, probably from riding a large motorcycle. He didn't look like the horsey type. Nor remotely Portuguese, for that matter. "Major Investigation Team," she concluded.

Fuck. Funny word, that. So gloriously versatile, and yet so meaningless as a result. I distinctly remember my father, on slicing through his thumb with a bandsaw, proudly honoring the word by using almost every variation in a single outburst. "Oh, fuck me!" he exclaimed. "Shirley, get me a fucking bandage! Shirley? For fuck's sake, where the fucking fuck… Well, find the fuckers! I don't give a fuck what you're doing—look at my thumb, I've fucked it right up! Owww, *fuck it!*"

Anyway, "Very pleased to meet you," I lied, politely. Lowry took my extended hand and shook it more energetically than his demeanor might have led me to expect. "Likewise," he said, throat full of gravel, accent distinctly Home Counties.

Diaz's shake was tauter, more powerful. "Morning." He smiled, revealing a missing incisor and nothing about his genealogy.

"Do you know why we're here?" Lowry asked, presumably hoping I might save him some time and confess.

"I'm afraid I don't," I replied, giving them each my best attempt at hope-I-can-help bemusement. "What can I do for you?"

Lowry, expressionless, flipped a glossy seven-by-five print from his jacket pocket and angled it in front of me. Shapeless black blazer, forced smile, blue velour drape. School portrait. "We're investigating the disappearance—" it was an altogether different feeling, almost reassuring, knowing where the sentence was going this time, even if forewarned did not necessarily equal forearmed "—of Erica Shaw and Sarah Abbott—" a second photo slid out from behind the first, with all the pizzazz of a cheap card trick "—both of whom have been missing since February."

This was awkward. Green certainly knew the identity of the half-dressed urchin she'd encountered yesterday; indeed, she took a peek at the picture and then, just to emphasize my predicament, nodded to Lowry and in turn to me with an almost playful explain-that smile. Denial, therefore, was not an option, unless I wanted to spend the remainder of the morning in the back of an unmarked car, waiting for the rest of the force to come and dig up the garden.

The other option, facilitated by the revolver hidden in my waistband, was to take more affirmative action and do the digging elsewhere. Which would lead, inevitably, to a similar conclusion.

After a moment's deliberation, I chose the third: don't try to hide the recognition; display slow-dawning confusion; express innocent alarm. "Missing?" I whimpered, perhaps overplaying the meekness a little since it raised one of Green's eyebrows quite noticeably.

"Do you recognize either of those girls?" she asked.

"Well, obviously," I replied, pointing to Erica's portrait. "Else you wouldn't be asking. What did you say her name was?"

Green rolled her eyes and quietly shook her head, seemingly having heard this one before.

"Shaw," said Lowry. "Erica Shaw."

"She told me it was Mary," I muttered. "I suppose you're going to tell me she's fifteen, as well?"

The chief snapped the photos back into his pocket with a

flourish. "She's not fifteen." He smiled. "But apparently she *is* alive and well, which makes it all the more imperative that we talk to her. Is she here?"

I took *here* to mean *here among us in the driveway*, so there was a valuable ring of truth to my "No, I'm afraid she's not."

"How well do you know her?" Diaz. West Country, maybe?

"She told me her name was Mary," I repeated.

Green bowed her head to hide a wry grin.

Diaz tried again. "How *long* have you known her?"

I forced my eyes top-left and my hands by my sides and did some quick mental arithmetic. "About thirty-seven hours," I guessed.

Green was the only one whose lips didn't move when she counted. She was also the first to arrive at the answer, but she kept quiet and let Lowry work it out for himself.

"Nine o'clock, Friday evening," he deduced. Give the man a lollipop. "And, what, you met socially, or…?"

Yes, socially sounds good. Feel free to prompt me all you like. "I met her in Murphy's," where the students pass through three hundred at a time, no one stays for more than one drink and all the girls look exactly the same. Because no one's looking at their faces. "Two bottles of wine and I'm anybody's. Dark bar, short skirt…you know what it's like."

Lowry's hands wandered to meet front and center, fingers furtively turning his wedding ring as he blankly shook his head.

Green chewed her lip introspectively.

Diaz nodded. "So she stayed here Friday night, and then what?"

"And then I took her to the bus station, and she went home."

"Home being...?"

"...where she lives," I confirmed. "A dwelling of some kind. A house, maybe, or a flat." All three fixed me with an impatient stare. "I don't know," I said. "In the city somewhere."

"Okay." Lowry nodded. "When are you seeing her again? Maybe you've got a number for her?"

"No, apparently if I can't call her, I can't call her at the wrong time. Which is another way of saying I'm a disappointment when sober."

"Convenient."

"Yes, for her." I might just get away with this.

Might.

Lowry looked up at the house, across to the barn, behind him to the garage. "So, like you said, no reason to assume she's here right now..."

I laughed. "I'm not keeping her chained up in the basement, if that's what you mean."

Green glanced round at the house, narrowed her eyes. "Basement?" she mused.

"I don't have one," I said. "You're welcome to have a look around, though," I suggested, urgently mentally ransacking the place to make sure I meant it. "I'm sure DS Green has some curiosity she'd like to satisfy, too. Perhaps she could, um...kill two birds...?"

She studied my face, swallowing a game smile.

"Trust me," I said, none too subliminally, "I really don't mind. My house is your house. Door's open. The garage opener and the van keys are on the hook in the hallway. Beer in the fridge. Knock yourselves out."

Green and Diaz stood in silence for a moment, eyes boring tunnels into me as Lowry nodded in pensive approval. Finally, the inspector turned to his sergeant and commanded, "Come on, Eli. Get that twat out of the car and let's get this over and done with."

I wished I could share his optimism.

○   ○   ○

"I'd like to apologize again for DI Fairey's behavior yesterday," said Green, returning to her scrutiny of my face once the murder detectives were out of earshot. "I just hope you're not one to hold a grudge, because those guys need all the help they can get, and I'd hate to think we'd shot ourselves in the foot where Sarah Abbot's concerned. This isn't a trivial matter."

"I agree entirely," I assured her.

"Then why," she asked matter-of-factly, folding her arms across her chest and leaning casually against the car, "did you just string us a line of utter bullshit?"

She had a strong poker face, I'll give her that. I erred on the side of caution and gave a simple, "What do you mean?"

"Oh, come on," she groaned. "Bit of a coincidence, isn't it? Girl goes missing for two months, presumed murdered, and I just happen to find her in your house, where I'm questioning you about—what was it?" She propped her chin in mock deliberation. "Oh, yeah. Kerry Farrow, missing, presumed murdered."

"Hey, that's not fair," I reminded her. "You said yourself that prostitute business was a stitch-up."

"No, I bloody didn't!" she gasped. "A product of unreliable information, maybe, but we don't just pluck names out of a hat. I'm not *that* fond of paperwork! You know—" she waggled a correctional finger "—I'm a lot more straightforward than you give me credit for. Protect the innocent, serve the public trust, uphold the law. Like Robocop, only less... metally."

"Isn't that what you all say?" I laughed.

"Probably," she replied. "But whatever, now we know she's alive, Erica's got some serious questions to answer, not least of which is how often she goes out drinking with a dressing gown and curling tongs."

Oh, shit. Since even I hadn't believed a word I'd said, I'd fully expected her to find a hole in the plot. This was a chasm, though, and she filled it with a glare to wither a charging bull.

"And," she continued, "I'm sure if you think those questions through, you'll see sense and help us out, because hiding her makes you complicit either in something she did or something she knows, and whichever it is, it's going to land you in a whole heap of shit. I know you know more than you're saying, and I know you don't want to cause yourself any unnecessary problems, so you'd better start playing along before anyone gets the wrong idea about you. Or before you get yourself hurt."

I gave her a purse-lipped nod I hoped was compliant but nonconfessional. "Of course." I smiled. "I'll help you in any way I can."

Green didn't reply. Her stern expression didn't falter. She

stood stone still, her eyes fixed on mine, and I was dimly aware that she was waiting me out. It took me a good ten seconds to catch up.

"Wait," I said, and when she took a breath I realized she hadn't been doing that, either. "What do you mean, *get myself hurt*?" No reply. "*Something she did?* Are you telling me you think she killed her friend?"

Green gave me a tight shake of the head and said, "I'm not telling you any such thing." She glanced over her shoulder, satisfied herself that we were alone. "I *am* telling you," she told me, "that not being convicted of stabbing your stepfather with a pair of scissors isn't the same thing as not having done it."

I was getting used to the stomach flip of doom by now, but the brain freeze was a new one on me. "I'm…" I'm…I'm what, surprised? Really? "I'm sorry," I stuttered, "she did what?"

"Right in the arse, just after he broke her mum's nose. A temporary derangement of the mind, the witch doctor said." She shrugged. "Far be it from me to second-guess him, but I think it's only right that you know." *Just enough rope to hang yourself.* "I've only got your best interests at heart," she said, smiling unconvincingly.

I blew out a cartoonish sigh of relief. "Right," I said, without any hint of sarcasm whatsoever. "So you really are the good cop, then."

She gave a cynical half laugh and offered me a Lucky Strike. "Shades of gray, big man," she said. "Shades of gray."

CHAPTER
SIXTEEN

"When's your birthday?"

"Pardon?"

"Your birthday." Erica took my empty plate from the table and placed it beside her own on the countertop. "When is it?"

"It was three weeks ago. Why?"

She scraped her leftover beans and bacon rind into the bin. "You didn't mention it."

"I didn't see that it was relevant."

"What did you get?"

"What?"

"What did you get for your birthday?"

I swallowed the last of my tea, suspicious as to where the question was leading. Specifically, I suspected I was in for another round of abuse. "Nothing springs to mind," I said.

"What, you mean you can't remember, or you actually got nothing for your birthday?"

"I didn't get anything, no."

She carefully set the plates in the sink, staring morosely in after them. "That's depressing," she said.

"Not really, I'm used to it."

"That's even more depressing."

"Is there a point to this?"

Erica shrugged as she turned on the taps. "Not really," she conceded. "Only that, since you're the last person I'm ever going to see, I suppose it'd be quite nice to know a bit more about you." She slashed her hand through the running water, hissed in a breath, opened the cold tap a touch. "I'm sure you can't blame me for being curious. I mean, it's just you and me now, right? And I'm pretty sure neither of us knows how long I've got to enjoy it." She looked over at me with an unexpected smile. "I know what the date is, you know. How long I've been here. It's funny, I can remember the hour before I met you like it was this morning, but it feels like I've been here years, not weeks." She laughed at the thought as she squirted detergent into the sink; she watched the bubbles rise for a moment before turning off the taps and flicking the scourer sponge into the water. "And the worst thing is, I literally walked right into that detective yesterday, and I just smiled sweetly at her like I didn't have a care in the world. And of all the stupid things, I did it entirely for her. I'm going to spend the rest of my life in a cage, just so you wouldn't cut the head off someone I don't even know." She chuckled to herself as she savagely scrubbed the plates. "Funny, I suppose I'm better off in here in that case. I'm hardly going to get far in life with survival skills like that, am I?"

"Don't talk crap," I said. "There's no such thing as a selfless act. You did it for yourself, not for her—you did it so you wouldn't have to take responsibility for what might happen to her. You knew you had no choice and look, you're still standing here. You never know, maybe the odds'll be stacked in your favor next time."

"Is this just a game to you?" She slammed a plate into the drainer and whirled around to face me, spraying suds across the floor. "Because, you know, disappearing back upstairs like a good girl and listening to the only person who's ever likely to find me just get into her car and drive away really doesn't feel like a game to me. And let's just talk about this *next time*, shall we? I don't think you ever planned for me to be here this long. Is that right?"

I hadn't realized it was quite that obvious. "What makes you say that?"

"I'm glad you asked me. Since I've been here, you've made three alterations to my room. You've installed a microwave so I can feed myself, a curtain so I can wash myself in private and a camera so you can watch me wee without having to keep walking backward and forward across the drive all day. And more to the point, I've just watched Kerry come and go in the space of what, a week? And yet, like you said, I'm not only still standing here but you've gone out and bought me a whole new wardrobe. For all I know, I could still be standing here when I'm eighty, and whether that's preferable to you just wringing my neck and being done with it...well, I really don't know. Have you finished your tea?"

"Yes."

"Well, I'd suggest you bring me your mug if you want it washed. It won't walk over here on its own."

I couldn't be bothered to argue.

———————

Erica went ahead and cleaned the whole kitchen. I watched her from the table as she scrubbed down the cupboards, scoured the oven, swept and mopped the floor. She worked in silence, without so much as a resentful glance in my direction. When she was done, she let her shoulders drop with a satisfied sigh and a muttered, "There."

I didn't know what to say. I imagined I should thank her, though I was mildly confused as to why; after all, I hadn't asked her to do it. Fortunately, she took the burden from me.

"I guess I'll go back to bed," she said. "Unless there's anything else you want me to do."

I was sure the sensible thing would have been to agree, but I was overtaken by a strange impulse. "Actually," I replied, "there is. I'd really like you to go through to the sitting room and make yourself comfortable. I'll be there in a minute."

She narrowed her eyes in suspicion. "When you say *comfortable*—"

"I mean take a seat, put your feet up, relax."

She was clearly unconvinced, but did as I'd asked.

When I followed her a moment later, it was with a reasonable Rioja and two crystal glasses. I found her perched precariously at the very edge of the sofa, her hands clasped in her lap. She was perfectly still, following me with her eyes the way a mouse watches a circling hawk. I opened the bottle, habitually leaving the cork on the screw, and filled both glasses before sinking into the armchair at her side.

"What's this?" She frowned.

I took in her uneasy pose, her look of indignation and uncertainty, and forced a smile. "Erica," I said, "I'd like to ask you something."

She raised a quizzical eyebrow. "If you're about to propose…"

I stifled a laugh. "Well, I was going to, but now we're sitting here, and you're giving me icy hostility, I'm thinking I'll save it for another day."

"Probably for the best. You know I'm way out of your league."

I smiled as I watched her sitting there, nervously clacking her nails together, her eyes wandering to the wineglass on the table. Ah, the hell with it. "To answer your question, I don't have the kind of relationship with anyone that might inspire them to mark my birthday," I said.

Her perplexity was more than apparent. "I can't imagine why that might be," she quipped.

"It doesn't depress me that I don't get birthday presents. I've got all the material things I want. Although I'd maybe like to have received a card, just to show that someone, somewhere was thinking about me. I don't care who, just someone whose first name isn't Detective."

"Are you serious?" She looked nothing short of stunned.

"Erica, believe it or not, sometimes it's tiring being the only one who gives me any thought."

"Well, if it's any consolation, I'm sure *I* was thinking about you on your birthday."

"Yes," I said, smiling, "but you were only thinking about whether to go for my eyes first, or start with a kick in the balls."

"Yeah, that about covers it." She laughed. "Just so you know, I've decided to go with both at once, in a kind of pincer movement." She took a sip of her wine, cradled the glass in her hands as she tucked her feet under her and settled back into the sofa.

"That'd probably do it," I agreed. I was instantly certain I'd live to regret that remark, though I immediately trumped myself with my next offer. "Okay," I said, "what else do you want to know?"

She studied me for several long moments, amusement writ large across her face. "What, anything?" she asked finally, her voice tinged with doubt.

"Yeah, why not? Anything you like."

"All right, then," she replied, her smile fading in a heartbeat. "Why?"

"Why what?"

"You know what. Why this? Me, Sarah, Kerry…?"

Perhaps *anything* was too strong a word. "Low self-esteem and an Oedipus complex," I suggested.

"Oh, come on, you can do better than that."

"Yes, probably, but you're missing the point. You said you wanted to get to know me better, not psychoanalyze me."

"Well, what the hell do you expect me to say? 'What's your favorite color?'"

"If I'd known I was going to have to come up with the questions as well as the answers…"

"Fine," she snapped. "Forget it. I obviously don't have a

right to know what's going to happen to me or what I've done to deserve it…"

"And who does? Think about what you're saying, Erica. Those are two of mankind's greatest unanswerables—'why am I here, and how long for?' You're hardly unique in not getting to the bottom of them."

"No, you're right, I'm not. But then I'm not out in the big wide world wondering whether I'll get hit by a bus tomorrow, either. Don't try telling me this is some potted version of real life in here because it's exactly the fucking opposite. There's only one variable here, and that's you." She punctuated her point by draining her glass, then reached sternly over to the table and refilled it. "Fuck it," she concluded. "At least I know I'm *not* going to get hit by a bus tomorrow."

"That much I can promise you," I replied.

She took on a certain calmness then, releasing a heavy sigh into her wine and regarding me with dark curiosity. "Can I ask you a question about Sarah?" she said softly.

Absolutely unquestionably no. "Yes."

She hesitated, furrowed her brow in concentration as though playing the words over in her mind. When she opened her mouth to speak, they tripped on her tongue. Finally, she closed her eyes, took a breath and forced them from her lips. "Did she suffer?"

I flirted with the idea of diverting the question, but quickly surmised that there was no sense in avoiding the issue; after all, Erica was an eyewitness. I was, however, taken roughly by surprise and left more than a little perplexed by the tact of my own response. "No," I assured her. "She never even knew I was there."

O   O   O

As Erica drained glass after glass, so her line of questioning wavered to the point at which she simply wanted to be told something she didn't already know. As the afternoon progressed, she became increasingly captivated and enthralled by tales of my various adventures across Europe and the Balkans. The abridged versions, naturally.

When she returned to her room at dusk, she was staggering drunk, cackling raucously at each misplaced step and leaving a trail of travel books dropped from the bundle clutched haphazardly to her chest. She was immediately horizontal on the bed, watching the room spin, clawing at her clothes in an aimless attempt to remove them. I saved her hapless fumbling and helped her with the buttons; she graciously and passively accepted my assistance, albeit while giggling her way through such choice phrases as "Fuck off, I hate you," and "You're a sick bastard and I hate you," and "I hate you so much it makes me wet as a fucking otter's whatever," and "If you touch my tits, I'll kill you." Happily, she was lucid enough to roll herself under the covers, and was asleep before I closed the door on her day.

My mood was briefly light as I strolled back into the house. Once inside, however, I was grateful for the return to peace and quiet, since it afforded me the opportunity to contemplate the first phase of my acquittal.

CHAPTER
SEVENTEEN

I don't know what I expected from Annie: wariness, probably, or the door slammed in my face, or at the very least some small spark of surprise behind her vodka-frosted eyes. Had I afforded the question anything like careful consideration, then given the early hour I might most reasonably have expected to find her asleep, or perhaps steaming off the scent of some unsuitable suitor. But no.

Annie was on the telephone, a bulky, old-fashioned cordless handset tucked into the crook of her neck, interrupted words fidgeting impatiently on her lips. She was carrying two mugs of tea in one hand, and she passed one to me with barely a glance as she stepped aside to passively invite me in. Then her back was turned, and she was pacing off across her average little living room, as gray as the average ghost in her average leggings and her average cardigan, ruffling up the corner of her average hearth rug with her average furry slippers.

"I don't understand," she said.

She wasn't the only one. I sniffed cautiously at the tea, wondering just how long I'd been procrastinating inside her garden gate before scraping together the courage to knock at the door. Long enough for her neighbors to report me as a prowler? Hopefully not. Long enough for them to register my presence? That could work, I thought, although it did raise the unattractive prospect of having to explain Annie to Rachel should this whole scheme go tits-up. The mug, meanwhile, was hot, and its contents smelled like...well, tea. I dropped my keys onto the tall table beside the door and perched on Annie's settee. It was plush and welcoming and well-sprung. The last time I'd been in this house, with Annie tucked in her bed and dead to the world, I'd spent all of my willpower fighting the temptation to curl up on these cushions and dream away the dregs of a disastrous evening. In retrospect, not crossing paths with Kerry Farrow would certainly have spared me the stress and inconvenience of this ridiculous situation; an appealing prospect were it not for Rachel, the inevitable price of my good sense. A time machine and a blanket would serve only to erase her from my life, and I wasn't sure that was an entirely fair trade.

"My niece," Annie announced, idly waving the phone at me. "She's fucking high. Listen..." She fumbled with the speaker button, and then set the handset on the coffee table to let her barely adolescent-sounding niece speak for herself while she sipped her tea:

"...it's just what Amy says, although she doesn't like foreigners anyway, but then I'm not likely to get eaten by a shark in a swimming pool, either, but I still couldn't go in one for ten years after I watched *Jaws*, even though no one actually got eaten in a swimming pool in *Jaws*, they were all in the sea, and thinking about it, I *did* go in the sea in Australia, and there was a boy I got off with called Brad who worked at the beach bar, who reckoned his uncle got bitten by a shark while he was *in a boat*, which I didn't really believe, but *that* happened in *Jaws*, as well, although apparently if they *do* bite you they hardly ever eat you because humans taste fucking horrific to them, which is all well and good, but I'd rather they found that out by biting someone else, like Brad, actually, because he stole all my travelers' checks, so it was a pretty shit holiday in the end, apart from not getting eaten by a shark, and then so anyway, we were in the McDonald's, and then I was in a car, I think, or maybe a van, I'm not sure, but it was bumpy, and we were like…kept turning left, because I think we got lost, and then somehow we ended up at the beach and it was three in the morning, and Lucy didn't have her top on and these two creepy-looking guys were standing in front of her and she was jerking them off in—"

"Jesus Christ." Annie snatched up the phone from the table and darted away to the kitchen with such startling speed that I expected to see her outline in dust where she'd been standing. I drank my tea, which was lower in sugar and stronger in flavor than I'd normally have brewed for myself, and muffled the cacophony of horror from the kitchen beneath my own dizzying reflections on the terrors of being in any way responsible for the welfare of a vulnerable young woman.

It was the work of a fleeting moment to conclude that I didn't have anything resembling a long-term plan for Erica, nor was I going to formulate one with Annie making all that noise, and so I gave up trying to think and counted her Wade Whimsies instead.

———————

There was silence for a long minute after the shouting stopped. Finally, Annie stalked out of the kitchen, her jaw set, the corners of her eyes lined and red. She snatched my empty mug from the table and retreated; I listened to the roar and bubble of the kettle, the jangle of the spoon, the dry sniff and the hitch in her breath as she forced a deep sigh and counted to ten. I counted with her. When she reappeared, there was a calmness in her face and a sashay in her walk. She set my tea gently in front of me and folded herself into the armchair opposite, girlishly tucking her legs under her and cradling her mug protectively in her lap.

She regarded me curiously for a long moment. Then, "The police came," she said, matter-of-factly. "They were asking questions about you—did I know you, *how* did I know you, when had I seen you, had you been here, when did you leave, where did you go…" She paused, gave an expectant shrug; I opened my mouth to respond but she cut me off. "I told them what I knew. I said you were my knight in shining armor, that you saw me being mugged and came running to save me. I said I thought the little cockchops was after my iPhone, not that he'd tried to rape me, 'cause, you know, the last thing I needed was the fucking Spanish inquisition. So I said you drove me home because I was shaken up, we had a couple of drinks and you took me to bed. I told them I didn't know when you'd left, and I hadn't heard from you since, and you didn't make me any promises, either." She blew across the top of her mug and sipped her tea. "It was the best I could do at short notice," she said, hoiking herself up to fish in her cardigan pocket for a pack of menthol Marlboro cigarettes. "But honesty's the best policy anyway, really, isn't it?"

My tea was sweeter and weaker this time, as I preferred it. "Did they ask you about…Cockchops?"

She was surprised by the question, and she peered suspiciously at me as she lit a cigarette and reached for an ashtray from the coffee table and sipped her tea and thought about how and whether to answer. "I told them I hadn't seen his face," she said finally, blowing a long plume of blue smoke up to circle the ceiling fan. "But that's not really relevant, is it? They tried to be discreet about why they were here, but it was pretty obvious. I'm sure you had nothing to do with that girl disappearing, because if you were Jack the bloody Ripper then you had the perfect opportunity to chop me up that night, didn't you? You're in my house in the middle of the night, and I'm passed out drunk and you don't stab me, rape me or even touch me up as far as I can tell. If all you did was have a good look when you put me in my nightie, those are some pretty poor serial-killing skills."

"I did peek ever so slightly," I replied, honesty being the best policy and all.

Annie's cheeks flushed crimson, and she hid behind her tea again. "Dirty bastard," she said, but there was a coy grin in her voice now. "I'll let you off, though. You saved my ass, so I suppose you're entitled to look at it if you want."

"Well, it's a perfectly nice one, so I'm glad," I assured her. It was, in all fairness, the least average of her attributes.

She chuckled a perfect pair of smoke rings and nodded a theatrical thank-you. Then the humor left her eyes again, her smile thinning until only the dutifully appreciative center remained. "So listen," she said, "I've got to go to work in ten minutes, so whatever favor you came here to ask me for..." She finished with a flourish, whirling a hurry-up hand, her cigarette drawing smoky spirals across the space between us.

The change of pace took me aback. I tried for an indignant gasp, but in my red-handed surprise it came out a guilty laugh. We both knew that a protest would be a waste of our collective time, and she'd given me a tight deadline. I conceded, because honesty's the best policy. "I need a place to pretend to sleep for a couple of nights," I said, feeling a sudden pang of anxiety as it occurred to me that I was really rather depending on her to be an agreeable Annie.

She fixed me with a dark stare as she charred the hot half of her cigarette in a single breath. "Yeah." She sighed smokily, crushing her butt and draining her tea and clattering her ashtray and mug back onto the table. "Well, it's nice to be needed, I suppose. For future reference, it's slightly less than flattering when a man only wants to *pretend* to spend the night with you, but well, that's just the story of my life, isn't it? 'Ask Anne-Marie, she won't mind. Good old Agreeable Annie,'" she trilled. "Accommodating Annie. Annie Fucking Alibi."

Good, we were on the same page.

CHAPTER
EIGHTEEN

I'd made her late for work, so Annie put her foot down. She had an old Renault Twenty, which, coupled with the way she drove it, demoted her backside to the second least ordinary thing about her. It was a heavy, bluff machine, but she kept it barreling along at a startling pace. Momentum, rather than outright speed, seemed to be the key; she barely exceeded sixty miles per hour, but she barely subceeded it, either. She threaded the big car deftly along narrow lanes lined with unruly blackberry bushes, hands loose and comfortable on the wheel, feet scarcely troubling the brakes, throwing it into bends like a fighter jet and fearlessly playing chicken with oncoming traffic. As strong as the urge was to claw desperately for the grab-handle above my head, I remained polite, stowed my damp hands between my knees and focused on my breathing.

"Promise me again," she said, the car thumping and shuddering as she bounced two wheels across the rutted verge to miss a Land Rover.

"I promise," I promised.

"Because if anything you do comes back and bites me on the arse…"

"Can't happen," I assured her, and, "Like I said," somewhat less convincingly, "I'm not going to do anything you wouldn't approve of." It was probably a lie, but on the other hand, I knew Annie only marginally better than she knew me, so there was always a chance that she was perfectly open-minded. One can always hope.

"Yes, well, I don't see how you could possibly know that," she observed, "but I suppose I'll have to give you the benefit of the doubt, won't I, because otherwise there's no way I'd ever agree to help you out. Is there?"

I…

"For the record, I approve of a lot of things, and you think I'm always going to feel like I owe you something and so I can't refuse to help you, but—"

"You don't owe me anything."

"Right, well, fine, but in any case, I'm helping you because I feel like I owe you something, *and* I think you're basically a good person, or at least you're trying to be one, so if you make a fool out of me, all bets are off. Okay?"

"Understood," I said, although it came out half-formed and trembling as she stamped on the brake, banged home second gear and pitched the car into a tight ninety-degree right, clipping the ditch at the apex and jumping out of the throttle to snap the tail into line on the exit.

I gave in to instinct and grabbed the handle. Annie laughed. She had, I noticed, the smile of a Hollywood vampire, extraordinarily straight save for fashionably proud upper incisors. I suppressed a sudden nonsensical urge to bite her. Then the hedgerows shrank away, and the windshield was filled with nothing but morning-blue sky seaward to the horizon, and for half a dazzling moment, I just thought *fuck it* and said, "Skip work. Let's go buy matching bikinis and sit on the beach all day."

She did take me to the beach, but she left me there alone and without a swimsuit. She said, "Keep the key as long as you need it," and, "Have a good night if I don't see you." Then she leaned across and kissed me on the cheek and told me to take care of myself.

"I'll see you in a day or two," I said, and smiled, because that's what being liked by Annie made me do, in a strange sort of way.

I strolled down close to the shore as she drove away, and sat on the sand and watched the shadows of the fishing boats shorten until my goose bumps began to chafe on the chill wind blowing through my shirt. Then I got up and sought shelter on the promenade, where I mistakenly asked a drunken French tourist for directions.

Eventually, having failed to understand the navigation function on my mobile phone, I bought a paper map and a foam cup of burnt tea from neighboring souvenir stands, and so equipped, and cursing the half pound of seabed in my socks, I set off in search of a train.

I sat across the aisle from a young woman. She was somewhere in her early twenties and had smooth, fair skin and

blond hair like Rachel's in a neat knot. Her face was unlined
by weariness or cynicism or indeed anything save for a faint
pair of symmetrical scars close to her hairline, perhaps the
mark of a little girl and an excitable puppy hammering out
their mutual inexperience. She wore Dunlop tennis shoes
below intricately turned ankles and a pinstriped A-line skirt.
The low cut of her waitress-issue blouse bared a neck that
was all cords and arches, like a Victorian suspension bridge.
Her eyes were closed to the sunlight flickering past the window, her ears plugged with tiny white buds, slender fingers
tapping a steady moderato beat at odds with the easy sway in
her shoulders. I couldn't hear the music, but as I watched, her
body coiled around a deep breath, and the rhythm accelerated
through the flat of her hand, and then her hips rocked to four
powerful chords, and her head dropped loose on her shoulders, and she squeezed her knees together and drew in her
feet, her calf muscles tautening and her ankle bones turning
and the tendons in the back of her hand thumping time and
the cords of her neck pulling the skin tight over her collar-
bones as her body snaked through what I heard in my head as
Hugh Burns's guitar solo in "Baker Street," clear as day. And
though confined to her seat, she danced unselfconsciously and
without restraint, and every small movement in every small
part of her—the *life* in her—was the most beautiful thing I
thought I'd ever seen. I wanted to cup her gently in my hands
and carry her home and keep her forever but, mindful of the
probability that she might have other ideas, instead I closed
my eyes and turned up the music in my head and, in spirit if
not quite in body, danced with her instead.

An hour and something later I was in the city, hiring a bland Chevrolet in the name of Henry Sutton. To a casual, squinting observer blessed with imagination enough to picture him without a foot-long beard, Henry bore me quite a remarkable resemblance. In addition to his rugged good looks, Henry also had a pleasing tendency to leave his satchel unattended when he strolled off to the toilet on the train. I don't know how long it took him to discover his wallet missing, and then to fail to find it at the station and eventually get around to canceling his debit card, but thanks to a quick stop for a padded envelope and a book of stamps, I'd hazard a guess that I'd already posted it back to him.

Hammer down, but not too far. Speed limits observed to within acceptable tolerances. Temptation to blow whole plan on visit to Rachel resisted. Home within an hour.

I made two slow passes of the mouth of my driveway, looking for any sign of anyone or anything in the trees. On the third approach, I stopped at the gate and stepped out of the car. Sniffed the air. Listened to the breeze. Closed my eyes and felt for the tickle of surveillance across the hairs on the back of my neck.

Nothing. Alone.

I rolled the car through, closed and padlocked the gate behind me. Drove on up to the house and parked in its shadow, close to the front door and with a clear view of the barn and the field behind it. Nothing out there moving, glinting or lying conspicuously still. No one watching. Business as usual.

———————

"My head feels like a…tractor? Or something? I don't even know what I'm… Did you put me in bed last night? You could've just left me on the sofa. I was out like a light, I wasn't going anywhere. Wait…you'd better not have felt me up, you pervert."

I flipped a tenth pancake onto the plate beside the stove and carried the stack to the table. A green shadow passed over Erica's face as I slid it in front of her with a flourish. "Try and get some down you," I suggested, sliding one onto my own plate and rolling it around a liberal sprinkle of lemon juice and sugar.

She made a strange gurgling sound and shuddered like it was ten below, but to her credit, she made a good effort. She got four down with maple syrup before she heaved mightily into the kitchen sink.

———————

I gave Erica half an hour in a lawn chair, to get some fresh air into her lungs and some sunlight onto her skin. Then I sent her back to bed to sleep off her hangover. She didn't argue.

I left her aspirin and a bucket of ice, Coke to rehydrate her and to put a bit of sugar back in her blood, a selection of biscuits and a choice of microwavable pasta meals to get her through the night. In return, I collected her dirty laundry, two or three small items of which found their way into a plastic bag in the trunk of the rental car.

Then I slept.

———————

As it had been on a dozen other evenings, the Abbott family home was in darkness when I cruised by on the stroke of sunset. At this time of year, it was also nicely secluded; whether through grief or just plain laziness, the Abbotts had allowed the garden to run its natural course, resulting in a tall and unruly screen of apple blossom and nettles on all three sides.

I stayed pressed to the fence on the approach to the house, so as not to flatten a knee-deep trench across the lawn. The trade-off was a dozen nettle stings to the face, prompting me to wonder whether suffering for one's art was in any way preferable to no art at all. I concluded that, whichever the case, I'd definitely rather be elsewhere.

Sarah's key, salvaged from my collection, ratcheted smoothly into the lock on the back door. I left my muddy boots on the mat outside and slipped into the terra-cotta–tiled kitchen. Even in the encroaching darkness, it was clear that all was not as I'd left it, but happily the table hadn't been taken into evidence, and there was no sign of the Abbotts having done anything drastic, like move out. Indeed, there was little sign that they'd done anything at all. The worktop was greasy beneath dirty dishes stacked close to toppling; those at the top slick and saucy and stained from repetitive rinsing, those at the bottom fossilized and destined only for burial. Loosely knotted carrier bags, bulging with mouldering food waste, formed a bitter-smelling pyramid in the corner by the door. On the far wall, between the door frame and a defiantly empty corkboard, an elaborately painted narrowboat slid between the snow-covered banks of a fenland canal at the head of a calendar unturned since February.

My route to the foot of the stairs took me by the sitting room door, where I paused to peer into the gloom. Four sticky-rimmed mugs and a *heat* magazine on the coffee table. Sideboard artfully arranged to present as the room's focal point a dozen wood-framed and candle-flanked photographs of a daughter missing, presumed Out There Somewhere.

Perplexed, but nonetheless encouraged, I climbed the stairs two at a time and took to the landing, where the door to the master bedroom was ajar. I gave it a nudge with my toe. The Abbotts' bed was empty and unkempt. Someone had recently bled in it. I retreated, crossed the landing past the box room and the bathroom to the one closed door in the house. I tucked my hand up inside my sleeve and used it to drop the handle; let the door swing silently into the darkness. And then I breathed a sigh of relief as I discovered that, like her parents, Sarah's Lilac-on-*Lion King* boudoir was all but frozen in time.

Sixty-five hand-stuffed teddy bears cast a cockeyed collective glare to one side of me or the other. They'd suffered the loss early on of one of their brethren, a fallow creature abducted to a life of unaccustomed wetness soaking up tears and snot on Carol Abbott's pillow. A small brown cub with felt fur and articulated limbs had joined it as an afterthought, perched in perpetuity atop her bedside table, posed within comforting sight of its elder such that the two might keep one another company on these long, empty-bedded nights.

Otherwise, only the ordinariness was extraordinary. The room smelled of vacuum cleaning and furniture polish. The dresser and windowsill had been recently emptied, dusted and recluttered. The bed had been made, but with little gusto and no attempt at a hospital corner. The wastebasket was still half-filled with Diet Coke cans and used tissues. The clock on the bedside table had been advanced to British Summer Time. According to her bedroom, Sarah and her diary were simply out for the evening.

That such stoicism made my life easier was not lost on me, and in gratitude I worked quickly and tidily. From Sarah's hairbrush, her pillow and the collar of a jacket crumpled at the foot of her bed, I was able to fill a small Ziploc bag with strands of fine golden hair. From under the bed, rumpled against the skirting board, I rescued an unwashed black silk thong. Finally, from inside the balled-up pair of tights in the middle drawer of the dresser, I retrieved half a pack of Marlboro Lights and a Zippo lighter engraved with the initials SJA. Perfect.

Now for the hard part.

CHAPTER
NINETEEN

By day, the Milton Cross estate is an oppressively dreary but otherwise unremarkable warren of sixties-built concrete council flats. Left to its own unsurveilled devices, it's a hive of inactivity, populated by prospectless drones whose eyes rarely find the motivation to meet. There's no church hall, no coffee mornings, no kiddies' play dates. No one's door is always open. It's the very antithesis of community.

At night, however, Milton Cross takes on the kind of delinquent vibrance that charms trolls from beneath their bridges across the breadth of the city. They arrive in fleets of old BMWs and absurdly pumped-up little hatchbacks, and they head for the houses with the open front doors, the window frames rattling to the beats of identikit dubstep party albums, the porch lights glowing weakly from within glass bowls dark with the husks of visitors past.

The ground-floor flat I was interested in, however, had no porch light, because I'd already removed the bulb. In the ten minutes I stood in the shadow of the stoop, four mini-skirts and two tracksuits passed within fifteen feet, and none turned so much as a hair in my direction. The windows of the apartments opposite were dark, the curtains drawn and untwitching. It was clear that the proverbial casual observer wouldn't be requiring any comforting cues tonight, invisible as I apparently was.

The flat, however, was empty. The windows were cold and unshuttered, the strewn contents of the living room settled and lonely and cloaked in darkness. Happily, at least, they were also the typical detritus of a lone male tenant, and judging by the lingering smell of microwaved gravy, one who had recently been in residence.

His name was Mark Boon, and I'd been looking for a reason to return his wallet since retrieving it from the scene of his attempted assault on Annie's undergarments. I had very little doubt that his absence at ten minutes to midnight on a Monday was similarly attributable, and so I added it to his list of offences, along with not having the common decency to be at home when I came to kill him.

———————

I hoped Mark wouldn't have to wait for the clubs to close before finding some hapless, legless student to terrorize. I suspected he probably would, though, so rather than hide in a hedge, I elected to wait fifty yards up the road in the car, with a flask of tea and the *Classic & Sports Car* classifieds.

It was a little after three when he finally appeared, agitated and hurrying, hat pulled down, collar turned up, balled fists making torpedoes of his jacket pockets. Every half-dozen strides, he snapped his head around to check over his shoulder, and his eyebrows flashed shock-orange in the sodium glow of the streetlights.

I squeezed my hands into new, tight leather gloves and hooked my rucksack from the passenger seat. Unzipped the front pouch and took out the ceramic lock knife I'd pressed into Erica's clammy right hand shortly after she'd passed out.

By the time Mark was fifty feet from the car, I was out and across the road and walking away, bag over my shoulder, blade in my back pocket. He'd have seen me, for sure, but a retreating stranger fumbling for a set of keys would be no match for whatever threat lurked over his left shoulder. Indeed, I probably already appeared *too* unthreatening, and so I injected a purposeful sway into my stride and stumbled over every fifth footstep, setting a meandering trajectory for a spot directly opposite the cracked and crumbling path to Mark's front door and pacing myself a fraction slower than him, now forty-five, forty, thirty-five feet behind me on the opposite side of the street.

My timing was perfect; I reached my destination five paces before Mark reached his, offering him a front-row seat as I dropped my keys on the ground, tripped over my own foot and staggered into a hedge. I heard his feet scuff the pavement as he turned sharply onto his garden path, making no attempt to help me up, just as I knew he would. And now he'd expect me to scuff around in search of my dropped belongings, and he certainly wasn't going to risk a backward glance for fear of making eye contact with a big, angry drunk whose fall we both knew he'd pretended not to notice. The payoff was swift and inevitable.

Mark was thirty-five feet in front of me, turning the key in his lock. From a sprinter's crouch, keys in pocket, I covered the gap in six strides and was on him as he cracked open the door. He never even knew what hit him.

———————

I had a speech prepared, but as tends to be the case when I go to the trouble of rehearsing my lines, Mark didn't stick to the script.

My entrance was perfect; I caught him a swift jab to the kidneys and straight-armed him through the door into the murky flat. After that, though, the plan went south. The floor in Mark's hallway was laid with cheap laminate, over which he'd placed a thin, scruffy rug emblazoned with the image of a large marijuana leaf. The first thing he did was yelp and the second was try to run, which had the sole effect of rolling up the rug until it caught between his feet, at which point we both tripped over it.

With my grip loosened, Mark made a break for freedom, though inexplicably he ran forward into the gloom rather than back out to the relative safety of the street. Perhaps he thought he could reach a weapon, or that having lost control of him, I'd scurry away with my tail tucked. Either way, he was about to be disappointed, because I had a handful of hemp and an impulse to whip him with it.

He'd staggered no more than eight feet into the lounge when the hastily flung rug coiled around his ankles and brought him sprawling back to the floor with a winded grunt. He was up again faster than he fell, but this time I was with him, hooking his right foot with my own and kicking it high, flipping him horizontal with nothing but gravity between his head and the floor five feet below.

Well, gravity and a coffee table.

He hit it face-first, the edge chopping him across the eyes and the bridge of his nose. Unfortunately, I'd already committed to a calming stamp above the shoulder blades, and the resultant folding of his neck made a rather ominous crunch. By the time his head ricocheted to the floor, it seemed only loosely connected to his shoulders. He'd be out for a while, I thought.

I kicked the door shut and stumbled and tripped my way to the window to draw the curtains, then picked my way around the wall until I found a light switch. There was only one bulb, but it was naked and bright and threw sharp shadows across the wasteland that was Mark's living room.

He didn't have much in the way of furniture; an uncomfortable-looking leatherette couch and two threadbare armchairs had worn twelve holes through the brown cord carpet. An expensive-looking hi-fi stood on an upturned milk crate below a vast wall-hung television, cables dangling and snaking from one to the other to the Xbox on the floor. In the corner, a tired old flatpack bookcase listed five degrees to starboard under the weight of half a dozen video games and the combined works of Barker, King, Herbert and Straub.

What Mark did have was pizza boxes, and beer cans, and biscuit wrappers and socks. Sticky, stained mugs and crusty dinner plates. Empty supermarket carrier bags scrunched into nooks and crannies. Envelopes torn just enough to check the letterheads, then discarded unopened.

The bedroom was scarcely any better, and it smelled like a tomcat, but I did at least find some clean bedding at the bottom of the wardrobe. I stripped Mark's bed, carefully parceling the sheet so as to preserve any flotsam and jetsam. Then I carried it through to the living room and arranged it semitidily on the couch, tossing his pillow on top and punching a head-size dent into it before covering it haphazardly with his duvet.

I spread a clean sheet on the bed and fished Erica's laundry out of my bag. There were three pairs of knickers, and one pair was more visibly distressed than the others, so those were the ones I turned inside-out and rubbed all over the middle third of the sheet before tossing them to the corner of the room. I balled up a second pair and left them on the bed, which I topped with a soft blanket. Then I delved into the small selection of beauty products in my rucksack and liberally fumigated the room with cheap body spray, most of which ended up in my mouth.

Some time later, after I'd stopped sneezing and coughing into my elbow, I pulled the bed six inches from the wall and dropped behind it Sarah's thong and a newly bought hairbrush, around which I'd woven strands of her hair.

Then I gathered the remaining bundle of laundry and the bag of cosmetics and followed my nose to the bathroom. Surprisingly, it was reasonably clean and tidy, at least until I threw Erica's clothes on the floor and emptied the bag in a sweeping, clattering arc across the sink and bathtub. The only thing I picked up was her toothbrush, which I placed at the back of the sink, near the cup containing Mark's.

Satisfied that my staging was just the right side of conspicuously chaotic, I turned off the light, retrieved my bag and crossed to the tiny kitchen. I didn't have to hunt for the knickknack drawer; there was only one set of drawers, and therefore only one second-drawer-down. I used Sarah's cigarette packet to nudge a cigarette packet-size hole among the knickknacks. Then I half closed the drawer and returned to the living room, where I carefully placed the cigarettes and Sarah's Zippo in the center of the coffee table. A discovery, a presentation, a challenge. *What are these doing here, Mark? What did you do to Sarah?* For a seasoned *Columbo* viewer it might have been a signpost too far, but you never know, it might just work. After all, nothing demands suspension of disbelief quite like real life, does it?

Whatever. Best I could do. Frankly, I was by now more concerned with Mark, whose breathing appeared dangerously shallow. My plan to stick the knife between his ribs relied on him being conscious and upright and more or less able to pump blood to his own extremities, but he was out like Evel Knievel, his pulse had joined him on the floor, and there was no way on God's green Earth I was going to get him vertical, let alone hold him up one-handed long enough to stab him.

Not for the first time, I settled for a quick and dirty gash. He didn't have any color left in his upturned cheek, but I expected it was already starting to pool in the other, so, blade opened, I tugged off his hat and took a handful of orange-orange hair and lifted his head. His neck gave the faintest creak of resistance, and then, with a hollow pop, gave out completely, his shoulders slumping and his face swiveling around to stare up at me, thirty degrees beyond dead.

I didn't have a Plan C.

CHAPTER
TWENTY

The sun was coming up by the time I slotted the car keys through the hire company's letterbox and ambled back to the station. It was a spectacular dawn of pinks and golds and endless glittering blue, and I was content to tune out the chitter-chatter of wheels on rails and quietly watch it slide past my window.

At the end of the line, I disembarked into fresh, clean, wide-open air and followed the sound of crashing waves and tinkling bells to the promenade. The air was already warm, but the breeze from the sea had a bite that made me turtle down into my jacket. My eyes were already stiff and heavy, my skin tingling with fatigue. My mouth tasted disgusting. I didn't linger.

A hundred yards along the seafront was a taxi stand, and a minicab delivered me to the village store a quarter of a mile from Annie's front door. The driver made a token early attempt at pleasantry, but he clearly knew the comedown from an all-nighter when he saw it, and so passed the twenty-minute drive in respectful silence while I dozed. I gave him an unremarkable tip and fussed over nothing in my rucksack until he'd driven away. Then, whistling tunelessly and with a pint of milk and whatever newspaper I'd just purchased held comfortably on display for the benefit of any nosy neighbors, I strolled on back to the house.

I don't know what I expected from Annie; relief, maybe, or indifference, or a pang of foolish regret. Given that it was bang on the dot of 8:00 a.m. when I turned the key in the lock and let myself into her cottage, I might most reasonably have expected to find her on the telephone, trying to eat some toast and finish her makeup and get to work on time. But no.

The house was silent and cool and hours-gone-by still. The curtains were drawn. There was no mug on the table, no cereal bowl with a half-inch puddle of grainy milk in the bottom. I kicked off my shoes and dropped my bag and padded through to the kitchen. The sink was empty, the worktops clean. The dishes on the draining board were bone-dry.

I left the milk and paper on the counter and resurveyed the sitting room. Nothing seemed out of place. I turned my ear to the ceiling, hoping to detect a creaking board or a running tap or a twanging bed spring. I heard the fridge compressor kick in, which made me jump out of my sleep-deprived skin, but that was all.

Tentatively, hearing alarm bells at the back of my neck, I headed for the stairs. No reply when I called her name, so I went on up. The bathroom wasn't spotless; there was a towel on the floor and toothpaste in the sink, and the screen around the shower end of the bath was streaked with water marks, but the tub was dry and the air settled and the toilet seat ice cold. And so I moved straight on to Annie's room. And that room was nothing at all like the other rooms, because in that room, Annie'd made a hell of a mess.

I smelled it before I opened the door, but I went in, anyway. Her quilt was on the floor, feverishly cast aside. At the foot of the bed, one of her shoes lay forlornly where it had fallen beside the trailing edge of the sheet, rumpled and untucked, once bright white but now mostly crimson, a dark, wide stain creeping out from the sorry heap of rags at its center.

Annie was most definitely gone.

I closed my eyes and waited for my heart to leave my throat. Then I took stock.

She'd used a T-shirt and a cashmere sweater to try to stem the flow, and they'd been saturated. Beneath the sheet, the mattress was spotted but relatively unharmed.

The room smelled plummy and a little floral, with a sweet oaky undertone. Hints of caramel and…toast? I wasn't sure, but I guessed at a Merlot. Judging by the size of the stain, there wouldn't have been a drop left in the bottle.

I crossed to the window to peer out between the curtains. Annie's Renault was nowhere to be seen, of course. I'd missed her, that was all.

I bundled up the ruined laundry and took it down to the rubbish bin in the kitchen. I threw the duvet cover and pillowcases and an armful of clothes I found on the floor into the washing machine, and then, for the second time in six hours, I went in search of clean bedding. I found it in a small airing cupboard in the spare bedroom—a matching set, dusky pink and soft as a kitten. By the time I finished dressing the pillows, I was already lying down, and seconds later I was dead to the world.

———————

The sunlight was almost horizontal through the gap in the curtains when I finally woke. The alarm clock on the bedside table told me it was just after six. I couldn't remember the last time I'd managed nine hours' sleep, and I marveled at how rested and ready I felt. None of which encouraged me in the slightest to move a muscle, because the house was still warm and quiet, and the mattress was pillow-soft and foam-topped, and the sheets were so gentle they were barely even there, and so I couldn't remember when I'd last felt as comfortable, either. At least until I felt the next thing I felt, which was a block of ice on the back of my leg.

I startled upright, which woke Annie, which I tried to process but couldn't. I just watched her stretch and yawn and twist around and squint up at me and say, "What's up?"

"How frigging cold are your feet?" I blurted.

She gave a lazy smile and a long hum of sleepy contentment and settled back into her pillow. "Sorry," she murmured. "Bad circulation and…"

She had bed hair. She looked pretty. I rubbed my eyes. No change. "You look pretty with bed hair," I said.

"Fuck off," she replied. "You know where the kettle is. Get it yourself."

I laughed. Now that she mentioned it, I could add hunger to the list of superlatives. My stomach was emitting the kind of rumble that would bring a seismologist back early from lunch. "I'll get some dinner on," I said.

"Breakfast first," she muttered. "Stick to the routine, it's time-honored."

Because it was six in the fucking morning.

———————

"You bought the *Daily Mail*? What the hell kind of monster are you?" Annie threw the newspaper onto the dining table and sat down beside me in the Hello Kitty T-shirt she'd worn to bed.

"Honest mistake," I assured her.

She took a bite out of her toast and daintily chased the crumbs away with her little finger. "I guess you had a busy couple of days," she said. "I couldn't wake you up for love nor money last night. Are you feeling okay?"

"I'm feeling awake." I laughed. "That's the second time you've asked me that."

"I was worried," she smarted. "I thought you were in a coma until you started thrashing about and panting. Then I thought you probably had swamp fever or something. I thought I was going to have to call someone to come and take you away and...put me in quarantine or something. Did you get everything done that you needed to?"

I smiled and nodded and gulped my tea. "I'll be out of your hair in a minute."

"That wasn't what I meant," she tutted.

"I know," I teased, "but…" But I hadn't attended to Erica in thirty-six hours.

"But?"

"I haven't fed my cat?"

Annie laughed so hard she choked on her toast.

———

She made me keep her key. "You never know when you'll need it," she said, and slipped it back into my pocket. "But ring first, in case I've got a man here."

"Got it."

She giggled again. "As if that's ever gonna happen!" Then she led me out into the sunshine and made a show of embracing me longingly in full view of the neighbors. "Acting face," she said. "Pretend you're here for the hot booty action." Which set me off again.

"Take care, Annie." I laughed. "Don't do anything I wouldn't do."

"How hard can that be?" she said, and squeezed me tight. "Don't be a stranger, Stranger."

○   ○   ○

Missing Annie was a new thing. I wasn't sure how I felt about it. Never having had or needed or wanted a friend before, I'd never known what I'd been missing. The notion that it might have been Annie was as startling as my longing to return to Rachel; a painful urgency that ambushed me at the edge of the village and burrowed deeper into my chest with every red light and stalled junction for forty miles.

Inevitably, though, the closer I got to home, the more pressing the problems awaiting me there became, and by the time I turned into my drive, my gluttonous head was sick from gorging on my predicament.

First things first: Erica. Satisfied that there were still no binoculars in my begonias, I clattered into the basement with my hands held high in apology, only to find her dozing with a book in her hand.

She stirred as I let myself into the cage, and greeted me with a yawn that could scarcely have been more indifferent. "Morning," she mumbled.

"How are you?" I asked her, fortunately biting back the explanation our respective roles dictated I didn't owe her. She'd stopped me in my tracks somewhat, and my words were coming out fussy and nervous.

"I had plenty to eat," she said, indicating the dishes neatly stacked on her tray beside the door. "But the toilet's blocked. It needs plunging or something."

I had to concede that I probably deserved that. "Right." I nodded. "Is there anything you want me to get you?"

She shrugged. "I've got a headache," she said.

Imagining that she was biding her time, I fetched her half a pack of paracetamol and a jug of ice water and collected her mug, since I was about to put the kettle on.

I returned with a cup of tea, a box of tea bags and an unopened bag of sugar, which brought a tear to her eye. I asked her whether she needed anything else. She said a teaspoon would be handy.

I fetched her a spoon and, as an afterthought, a packet of shortbread biscuits. Mindful of the dangers of boiling water in a microwave, I took the kettle, as well. This guilt business was becoming expensive.

CHAPTER
TWENTY-ONE

"It's just like being at the seaside." Rachel laughed as I took her hand and helped her out of the Jensen onto the soft sand of the car park. "Only...you know...without the sea."

"And the tourists and the screaming children," I agreed.

She smiled at the sun and buried her toes. "Where to now?"

The picnic site was deserted. Before us, a sea of heather stretched back the quarter mile to the road and the tight rows of slender pines beyond. Above, a deep blue sky scattered with great billowing cotton-wool clouds, each with its own distinct arrangement of deep-set eyes, elfin ears and pointed nose. And behind us, twenty square miles of leaf and bark and shadow. I knew which one I'd prefer. "You choose," I said. "It's your day."

"Right answer." She smiled, reaching out for my hand to steady herself as she slipped into her shoes. "I hope you're feeling fit."

"As a fox," I replied, enjoying a glimpse of the small of her back as she bent down to tie her laces. "Why, what have you got up your sleeve?" I grimaced at my choice of words; fortunately, there was no icy stare to meet them.

She simply stood, turned to me and, with a sly grin, said, "You'll just have to wait and see." And with that, she led me into the wood.

———

"So." She squeezed my hand. "Is this where you bring all your lady friends?"

Ha. "If only you knew." Sorry, it just slipped out. "Wait," I protested, before she had time to take it in. "What do you mean, *all*?"

"Right." She laughed. "If only I knew. So tell me about it."

"There's really nothing to tell," I assured her, so awkwardly failing to strike a convincing tone that all I could do was hope she'd accept a change of subject with good grace, and then quietly forget about it. "Ask me another," I said.

"Who's your favorite Bond?" she replied, without so much as a sideways glance.

Easy. "Roger Moore."

"Really?" she chuckled.

"Those were the ones on TV when I was a kid. Where I grew up, Roger Moore was how you knew it was Christmas."

A moment's silence like raised eyebrows. "Yeah, mine, too," she admitted. "*The Spy Who Loved Me*'s my favorite."

"That's the one with the Lo—"

"The Lotus that's a submarine, yes." She laughed and curled her arm around mine and gazed up at the sparkling canopy.

"I've always wanted one of those," I mused, and I smiled, too.

Rachel clung to me as we walked, but I felt I needed the support more than she did. My head swam with anxiety at sharing this personal space; an exhilarating novelty, and I leaned into her, held her hand to keep her close to me, to pin my pulse to its sweet allegro rhythm. I listened for hours to her lessons in wood lark and nightjar and will-o'-the-wisp; Spanish catchfly and perfect meringue and the elusive military orchid. She talked about the leaves on the trees and plucked tiny flowers from the ground. She stopped dead in her tracks at the sight of a doe, pressed a finger to my lips as it mirrored our petrified pose; stifled a joyous laugh as it bounded away, white tail bobbing from tree to tree amid a cacophony of crackling brush. And as we crossed the expanse of knee-high grass where four woods met, she simply settled her head on my shoulder and sighed.

"You want to know something really strange?" she said.

"Yes," I replied. It couldn't be any stranger than what I was feeling.

It was, of course. "I honestly can't think of anywhere in the world I'd rather be right now than here, with you." And then, in a missed heartbeat, she was looking down at me, sprawled in confusion at her feet. "Christ—" she laughed "—are you okay?"

If ever there was a loaded question… "What the hell was that?"

"A rabbit hole," she said, probing the ground with her toe before cocking her head at me with a mocking grin. "I guess we should add those to the list of fearsome predators. Is it comfy?"

"Very." I felt the soft grass curl around my face and the

warmth of the sun wash over me. If I had any inclination at all to get up, it evaporated as she lay down by my side. "Don't get too settled," I warned her. "It'll be dark soon."

She wriggled closer, nudged up against me and flashed a mischievous grin. "I know."

We lay in silence as the sun dipped behind the trees, streaks of orange and blood-red lingering in its place before they, too, slipped quietly over the horizon. And then the sky was gone, and a blanket of stars spread one by one across the endless black void.

Finally, at first sight of the half-moon, Rachel rolled to her knees and took both of my hands in hers. "It's perfect," she whispered. "Come on." She stood and pulled me to my feet, beckoning me with her as she turned and walked away.

I watched her for a moment, hips swaying as she waded through the grass. She didn't look back, though she clearly sensed me behind her as I began to follow. She said nothing as she veered right from our original path, heading up into the denser forest where the trees rose up from a carpet of broadleaf fern.

"You know what eats all the rabbits in these woods?" she asked.

"Yes," I said. "Weasels."

"Stoats…"

"Same difference."

She laughed. "Well, yeah, if the weasel's been to the gym I suppose it might just—"

"Get to the point." I smiled.

And then as Rachel reached the tree line she spun around to face me, halted me with two firm hands against my chest. "Do you know how the stoat catches his rabbit?"

"He saps its will to live via the medium of modern dance."

"He hypnotizes it." She laughed. "He fascinates it. Puts it into a freaky trippy trance." She backed away from me, a sudden darkness crossing her face in tune with the shadows that folded in around her. In one swift movement she grasped the neck of her flimsy jumper, pulled it up over her head and cast it aside. "And when the little rabbit is all cross-eyed and dizzy..." She kicked off her shoes, reached around to unbutton her skirt, stepped neatly out of it with a defiant smile as it dropped.

I felt myself sway as the starlight played across her skin, the soft curves of her dark silhouette both luring me in and rooting me to the spot. My head was a mass of sparks and short-circuits, my spine coursing with electricity. I heard myself speak, felt my hands move. "Okay," I said. "I'll bite." I unbuttoned my shirt and tossed it into the brush. I fumbled my belt open and shook free of my trousers. I shivered as the night air tightened my skin and wrapped me in goose bumps.

Her smile gave way to a throaty laugh as she stepped back among the shoulder-high ferns, shrugging out of her bra as they closed around her. "What makes you think you're the stoat?" she said. The current surged as she dipped briefly from view; she straightened to throw her underwear onto the pile. "Your turn," she instructed me.

Any stirring I'd felt abandoned me as I cast aside the last remnants of my clothing. I could barely see her, but in that moment I felt her eyes all over me, along with those of every owl, moth and bat that might be lurking in these woods. The sensation unnerved me, and I dropped my shoulders, willed my hands to fall to the rescue of my modesty. They slapped uselessly against my thighs.

"Good," Rachel said. And then, with a loud, joyous giggle, she brought my mind crashing back down into sharp focus. "Now close your eyes and count to ten." She laughed. "And catch me if you can."

I plunged into the maze of ferns, and within seconds I was in almost absolute darkness. The supple branches bent easily before me, the leaves barely tickling my skin as I carved a blind trail.

At thirty paces I paused, straining to detect any sound that might betray Rachel's position. From ahead and to the right came a faint rustling of foliage. To the left, a brief, distinct cracking of twigs. I gambled and broke right and the faint rustling became a thunderous crashing, accompanied by a loud, playful laugh. A nervous glee welled up inside me, spilled over into a grin as I increased my pace, lunging after what was now a sprinting quarry. I heard her spin around and dart to the left; I bolted after her, those branches she disturbed still springing back to meet me as I scythed through them. I could hear her panting, her feet pounding right there in the blackness before my eyes, a mere arm's length in front of me. I tripped as I reached out, hit the ground so hard that I'd bounced to my feet before the pain had a chance to register.

The silence was so profound that it rang in my ears. I stood stock-still, just waiting and listening, willing Rachel to give herself away. It was a short wait; with a loud and deliberate clearing of her throat, she signaled herself no more than thirty feet in front of me. I bolted, covered the ground between us in half a dozen strides, but arrived in empty space; immediately, I heard her cross at speed behind my back, trailing a playful giggle. I whirled around to give chase, but no sooner was I behind her than she was gone. I dug in my heels, skittered to a halt, and she was behind me again, sprinting back toward open ground. Her shape was just visible enough against the moonlight beyond the wood; seizing the advantage, I took off at a savage pace, slashing the ferns aside, my feet barely touching the ground. I locked my eyes onto her back, let my remaining senses guide me through the trees as I gained on her in great soaring bounds. And then she fell.

I swooped, leaped onto her with an instinctive growl. And again, I fell only on myself. I crumpled and rolled, a thousand shards of dead wood tearing at my back as I grated to a halt. I caught her at the corner of my eye as I scrabbled for grip, clawed myself up from the floor. I certainly heard her; wood snapping, leaves tearing, hooves thumping the—

"Oh, shit" had barely escaped my lips when, for a split second, I was face-to-face with my quarry. It looked as surprised as I was, eyes wide and mouth agape as it pirouetted, hind legs scrabbling for grip before they left the ground.

I didn't even make it upright. Seventy-five pounds of roe deer hit me square in the chest, knocked me clean off my feet and barrel-rolled over my head. I lay stunned and winded as it slammed into the undergrowth behind me, legs thrashing, hooves clattering together in its panicked attempts to right itself. Thankfully, as it did so, my prayers for it to continue on its chosen course were answered; it neglected to turn and run back over me.

I lay still for a full minute, regaining my breath, allowing my heart to return to some semblance of its regular rhythm. The shock faded rapidly, replaced by an almost delirious amusement tempered only by the throbbing pain in what seemed to be every one of my muscles. I felt little inclination toward getting up.

My lack of motivation, however, passed in a heartbeat when Rachel called my name. She was close; I listened carefully to the sound of her feet, determined to ensure that she had but two before resuming the hunt. She was moving slowly, heading back into blackness. I rose to follow, walking at first, swiveling my hips and stretching my shoulders, shaking the pain from my arms.

I gradually picked up speed, settling into a stealthy canter; I was confident of her position now, my ears taking the bulk of the strain, homing in on the crystal-clear sound of leaf against skin.

She yelped as she heard me approach, broke into a flat-out run. I had her then; I could hear her breath, smell her skin, taste her perfume as I bore blindly down upon her. And I was close enough to reach out and touch her when, despite the assertions of my ears and nose, I felt her behind me. My heart skipped into my mouth, and my insides rolled over, and I ploughed backward into a five-foot fern as I spun around to face her. I saw her shadow flash across in front of me, heard the snapping twigs and swishing leaves as she passed. I heard her above me and felt her beside me when I knew that she was circling right behind me, and the realization that I'd been chasing an echo sparked a fireball of panicked confusion in my head. That was when I lost it.

I abandoned my sense of irony and made a beeline for the tree line, eyes focused on the exit, ears filled with crackling bracken, nerves coursing electric; every hair on my body stood to attention, my spine tied in knots, breath coming in short, inefficient gulps. She gained on me effortlessly, so that I could all but feel her breath on my back as I exploded from the cover of the ferns. I lost all balance then, was briefly airborne as my body outpaced my buckling legs, and I sailed headlong into the floor. I rolled onto my back, scrabbled crablike across the last twenty feet into open air, my own rasping breath ringing in my ears as I collapsed, prey, defeated, ready for her to pounce.

"Christ, are you okay?"

I heard myself yell out, felt all of my organs simultaneously fail as her voice floated down from behind me. I spun around to face her, standing there knee-deep in the grass, the moonlight through the treetops casting a spiderweb glow across her skin. "Jesus," I stammered. "You made me jump."

"It's creepy in there, huh?" She smiled, brought out her hands from behind her back as she glided silently to me on the balls of her feet. "I picked you a flower," she said.

I slumped, closed my eyes, let my head fall back and tried in vain to steady my breath as she knelt down beside me. As much as I yearned to watch her as she trailed soft petals across my chest, inside my head there was daylight.

CHAPTER
TWENTY-TWO

It was past one in the afternoon when I got home. Having not eaten in twenty-four hours, I was ravenous. I threw a frozen pizza in the oven and gorged on chocolate digestives while I waited.

With the pizza baked, I wandered through to the sitting room and relaxed on the sofa, feet up on the coffee table, plate on my lap. My hips ached in protest at last night's cold, hard bed. I reached for the TV remote, but my hand stopped short as I realized what was on.

———

"I can't believe you left me on my own again."

"Erica, I'm s—"

"Do you know what I had for dinner last night?" She stopped pacing and fixed me with a furious stare. "Do you?"

"I was—"

"Rice Krispies with tap water. And do you know what I had for breakfast?"

"I—"

"Rice Krispies and tap water. And I bet you can guess what I just had for lunch…"

"Look, I—"

"Where the hell have you been?" She stood perfectly still, hands on her hips, anger radiating from her in hot waves, burning my cheeks.

"Erica, I was out longer than I expected," I said. "I'm sorry."

"Really?" She shook her head with a derisive laugh. "This has got to stop. What if something happens to you? What if you have an accident and end up in hospital for days, or weeks or months? What if you don't come home at all? Have you thought about that? You said you didn't want me to starve to death, right? Well maybe you ought to think about some kind of contingency plan, because at the moment you're not just being inconsiderate, you're being downright fucking selfish and irresponsible. And what the hell are you saying sorry for? You don't even know what it means."

Up until that moment, she may have been right. Chances are, I wouldn't have even understood the question. But as I looked into her fiery eyes, felt the heat of her anger and fear and, with a growl from my belly, her hunger, too, I felt a little bit like I did know what it meant. It hurt me to look at her. "I've made you some lunch," I said. "It's upstairs."

She finally dropped her stare and let out a deep sigh. "Did you bring me the extra-long fork, then?"

I unlocked the cage and swung the door open, stepped aside and waited. Erica stood firm for a moment, shaking her head and laughing incredulously to herself, clearly wrestling with the urge to continue her tirade. Finally, she shot me a weary glance and stormed out of the room.

I followed her across the driveway, watching her suck in great lungfuls of fresh, sweet air, her furious march reduced to a wistful stroll once exposed to natural light. She kicked at the gravel and flicked up her skirt and paused before the door to gaze up at the sun.

I ushered her inside and guided her to the sitting room, where my pizza was waiting. "Take your time," I said. "Watch TV if you want. I'll get you something to drink."

She sat bolt upright, hands clasped between her knees, surveying her lunch. After a moment she looked up at me with a half smile and said, "Thank you."

I took the cordless telephone from its cradle and retreated to the kitchen, where I browsed idly through the fridge for some time before noticing that it was virtually bare. I settled for a sandwich of sliced pastrami and plum chutney, and a cup of sugary tea.

I replayed every minute of last night in my head, from Rachel excitedly opening the door of her flat to the moment her fingers curled into her palm, and her head lolled to one side, and I curled up beside her and fell into a deep and contented sleep beneath the stars. I don't know how long I stared out the window, but my tea was stone cold by the time it occurred to me to drink it.

"What the hell happened to you?"

I jolted awake to catch Erica eyeing me suspiciously as she put her empty plate in the sink. "What do you mean?"

"Your back," she said, instructing me to turn around with a spiraling wave of her hand. "Is that *your* blood?"

The question disturbed me, its casual honesty a jarring reminder of the space I surely occupied in her mind. I felt suddenly exposed, inexplicably compelled to protest some semblance of innocence, however absurd. "As opposed to what?" was the best I could muster.

"Cut the crap," she said, spinning me with a forceful hand to my shoulder. "Oh, God, you reek of perfume. Do I even want to know?"

"It's nothing," I assured her. "I fell over, that's all."

"Take your shirt off."

"What? No." I poured my cold tea into the sink and switched the kettle back on.

"Does it hurt?"

"Yes." Now that she mentioned it.

"Come here." She was around me and unbuttoning my shirt before I had time to object. "You can be the big man all you like, but you can't see your own back. Unless you have no spine, obviously." She tugged the shirt down over my arms and turned my back to her. After a moment's silent examination, she laughed under her breath. "Yeah, right," she said. "Fell over, did you? Over what, Beachy Head? What the hell did you do last night? You smell fucking horrific."

I shrugged my shirt back up to my shoulders. "Right, well thank you for that diagn—"

"And you look even worse. You do realize you've got a

thorn bush growing out of you, don't you?" The shirt was all the way off this time, and crumpled at the far side of the kitchen floor. "Sit down, Uncle Fester," she commanded. "I'll find some tweezers."

———

Erica spent a full hour pulling thorns and thistles and splinters of bark and twig from my back. She was less than careful, digging at me far more aggressively than was called for. Occasionally, she scratched at an open wound, ignoring my hissed complaints. Despite her deliberate clumsiness, however, she was creditably thorough. She worked in silence save for the odd "Keep still," diligently removing every small trace of woodland flora to a neat mound on the table. Finally, she set aside the tweezers and stepped back to admire her work. "There," she said proudly. "You're tree-free."

I was markedly more sore than I had been when she started, and I was distinctly aware of several trails of blood trickling down my back, but I couldn't bring myself to criticize. Her shadow on me was warming, and I felt a certain disappointment that the services of her hands were no longer required. Was that the kind of thought uncles had about their nieces? I suspected it probably was, though it seemed a little inappropriate. "Thank you," I said, somewhat inadequately.

"I haven't finished yet," she replied, a hint of a smile in her voice. I listened patiently as she pulled soft cotton wool from crinkling cellophane and unscrewed the metallic cap from a glass bottle. With one hand she took the towel from the back of my chair and bunched it roughly around my waist. "Okay, lean forward, nice and still, deep breath. This'll sting a bit."

I obeyed with a smile and rested my forehead on the table, anticipating the first bite of the TCP, the strange and intense splashed-acid cold burn rendered almost pleasurable by its promise to heal. What I got, however, was a wave of searing pain so intense that my brain cringed, and my eyes fell out of focus.

Erica slowly poured the bottle of antiseptic over my back, careful not to waste any on unbroken skin. I let out a shocked howl as my skin tightened and my body convulsed, my face pushed into the table, the pain enough for me to wonder whether she'd gone the whole hog and struck a match.

For her encore, as I made a desperate grab for the edge of the table, she put down the empty bottle and took a firm hold of the towel. Holding it taut across my back, she collected the dripping disinfectant and dragged it back over my wounds, rubbing it in forcefully enough to repeatedly bounce my head against the oak.

"*Now* you're done," she said finally, draping the towel around my shoulders. And then, as I made a groaning effort to regain my sight, she laid a hand on my fiery back, brought her lips in close to my ear and whispered, "I hope she was fucking worth it."

CHAPTER
TWENTY-THREE

Control. Control control control. Drive.

I didn't know where I was going, and when I arrived in the city, I didn't know how I'd got there. All I knew was that I needed to take back control of my life, or I wasn't going to survive another week.

My back still stung. I'd ground my teeth until they bristled with every drawn breath, and my wrists ached from gripping the wheel so tight. I'd seen a hundred and ten from the Transit and the cab smelled of burnt oil and brake dust. I had a headache.

I sat on the corner of King Street, passing headlights sweeping through misty memories of an afternoon's pacing and nail-biting and struggling with the thousand and one thoughts fighting so noisily for space in my head that not one could make itself heard. I remembered a pimply-faced youth in a bright red polo shirt selling me a larder-size fridge for the basement, with a three-star freezer compartment and a trap-door shelf for bottles. I remembered not remembering what I was doing.

Control.

The girls came and went across the street, a parade of fake-fur collars and leather skirts, bare legs marbled and pale, eyes hollow and dark. They emerged from the shadows to lean through car windows; as each was whisked away, so she was replaced immediately by the next. They scrolled through almost hourly, their faces familiar by the third cycle. None looked twice in my direction as I sat entirely still in the darkness, all but invisible inside the van.

I watched them come and go, their expressions grow longer and the trembling of their knees more pronounced. I studied their posture, their energy, the alertness in their eyes, eliminating them one by one until, by eleven o'clock, I'd settled on the most favorable. And then, as I waited for her to reappear, a new face arrived and wiped the slate clean.

This one was perfect. She swayed unsteadily on her feet, the heavy hem of her coat swishing about her ankles as she whirled around, eyes darting nervously from one end of the street to the other, empty beer bottle thrown weakly into the bushes beside her. She was tall but narrow; between the woolen coat and the motorcycle boots, I imagined that her outfit must account for half of her weight.

I wasted no time; the van was fired up and at the opposite curb in an instant. Window lowered. Smile on face. "Hello," I said.

She flashed a nervous smile, checking each end of the street again before she leaned in close to the window. "Do you want to talk to me?" she stuttered.

She seemed particularly atypical up close, in that her face was soft and unmarked, her hair recently washed and her coat remarkably well made. Intriguing. I stepped out onto the pavement and stood aside, holding the door open for her. "Yeah, why not?" I shrugged. "Slide over."

———

"So...what do you want to do?" She looked more relaxed now that the van was moving and she had a cigarette lit, though the crack in her voice betrayed her true reticence.

"You tell me," I suggested. "You got any special offers on?"

"Hands are twenty, lips are thirty and you can do me for sixty," she said, without a trace of irony. "Or all three for eighty, which is the best bargain you'll get this week. Turn left."

Whilst I admired the simplicity of her pricing structure, I had to question its straightforwardness. She was charging twice as much to lie back and stare at the ceiling as she was to creatively choke herself, and she was adding a premium for splitting the workload. By my calculation, dividing the labor among all three departments should reduce the cost to thirty-six sixty-six at the advertised rates. She was charging a full retail markup. Astonishing.

She guided me to a narrow track between a field of allotments and the London line. Her coat was off before the engine. "So. Here, or...?" She looked at me with wide, expectant eyes, apparently awaiting further instruction.

"Well," I pointed out, "there's not a great deal of space in here."

"No." She frowned apologetically. "Sorry, I've never done this before."

Even better. "You can't be serious," I said.

She clasped her hands uncomfortably in her lap. "I know, they all say that, right?"

"They?"

"You know…working girls."

"All right, I'm confused," I said. "Are you not one?"

She shook her head without much conviction. "I'm a barmaid," she replied.

"Right. So, what, I pay you sixty pounds and you squirt me out a drink?"

"No." She laughed. "What I meant was, I'm not doing this for a career, or to buy crack or anything."

"Why are you doing it, then?"

"Because—" she sighed "—I just got laid off, and my boss is being an arsehole, and he says he can't afford to pay me, and I need the cash."

"Surely there are other bars?" I suggested.

"Yes, there are, but I'm not going to get another job and get paid before the end of this week, so my rent won't get paid, the electric meter won't get fed and neither will I. And before you say it, it takes longer to get any dole money than it does to get a job." She lit another cigarette. I flicked on the ignition and rolled down her window. "And of course," she continued, "there's nothing to say that I *couldn't* make a career out of this. I mean, if I can just shag for a couple of hours a night and make, like, thirty grand a year, I'm laughing, aren't I? I mean it can't be that bad, right?"

My mind wandered over to the hunting knife nestling in

the glovebox and the nylon straps attached to the other side of the bulkhead just inches behind me.

Christ, what the fuck was I doing? Did I really feel so powerless in my own life that I had to take this poor, vulnerable creature's to compensate? An act contrary to my every instinct, one that had already come close to ruining my life and indeed one that I consider a crime of pure, unadulterated cowardice? What the hell was I going to prove like this?

"Are you okay?"

"What's your name?" I asked.

She took a long drag. "Tammy."

"What's your real name?"

"Okay, Sammy." She laughed. "Short for Samantha. You can look at my driving license if you want."

I waved away the offer. "Samantha," I said, "have you given any thought to the type of person who's likely to pick you up?"

"Well, you picked me up," she observed.

"Exactly."

"What? You're hardly some fat, smelly old codger, are you? If you came up to me in a club and bought me a few drinks, I'd probably shag you anyway, so what's the difference?"

"The difference is, you've got no idea who I am. Nobody saw you get in here with me. That's a pretty big risk for sixty quid." *Take the bait, Sammy. It's not too late.*

She rolled her eyes with a weary smirk. "I'm not a child," she said. "I can take care of myself."

She didn't have a clue. I looked at her tiny hands and her skinny ankles, the uncertainty in her eyes outshining the defiance. With a sigh, I took out my wallet and dropped three

twenties onto the seat beside her; she smiled and tucked them
into her bag.

"Okay, good," she said. She was welcome to it; I didn't
mind feeding her for the week. Indeed, I was about to start
the van and drive her home when she hopped out onto the
mud and slammed the door behind her. "Come on, let's go."
She smiled, peering through the open window. "I haven't
got all night."

O   O   O

I tried to give her one last chance. She didn't belong here;
she was a child, for Christ's sake, desperate and out of her
depth, and she was all but instructing me to do her harm. She
didn't deserve what was going to happen to her, but she was
making no effort whatsoever to avoid it. Even as she slipped
her shirt over her head, I wanted only to see her safely to her
door, last chance, last chance, but God help me, the V of her
soft, pale belly *(cut it)* and the peaks of her hips above her low-
cut jeans, her little-girl jeans, so young, too young, no sense,
no idea, never known pain or death or fear, just endless idle
hope and bad fucking judgment—she was making it as difficult as she knew how. And sure enough, once she was naked
and giving me the hurry-up, the choice was no longer mine.

The first time I put my hands around her neck, I held on
until her grip on my wrists became weak, and her mouth gave
up on its contorted efforts to suck in air. And then my body
overruled itself and I simply let her go, sat back against the
sliding door and watched her gulp and heave as she crawled
to the wall and pulled herself upright. She fixed me with a

look of startled anguish, bare chest heaving as she struggled
back to life.

"I'm sorry," I said weakly. "I don't know what I'm doing."
I wasn't even sure which of us I was talking to.

"You," she gasped. "You—"

"I know." I nodded. "Too late for sorry, right? The damage is done."

She knew as well as I did that I couldn't let her go, but
she struggled to her feet nonetheless. She began to cry as she
staggered toward the back doors; she fumbled with the catch,
sobbing and heaving and hiccupping hoarsely until the offside
door swung open and ejected her into the mud. She landed
on her hands and knees, retching violently as the fresh air hit
her. I gave her a moment; I knew she wasn't going far.

The second time, I was firm with myself. I pulled her back
inside and straddled her naked hips and pressed my thumbs
into her windpipe, silencing her screams. I maintained my
grasp long after her hands fell away and her legs stopped
thrashing, after her disbelieving, panicked stare faded and
her eyes rolled back in her head. I held on through the faint
twitching, until my arms ached and my fingers cramped and
every trace of pink had vanished from her skin. And even
then, I held on some more.

And now, as I sat idly tracing her cold contours with my
fingertips, I felt no satisfaction at having shouted down the
voice in my head. There was no elation, no relief. In spite of
myself, I felt nothing but hollow.

CHAPTER
TWENTY-FOUR

"Hello? Anybody home?"

Saturday, 9:00 a.m. Rachel stood at the end of her bed in a pure white cotton robe, balancing a tray of croissants and coffee and rolling her eyes in amused impatience.

"Hi." I shook Sammy's dead eyes from my head, propped the pillows up behind me and cleared a space on the bedside table; she set down the tray and hopped onto the bed, straddling my knees and leaning in to kiss me.

"Did you go somewhere nice?" she purred.

"Not especially." The robe was loose and, with a little assistance from my index finger, afforded me a most pleasing view. "I am now, though," I said.

"Cheeky." She laughed, snatching it shut. Her sleeves rode up as she did so, exposing the prominent scars across her wrists. She saw me notice and quietly covered herself.

"Don't be so coy," I said, with just a trace of a sly smile. "It's too late, you've got nothing left to hide."

"No," she conceded. "I don't suppose I have."

I took both of her hands and brought them close to my chest; she chewed her lip nervously as I turned her palms upward and swept back her sleeves. "Tell me about these," I said.

She looked down at them awkwardly, let out a heavy sigh. After a moment's reflection, she smiled sadly and said, "I suppose that's my tribute to my little sister." She pulled them away from me, held them up for self-inspection. "Not my finest moment."

"What happened?"

She laid them back in my lap, tucked her fingers into my palms. "She was a year younger than me," she said. "We were inseparable when we were little. Everyone used to think we were twins because we looked so similar and Mum used to dress us in identical clothes. In fact, when we were old enough to dress ourselves, we still did it because we'd kind of cottoned on to all the extra attention. I think sometimes even Mum and Dad forgot that we weren't two halves of the same person. The only time we were apart was when we were at school, because she was in the year below me, but even then we'd slope off together at playtime, and eat our lunch together at lunchtime." She smiled sadly, gazing among the flowers patterning the bedspread. "Of course, all the other kids thought we were weird and unsociable, so nobody else wanted to play with us, anyway," she said, laughing. "Well, when I left school I put off going to college for a year while she finished her A-levels, because we both wanted to go to the UEA and study English. I did a year in Sainsbury's stacking shelves so I could buy us a little car, which turned out to be one of the last of the old-school Mini Coopers. Dad chipped in a bit. He was tired of being a taxi. Anyway, it was the coolest thing, British racing green, and it had wide wheelarches and leather seats, and a CD player. Although the speakers were a bit crap." Her face fell; she sucked in her bottom lip and fixed her eyes on the swell of my legs between her knees.

I released her hands, lightly traced the scars with my fingertips. I couldn't find anything to say; my desire for a happy ending to her story was outgunned by inevitability, and I felt suddenly nervous. But I let her go on.

"We'd found some people to share a house with, so the week before term started, we were moving all our stuff, which basically meant Dad hiring a van and doing all the work, and he was following behind us when we crashed. I can't remember anything about it, but he said I just swerved straight across the road in front of a tractor. No idea why."

Metal on metal rang in my ears and sent a shudder through my spine. "Jesus," I muttered, at a loss for anything more profound.

"Anyway," she continued softly, "whatever happened, all I can remember is standing in the middle of a garden with the greenest trees you can imagine. I mean just greener than green, not like anything I've ever seen, and all these colors everywhere that…well, that I just don't know the words for. Nothing on Earth, just…indescribable. I can't even see them in my mind now. And, well, Becky stood there right in front of me with this Oh-my-God look on her face, and laughing. And then…" She trailed off, disappeared inside herself for a long moment before finally looking down into my eyes and taking a firm hold of my hands. "And then I could just hear my dad's voice screaming, 'Rebecca, Rebecca, oh my God, Rebecca, don't go! Stay with me, Rebecca!' I could feel him

shaking me, but he'd already given *me* up for dead. With all
the blood and everything, he actually thought I was her, although whether it was just wishful thinking or not I'll never
know. And then Becky was looking at me and shaking her
head, like *don't leave me*. She was terrified. And I tried to
reach out to her, but I couldn't reach her, I was being pulled
back. And then I don't remember anything else until a week
later when I woke up in intensive care, and there was nobody
there because they were all at the funeral. It was the anaes-
thetist who told me she'd died. And when they did show up,
they were far more concerned with their own feelings than
they were with mine. I was a mess, and all they'd say was
'It's okay, Rachel, it's not your fault' over and over, only they
made it pretty clear that it was themselves they were trying to
convince. And then of course, when the police decided they
couldn't find anything wrong with the car, it just got worse.
They never came out and said it, but they didn't need to. All
they seemed to be able to see was a dead daughter and the
person who killed her, curled up in the corner crying all the
time and getting under their feet. It sounds ridiculous now,
I know, but that's how they made me feel. And I missed her
so much I can't tell you, I mean it was like losing an arm or
something, just this constant itch reminding you there's a big
part of you missing, and I knew she was having a far better time being dead than I was being alive, and I was certain that no one would miss me, so I got in the bath with a
bottle of aspirin and a carving knife. I ended up dying twice
in the space of two months, although the second time I just
had one of those hovering-on-the-ceiling things where I got
to watch the doctors scurry about and look like they gave a

shit. I wasn't out for long." She took another long look at her wrists, let out an exaggerated sigh. "And all I got," she said, "were these lousy scars. Oh, and—" she rapped her knuckles on the top of her head "—nice big bit of titanium, too."

"Christ. I had no idea…" what to say.

"Well, of course not," she said. "It's not like I wear it on a T–shirt."

I forced a smile. That she had been wronged saddened me, but my total helplessness had me teetering on the brink of rage. "Tell me it got better for you," I said.

"No, not really. Mum sat me down and bawled me out for scaring her so badly, and then she broke down and wailed about how badly she was coping with losing Becky, and how she couldn't go on living if she lost me, too, and how did I think I'd feel if it was the other way around, if it was her who'd killed herself eight weeks after my sister. She said I was just being selfish and yeah, I suppose I was, but then *somebody* had to think about me, right?" She reached over to the table and handed me my tea, then went back for her own. "Of course—" she shrugged "—I could understand the loss part because I was feeling it myself, but it was more of a logical thing than an emotional one. I knew they were suffering, but I just didn't…*feel* for them. Too busy worrying about my own problems, which probably makes me a psychopath or something, but whatever. It can't come naturally to everyone, can it?"

"Of course not," I whispered, although in truth I had no idea whether it was the right answer.

"So," she said, "I guess these scars are here to remind me that however hard it gets, there's always something better just around the corner, and I've just got to wait my turn. Third time lucky and all that." She smiled and sipped her tea. "And in the meantime, I've just got to make the best of it which, from where I'm sitting, it looks as if I am."

"Do you think so?" It was all I could muster.

"Are you kidding?" She laughed. "I hadn't been happy for nine years, and then you come along, and I'm walking around with a big, stupid grin on my face, sniffing flowers and smiling at babies like I've had a bloody lobotomy! For the first time I can remember, I feel like I've got something to look forward to. I don't know what you've done to me, but you're the first thing I think of when I wake up, and I go to sleep dreaming about you at night. I've known you three weeks, for Christ's sake. I'm losing my sodding mind!"

My head was spinning. I spilled my tea on her bright white bedspread. *Control control control.* "Jesus," I said, "I might not know much, but I reckon I know all about losing my mind." And I dealt with that the only way I knew how. After breakfast, I went shopping.

○ ○ ○

Six weeks had passed by the time the police showed up. There had been letters from the school, the occasional sounding of the doorbell, and by the end of the second week I'd unplugged the phone, so incessantly was it ringing. But by and large, I'd been left alone.

The neighbors, all of whom worked during the day and were therefore only home after dark, had been reasonably unconcerned at not having seen my parents. They had, after all, seen the lights on in the evenings and heard all of the usual neighborly noises—doors closing, television chattering, toilet flushing. To the casual observer, nothing had seemed out of the ordinary.

When they finally came, on the morning of the seventh Sunday, the smell led them straight to the woodshed. I watched them from the window as they walked brazenly inside, reemerging in seconds to throw up on the grass. Then I sobbed my relief into the perfumed armpit of a softly sprung policewoman, who fawned and gently shushed with perfectly practiced patience.

It was my father's mother who'd reported us missing, and it was said that when she learned of his fate her heart broke clean in two. Physiologically speaking, I found this hard to accept, but I came to understand the analogy over time. It was, after all, my father's broken heart that folded his legs and sent his head wheeling to its fatal union with the lathe handle.

In any case, my discovery couldn't have been more timely; it was a particularly harsh winter, and despite my best efforts, within a fortnight, I'd reduced the food in the freezer to half a dozen pastry cases. My hurriedly developed hunting skills, whilst improving daily, had only netted me three ducks and a gristly, decrepit fox, and by the end of the fourth week, the fauna had wised up completely.

It was around then that I'd turned my attention to Nicola Pye. She lived on the edge of the village and was in my class at school, and I was attracted to her not for her delicious-sounding surname, but for her parents' propensity for allowing her to play in the woods at dusk. She was also on the plump side and had a tendency to lumber, and as a bonus she seemed to exhibit precious little spatial awareness, all of which would have made her unsportingly easy to catch.

Would I have gone through with it had I not been found? I don't know. I'd doubtless been deliriously hungry enough to picture Nicola as one of those pork-cut posters you see in the butcher's shop, but I wasn't stupid; I realized that, like everything else I'd caught, little girls weren't made of sugar and spice and all things nice, but rather inedible fat, bone and stringy yucky dangly bits.

What I do know, however, is that my stomach had little say in the matter. Yes, I stalked Nicola in the woods because I was hungry, but I imagined her with an arrow through her neck because it tickled me. Always had.

My father, for all of his faults, wasn't a monster. He did his best for me, as far as he understood how, but his fate was foretold by the sadness in his eyes at the end of every day. He knew that he was going to die a broken man, that my mother was too feckless and flighty to stay and watch it happen, and that nothing he could do, either in life or in death, would have any bearing on who or what I was to become. He knew, as I know now, that I was born and not made. A product of nature, and nurture be damned.

CHAPTER
TWENTY-FIVE

So. Shopping. Harassed mothers in juice-stained joggers, struggling to control their young. Fat women with greasy hair and damp armpits, hoarding cake and store-brand diet cola. Teenage girls with braces on their teeth, giggling and holding hands as they tried on cheap jewelry. And there, among the rails of in-house designer evening wear, a tiny package of perfection.

She was four or maybe five, blue denim dress with matching buckle shoes and wispy blond hair to her waist. She clung for dear life to a giant stuffed rabbit as the tears streamed down her face. Sniffing and whimpering, she wandered slowly and aimlessly, scanning the faces around her for a spark of recognition.

Women glanced down at her with theatrical concern, looked around briefly for a match before going on about their business with a sympathetic smile. Men gave her a wide berth, mindful of the ease with which honorable intentions can be misconstrued. I, naturally, moved right in.

"Are you lost?" I knelt down in front of her, looked deep into her swollen blue eyes. Any wariness she may have possessed was crushed beneath a ton of despair.

She nodded, bottom lip quivering, eyelashes swatting at the tears. "I can't find my mummy," she sobbed.

"Well, look." I smiled. "You stay with me, and we'll see if we can see her, okay?"

She squeezed the toy to her face, nodded slowly and took my hand. I stood, meeting the suspicion on passing faces with a defiant, righteous glare. "What's your name?" I asked.

"Molly." She sniffed.

"What does your mummy look like, Molly?" I steered her easily toward the front of the store. "Has she got yellow hair like yours?"

A silent nod.

"And is she wearing a pretty dress like yours?"

"She's got a pink dress."

Away from the scene of the crime, barely a soul looked our way. "I like your bunny," I said. "What's his name?"

She gave it a long, affectionate look and a tight squeeze. "Bunny." She shrugged.

"Well, that's as good a name as any." I laughed. "Does he go everywhere with you?"

She nodded, heaved out a giant sob as we neared the automated one-way entrance barriers at the edge of the foyer. A security guard stood with his back to us, idly chatting to a middle-aged member of staff.

"Excuse me," I called. "Security!" He turned to face me, eyes narrowed in officious scrutiny. "Can you let me through, please?"

He unquestioningly waved his hand in front of the nearest barrier, which obediently swung open. I guided Molly through with a smile and a thank-you. Easy as that.

"Do you know your mummy's name?" I asked her, thirty feet from the door.

"Sally," she replied.

"And has she got a big green bag?"

"With flowers." Fifteen feet.

I pointed to the slender, tearful blonde flapping her hands at the customer service desk as the beginnings of an announcement rang out over the PA system. "Is that her?" I suggested.

Molly's face lit up. "Yes," she exclaimed.

I released her into a run as her mother turned to follow the assistant's stare and all but fell to her knees.

"Oh my God, Molly," she cried, folding the girl into her arms. She looked up at me, eyes filled with tears, and mouthed the words "Thank you." The relief and happiness in her face filled me with an odd, warm glow. All I could do was smile, and beat a hasty retreat.

Okay. Control. We can do this. It won't change what I did to Sammy, won't get rid of the spiny, glittery pressure behind my eyes, but I can at least try to even the odds.

I found myself in the market square, neither destination nor purpose clear in my mind but for the notion that dicing a shop assistant might not help me make sense of my feelings this time. People milled around me, hundreds of tiny universes flitting in and out of my own, each driven by its own immediate wants and needs. They darted from shop to bank to post office to shop, fueled by greed and necessity. Retail junkies. Slaves to the rhythm of supply and demand. I couldn't even bring myself to pity them.

I watched a withered, tweed-suited old man at the edge of the square, gazing sadly at the memorial there. He bowed his head to the list of his fallen comrades and crossed himself with an unsteady hand before turning to the task of crossing the street.

Cars were scarce but quick to appear; the roads through the center of town are narrow and confusing, more of a rat-run than a route. The younger and more able-bodied find no real challenge in not getting run over; those of a slower disposition, however, can quite easily find themselves stranded at the white line, staring down a mail van. With this is mind, I joined the old man at the curb and rendered my assistance.

I strolled down to the river and watched delighted children throw bread to the ducks and swans. Couples walked hand in hand, laughing and cavorting in the sunshine. A golden retriever leaped excitedly into the water to fetch a rubber ball, returning to shake out its coat over horrified passersby.

I strolled into the florist's shop, where I bought some yellow-and-white chrysanthemums and a pretty blue ceramic vase. The girl behind the counter said she wished someone would give her flowers. I smiled and bought her a rose. She blushed. Said I'd made her day.

Wandering up through town, I was accosted by a troupe of

Girl Guides panning for cash. Their leader, a squat middle-aged woman with a basin haircut, explained the need for a total refurbishment of the guide hut; I gave her my number and a promise to paint some walls. She and her troupe were remarkably thankful. I asked her whether Girl Scout cookies would be provided. She told me that was an American thing. "We'll see about that," I said, but I wasn't really sure what I meant, because I didn't fancy eating any of them. The troupe said they'd see what they could do. Apparently I'd made their day, too.

———————

The traffic parted magically before me as I hightailed it home, wind in my hair, fingers drumming the wheel, the Commodores on Radio 2. Birds swooped down from the trees to glide alongside me, chattering to the deer and the foxes and the rabbits lining the roadside, a thousand fluttering tails and bristling whiskers and tiny twitching noses all united in celebration. The midday sun slid proudly by in an endless deep sapphire sky, and I laughed so hard that I started to cry, though I wasn't entirely sure why.

I was still sobbing as I closed the gate behind me and wound through the dappled trees; parked the Jensen in the shade and strolled breezily to the door; scooped up the mail from the mat and threw open the downstairs windows.

I floated around the house on a cushion of air, the tension flicking off me in gobs as a million images cascaded through my mind, none staying long enough to be deciphered, but every one leaving wonder and excitement in its wake. I ricocheted from room to room, unable to settle. I made tea, then promptly forgot and opened a bottle of wine. I put the bottle down somewhere and forgot about that, too. I breezed into the kitchen to make some tea, and discovered that I'd already done so. It was cold, which put me off. I decided I'd open a bottle of wine, but couldn't find a corkscrew. In hunting for it, I found a bottle I'd already opened. I didn't put it down this time.

I lingered in the kitchen, tried to slow down the thoughts in my head. I grasped wildly at feelings of happiness, turned them around and over and inside out, struggling vainly to analyze them. The more I did so, the more I grieved for Sammy and Kerry and Sarah and the rest. I forcibly rejected them, allowed the mystery train of random thought to regain control. It felt like I'd been standing there ten minutes. The clock said two hours.

And yet this dizzying whirlwind of confused emotions was suddenly overshadowed by the return of that uncomfortable, nagging feeling that I was forgetting someth—

Shit.

———

Erica didn't look happy. She sat on the edge of her bed, knees crossed, hands folded together in her lap, fire and brimstone in her eyes. She watched me like a hawk as I let myself into the cage; her breathing was slow and controlled but her temples betrayed a pulse that pounded like a jackhammer. I chose not to ask how long she'd been sitting there.

"Hi." I smiled.

She didn't answer; she just stared.

"I brought you some flowers," I said. "Thought they might brighten the place up a bit."

She replied with a raised eyebrow and a slow half nod, watched me silently as I went to the sink to unwrap the flowers.

"I thought maybe later you might like to get out, walk around the garden or something." No answer. "It's a beautiful day. The deer are out grazing, I noticed." I rinsed and trimmed the stems, three at a time in two-inch increments. "We could have a barbecue later, if you fancy it."

When she finally spoke, her voice was hard and accusing and not two feet from my left ear. "You left me alone again," she said. I whirled around to face her, trying hard not to appear startled. She'd picked up the vase from the floor near my feet and was rolling it from hand to hand, testing its weight. Her eyes blazed with intent.

"Yes." I sighed. "I occasionally have to do tedious things like work and shop and take rubbish to the dump. If I lock myself in the house all day we'll soon be very hungry. I'm here now, though." I tried on an appeasing smile and held out my hand.

She blew a half laugh through pursed lips and wearily shook her head. She clearly wasn't buying my explanation, and I didn't blame her; she did, however, hand over the vase.

"Thank you." I smiled.

"Don't mention it," she snarled as she retreated to her bed.

I half filled the vase with water and dropped in the chrysanthemums, alternating the colors and setting them neatly in height order front to back. "There," I said, proudly holding up the arrangement for her to admire. "A little bit of sun-shine in a jar."

"Lovely," she said.

Of course, she didn't mean it. She wasn't even looking at the flowers. This, however, ceased to concern me the moment I turned around. I'd got as far as "Oh, come on…" when I noticed two things out of place. One was Erica, who was not on her bed as I'd anticipated but was in fact standing three feet in front of me with her arms raised. And the other was the microwave, which did not belong on my head.

CHAPTER
TWENTY-SIX

My back was damp. The left side of my forehead stung like I'd been nuzzling nettles, and a searing, splintering ache pounded through my skull. My brain was mostly white noise.

Slowly, timidly, I half opened my eyes. Intense halogen light speared through my head, elevating the pain from a staccato pulse to a constant, high-pitched whine. I took a moment to steady my breathing before trying again.

When I eventually managed to focus, it was on a diamond pattern in heavy steel mesh, bold against a background of dull gray concrete. I stared for some time, tracing the pattern with lazy eyes; after a while I could begin to turn my head, follow any one of a seemingly infinite number of paths across my field of vision. The one I chose wound tortuously floorward until my burning forehead touched sticky wet rubber but, curiously, I couldn't see where it led. There was a packet of aspirin in front of my face.

I figured I was in some degree of trouble; the warm wetness beneath me ran from my head to halfway down my back,

and out across my shoulders. I felt distinctly faint, and I surmised from the crackling sensation that my forehead had been
breached, though to what extent I was almost afraid to find out.

Tentatively, I raised my hand to my head and traced the
wound with my fingertips. The skin was rough and tacky,
the lump the size of a golf ball, but it felt more or less intact.
On inspection, my fingers were spotted rather than soaked
with blood. I ran both hands through my hair, checking for
further signs of injury. No one spot was any more tender
than the next.

There seemed to be no damage south of my neck. Fingers
and toes wiggled freely; arms and legs bent and swiveled at
my command. My breathing was free and easy, there was
no pain in my torso, and I could feel my hands patting and
prodding. I slipped them into the wet patch beneath my back,
drew them out and held them before my eyes. The liquid was
clear and odorless, very much like water. Whatever I'd done
to myself, it didn't appear to be life-threatening.

Relieved, I closed my eyes against the uncomfortably bright
lights, focusing on nothing but the deep red sunset that was
the inside of my eyelids. I relaxed my body, let my head loll
and the pain ebb away to a low hum, concentrated in an almost tangible ball at the back of my brain. I tuned out the
static and welcomed back a slow train of rational thought and
desirous images and random memories. I grasped at snippets
of reason and information and spatial awareness, a rapidly
expanding multidimensional jigsaw puzzle, the solution to
which I relied upon to drive my next move. I felt a surge of
anxiety as I realized I was trying too hard, so intent on finding all the pieces that I couldn't properly see the ones I had.

The pain exploded back out to the far reaches of my skull. I pulled myself back, took a long, deep breath, ejected the questions from my mind to make room for an answer.

And as I did so, everything fell into place.

The alarm rose in me so fast I thought it might spew from my mouth. I hurled myself against the cage door, and it deflected me with barely a rattle, bouncing me straight back down to the mat. I rolled to my feet and flew at it again, with the same result. Satisfied that the door was performing as intended, I quit while I still had my ribs. A cage is, after all, designed for the sole purpose of keeping things in.

I took instead to pacing frantically back and forth, struggling to ignore the blurred vision and screeching headache and concentrate on finding a way out. Of course, I knew that there wasn't one, and the result was merely an incoherent, profane babble. The plan was soon abandoned in favor of simple blind panic.

Having no idea how long I'd been unconscious, it was impossible to guess at what might be happening above my head. If she'd stuck around and called the police, they'd have been here and hauled me out inside twenty minutes. If she'd walked home and called them, it could be a couple of hours. If she'd taken my car and intended to simply leave me here, I guessed I'd know in six. The reality, though, was that I could have been out for two minutes or two days and I'd be none the wiser. Her clothes were gone, but they were already kept in bags. The chrysanthemums, though crumpled, were still alive—but then they'd lain in a puddle of water.

I picked up the empty vase and, though overtaken by the urge to violently throw it at the wall, I refilled it instead. I scooped up the flattened flowers and dropped them carefully inside; stood them on the back of the sink. I felt a little calmer.

With my temper settled, I attended to the pain. The aspirin packet was nearly full, and I swallowed a handful with a glass of water. I lay on Erica's bed to help it along; placed her pillow over my face and closed my eyes. At some point, I passed out.

Rehearsing the arrival of the police was a dead end. "Thank God you're here" wasn't going to cut it, given that I was imprisoned in a cell of my own devising, in a hidden basement underneath my own garage. And unless they sent a pair of unarmed beat bobbies, I wasn't going to be fighting my way out. I imagined I'd feign unconsciousness and take my chances jumping from the ambulance. It wasn't great, but it was better than "Damn, you got me."

And where the hell were they, anyway? She could have crawled home on her hands and knees and they should still have been here by now. It'd be dark outside, and cold. I hoped she'd closed the windows.

I toyed with the idea of plugging in the microwave; the clock would be reset to midnight, just as it was when I brought it down here, but I could at least monitor the passing of time. It was, however, badly damaged at the business end, and the last thing I needed was a fire.

Jesus, what if Rachel was trying to call? How long would it be before she started to worry? Who would she tell when she did? Would they come out here looking for me? And if they did, would they even find me?

And what if she didn't start to worry? What if she was waiting for *me* to call *her*? What if she believed that she'd scared me away, that I simply wasn't returning her calls? What if she reacted the wrong way? Would I ever know? And what would be worse—Rachel thinking I ran out on her, or Rachel finding out about this?

What if nobody knew I was missing? Would Annie ever notice? What if the bills went unpaid and the lights went out? What if I didn't turn up to paint the Guide hut? Would *they* come looking? Is that their job? I don't even know what fucking Girl Guides do.

The fridge was empty. No wonder she'd been pissed off. I'd already been hungry, but knowing this made me ravenous. My stomach was growling to wake the dead. The empty churning combined with the headache, the dizziness and the nausea made quite a concoction, and when added to the anxiety of incarceration it became almost unbearable. I curled up in a ball on the bed and awaited the onset of dry retching. Sometime later, I slept.

The camera was bothering me. It stared down defiantly from its perch, ten feet from the end of my nose. I knew where the cable went, and I knew that no one was sitting on my sofa staring at the television. Nobody was watching me. Nobody but the camera. I turned my back, stood stock-still. I'd have to watch my words. Don't want them to think they've won.

○　○　○

"Don't know when...I've been so blue...Don't know what's... No, okay, I know, but I never said I could sing, did I? If you don't like it, don't listen. I'm talking to myself, aren't I? Am I saying this out loud? God, this had better be a dream. I haven't had a cup of tea in...fucking *days*. You lock me down here with nothing but an empty glass and you expect me to—what, exactly? Freak out? How would you like it? You're not even listening, are you? No, I didn't think so. Typical woman. Me me me me me. I don't even know what I'm talking about. Shut up. Fuck off."

"Did you just tell me to fuck off?"

"Don't know when...I've been so blue-oo-oo-hooooo... Oh, for fuck's sake, man, either sing the whole thing or sing something else, but don't just repeat the same two fucking lines over and over and over and over and over..."

"Kisses for me… Save all your kisses for m—fuck."

○   ○   ○

I paced to the brink of collapse, my mind out of focus, my awareness of my surroundings ever dwindling. When I finally fell asleep, it was midstride; I barely noticed hitting the floor.

I woke to see Rachel crouched over me, hugging her knees and rocking back and forth on the balls of her feet, tears streaming down her face. Her words were muffled, indecipherable. I spoke to her, but I couldn't hear my voice, and I didn't know what I'd said. Her head bowed and she began to fall; I sat up to catch her, held her head in my arms but she was heavy and lifeless, a rag doll. I shook her, fearfully called her name again and again but it was too late; she was gone. My heart dropped out of my chest, and I struggled for breath as I held her to me, blood from an absent wound pooling in my lap. And then I caught a glimmer of movement from across the room, and I looked up into sparkling blue-green eyes filled with happiness and awe and profound overpowering relief, and for a moment my pain subsided. I gasped in wonder and giggled like a child. Until I realized that the eyes were Erica's.

I woke up bolt upright, a scream halfway out of my mouth. My head was pounding, and my stomach was spinning, and I dragged myself to the toilet in time to be violently sick.

I sucked down a handful of aspirin, swilled it around with a dozen glasses of water. I lay sprawled on my back with my eyes screwed shut, willing away the pain, Rachel's last breath playing on a loop behind my eyelids for endless, miserable hours. Or maybe they were minutes.

When the pain became bearable, I propped myself against the side of the cage and forced the pictures from my mind; stared at the bed and the toilet and the broken microwave and just waited. For exactly what, I neither knew nor cared.

———

The hunger soon gave way to a greater longing, a longing for fresh air and daylight; grass and trees and birdsong. A shower, a toothbrush and a change of clothes. A chair and a window and a soothing voice.

With longing came self-pity, and with self-pity came an acute awareness of the gravity of my situation. With that awareness came the embarrassment and shame of my own stupidity. And hot on their heels was anger.

It hit me like a bullet, exploding through my chest and sending white-hot splinters up and down my spine. I scrabbled to my feet, snatched up the microwave from the mat and launched it furiously against the wall. It dismantled itself impressively, a cacophony of shrieking metal signaling, if only to me, my renewed enthusiasm for finding a way out of this hole. I strode to the door, shards of glass and plastic crinkling underfoot and, returning the camera's soulless stare, I made my intentions known.

"Erica," I said, "I'm going to kill you."

———

Awaking later from a pain-induced sleep, and having finished off the box of aspirin, I found my sustained anger complemented by a startling clarity of thought. The white noise was gone, and with it the underlying panic; I saw everything in crisp relief and pin-sharp color, and for the first time I was able to fully take stock of my circumstances.

I'd been abandoned in a steel cage in a concrete basement under twelve feet of soil. The cage was designed and built to be impenetrable without cutting equipment or perhaps a mechanical digger, neither of which were available.

I had a mains water supply, at least until my unpaid bills began to cause offence, but no food. Unless by some miracle I was discovered, this would inevitably lead to my demise. However, should starving to death prove too much of a drag, I had the choice of a knotable curtain or a live electric current to help me along. A forcible exit, then, was out in favor of an untimely and undignified death.

There did, however, appear to be a third option; whether newly presented or newly discovered I couldn't say for sure. As much as it galled me, the more I stared at the cage door, the more I had to admit that it wasn't padlocked. And the greater my acceptance of this fact, the clearer it became that I ought to try the bolt.

Needless to say, the door wasn't locked.

CHAPTER
TWENTY-SEVEN

I held my breath as I crouched stone-still in the darkness, listening for the faintest sign of life outside the cupboard. Hearing none, I cracked open the wooden door a thumb's width and hunkered down to squint through the gap. Nothing. Silent and dark and a dry sixty degrees.

I flung the door wide and stumbled out into the garage. The van was just as I'd left it; clean, locked, alarm warning light flashing. As far as I could tell, everything else was in its place; lawnmower, barbecue, patio set, toolbox, garden fork... Garden fork. Better than nothing. I swept it into my arms from where it stood against the wall; cobwebs stretched and snapped and draped themselves over my fingers.

Armed, I set about finalizing my escape. I reached above me and pulled the emergency release for the electric door, popping the latch on the motor rail. After a preparatory deep breath, I threw the door up over my head, adrenaline coursing, fork poised in readiness for whatever might loom out of the darkness.

Whatever I was expecting, I was way off. Unfiltered sunshine blasted into my unsuitably wide eyes, painfully blinding me and knocking me off balance. I staggered out onto the driveway, all too aware that the swiftly advancing garden tool would be a red rag to any waiting marksmen. However, between swiping the sun out of my eyes with my free hand and steeling myself for the hail of bullets, I somehow forgot to drop it. Miraculously, I was still standing when I managed to squint between my fingers and take in what lay before me.

The driveway was empty but for the Interceptor. The house lay still, ground-floor windows open, front door closed, a lone pigeon perched quietly on the roof. And behind me nothing but trees, their branches nodding lazily in the gentle breeze, bark rustling to the rhythm of tiny squirrel claws. There was nobody out here but me.

———

The car didn't seem to have moved; the keys were still in the ignition, the driver's-side window wound down. The hood was cold. If she'd gone, it was on foot, and if she hadn't, she was here alone. I was starting to suspect the latter, and it made me uneasy. An ambush is an ambush, no matter how many hands it's laid by. And she'd already felled me once.

The possibilities for booby-trapping the house, and the scope for bluff and double bluff, were endless. Since she would surely have realized that I'd be expecting a trap, I was optimistic that she wouldn't have bothered with one. On the other hand, if she'd anticipated my line of reasoning and my intention to just walk in through the door, I'd be a sitting duck for a twelve-gauge and a ball of string.

By the time I had my hand on the door handle, the issue had become one of trajectory. If she'd rigged a makeshift pulley, with the door ultimately tied to a trigger across the hall, and if she'd expected me to expect it, would the gun be aimed at the door or off to one side? And in the case of the latter, which side?

After much deliberation, and shamefully late in the game, it occurred to me that the simplest option available to Erica would have been to leave me locked in the cage, and that the booby trap was in fact a figment of my concussed imagination. Unless, of course, that was what she wanted me to think.

"Fuck it." I twisted the handle and gave the door a gentle push, let it swing slowly open to reveal a quiet, empty hallway. Wielding the fork like a bayonet, I slipped inside, pausing to listen after every tentative step. Nothing to hear but the ticking clock in the kitchen and the big bass thrum of my pulse.

I edged toward the living room with one eye on the stairs, tingling in anticipation of the slightest movement. I could see before I reached the doorway that the room was empty and unspoiled. My books were still on their shelves, the cushions still on the sofa; the fruit bowl was full, dead-center of the coffee table. Good.

The kitchen, on the other hand, conflicted me. Whilst there was no sound from within, the back of my neck told me a different story and as I neared the door, I felt urged to back away. I stood entirely still, held my breath, strained my ears until they rang in my head. I stared at the reflections on the windows, the chrome toaster, the oven door. Nothing moved. I relaxed, told myself I was needlessly paranoid. And then I walked on in and proved myself wrong.

———————

"You took your time," she said. "Sit down, I've made you a cup of tea." Erica sat at the breakfast table, draped in low-cut chocolate satin and an arrestingly pleasant smile. Before her, steaming tea and buttered toast, miniature jams and Lyles maple syrup, a stack of American pancakes. A mobile phone I recognized as my own. And, most troublingly, a loaded .38 revolver—also mine.

My desire to skewer her with the garden fork grew in direct proportion with the dawning of its impossibility. She and I both knew that I'd never get within striking distance, but I tightened my grip on it nonetheless, finding some small comfort in the gesture of intent.

She laughed. Not her usual reflective, sad-eyed half sigh but the kind of ticklish giggle one might afford a newly trained puppy as it excitedly presents its paw. "Come on," she said, "don't be silly." She nodded toward her opposite chair as she spread blackcurrant jam onto a slice of toast. "Sit down and have some breakfast. I'll be sick if I eat all this."

"I'm not interested in breakfast," I said. It was an obvious lie; the grumbling from my stomach all but shouted me down as the thick smell of fried batter, until now having somehow eluded me, surged through my nostrils and set my mouth watering. I figured it wouldn't hurt to build up some energy before I skinned her alive, however halfhearted my intention to do so; nevertheless, for some stubborn reason, I stood my ground.

"It's a beautiful day." She smiled between bites. "We should get out and do something. Go to the park maybe, or the seaside. I haven't been to the seaside in years. We used to go to Cart Gap when I was a little girl. Me and Mum and Dad and my friend Marie. I always used to end up getting upset because my dad paid her more attention than me. He was always asking her if she wanted an ice cream, and if *she* wanted one then he'd ask me if I wanted one, too, and then he'd take her off to the ice cream van with him and tell me to stay and keep Mum company. Funny, I never really thought there was anything suspect about it until just now. I wondered why she stopped coming over to play." She laughed girlishly through a mouthful of toast. "Where the hell is Cart Gap, anyway?"

I was starting to feel self-conscious, standing here *en garde* in the middle of the kitchen while she airily daydreamed all over the table. "That's a lovely story," I fumed, "but the only place you're going today is back to your room."

The smile lingered as she dropped a new slice of toast onto her plate and dipped her knife into the jam. She spread it in one slow, careful swipe. "Oh, shush," she said. "Don't be such a bloody grouch."

A what? "A grouch?"

"Yes, a grouch. I've made you pancakes, and you're just standing there with a sour face, pointing your tool at me. You know, I don't think laminate flooring needs to be turned. You're not likely to grow anything, anyway."

My response didn't do me any favors. "It's fucking oak," I

snapped, which just made her laugh so hard that she had to put her knife down.

"Christ—" she giggled "—you really are angry, aren't you?"

Yes, I was. I slammed the fork into the floor, left it springing back and forth as I advanced on her. "Angry?" I roared. "Are you out of your mind? You hit me over the head with an oven and locked me in a cage for a week, you psychotic little shit!"

Her mood changed in a heartbeat and she was on her feet, the revolver in her hand and aimed directly between my eyes before I'd even reached the table.

As unsure as I was that Erica had the nerve to pull the trigger, I wasn't going to take any chances. She had, after all, had the nerve to brain me with a microwave, and I'd already been humiliated so comprehensively that face-saving was now viable in only the most literal sense. As such, I stopped in my tracks.

"You're damn right I did," she snarled. "You fucking deserved it, and not only that, you needed it, too."

"I did what?" I suspected that, if challenged, she could back up her first assertion, but, "I needed it? What, like a hole in the head? I mean, sure, I wasn't concussed before, but then I haven't got a pet pig, either, and I'm pretty sure I don't nee—"

"You've been asking for it for fucking weeks. You've been bumbling around with your head up your arse, not knowing what day it was and generally being a massive useless twat and, more to the point, neglecting your responsibilities, i.e. me. You're a shambles and a liability, and I'm not going to sit down there on my own and starve to death while you're off gallivanting around, doing God only knows what with

God only knows who without so much as bothering to re-member that I exist, you stupid, selfish, useless bastard. And you know what else? You weren't down there a week, it was forty-three hours. You couldn't even make it two days, for Christ's sake. Do you know how long *I've* been down there? Three fucking months, that's how long. Are you starting to get the picture yet? You want to ask me how fucking angry *I* am? No, I didn't think so. I suggest you sit the fuck down, right now, and eat your fucking pancakes."

Assured of her willingness to shoot me in the head, bereft of what might be deemed an adequate response and, strangely, more than a little aroused, I did as I was told.

After forty-three hours, which feels closer to forty-three days when incarcerated with only a brain injury for company, pancakes and maple syrup and hot, sweet tea make for an al-most religious experience. After ten minutes under Erica's watchful gaze, however, I was ready to crawl out of my skin. She stared at me unblinkingly, fingers folded together under her chin, eyes flickering between homicidal and hysterical. She didn't speak, even after I'd pushed away my empty plate, and for the first time in my life the silence made me uneasy. Almost as uneasy, in fact, as my next thought. "Erica," I said. "This may seem like an obvious question, but why are you still here? Why didn't you just…go home?"

She smiled thinly, turned her eyes to the table, chewed on her bottom lip as she considered her answer. "I nearly did," she said finally. "But then I couldn't."

"What does that mean? There's a car in the driveway. The keys are in it…"

"I know, and I threw all of my stuff in it and drove it right to my house, but…" Her eyes fell to her hands, now playing idly with the revolver on the tabletop. "It's my stepdad," she muttered. "She's moved him back in. I could see him through the front window, feet up on the table, reading the *Daily Mail*. That piece of shit beat the hell out of my mum and my sister and me for three years before we finally got rid of him, and I've been away for three months, and if you think the hours feel like days in that cellar, well trust me, the months feel like decades, and when I come out of there after *three months* I find everything back to the way it was, with that psycho fuckbag living in my house and putting his hands on my family, and I'm just not ready to deal with it yet." She pushed the revolver to one side, sat back in her chair with a heavy sigh. After a moment's silence, she looked me sadly in the eye. "I thought of all those cheesy lines about where the heart is and where you lay your hat and all that crap and, well, my life just isn't the same as it was three months ago, is it? I'm not the same person anymore."

"So, what, you hit me over the head to teach me a lesson and then just trot off back to your room? What the hell kind of a plan is that?" And why the hell am I pointing this out to her?

"Oh, I've got a plan, all right." She nodded. "I'll be going home, sooner rather than later, but not before you've taught me how to kill that fucking monster and get away with it, because God knows I didn't do a good enough job last time. And I'll tell you now, in the meantime, there are going to be a few changes, not least of which is that my room is now at the top of the stairs and to the right. You're going to fit a lock, to the *inside*, and after that you're not going to come in unless I say it's okay. You're going to stop treating me like a pet and show me some fucking respect. You're going to buy fresh meat and proper vegetables, and you're going to hand them straight over to me because, quite honestly, your cooking is sketchy as fuck. And most of all, you're going to get rid of this Rachel woman because she's fucking with your head."

I felt my shoulders rise, tasted bile in my throat. "What do you know about Rachel?"

"Know? Nothing at all." She smirked. "Except that she quite obviously doesn't know the first thing about you, and she's turning you into Bambi. Oh…" She sat up and slid my phone to me across the table. "And *she* wanted to go to the beach today, too."

I snatched up the mobile, but could only stare cluelessly at a list of truncated text messages.

"You told her you were away today," she continued. "But apparently she's got the whole week off and, well, from the color of the gas bill, it doesn't look like you were planning to go to work, either, so you told her to swing by tomorrow."

"If you said anything to her—"

"You'll what? Kill me?"

It would have been easy to say it, but in truth I didn't know what the hell I'd do. Words failed me.

"You know why I let you out this morning?" she said.

"What?"

"I let you out because you looked up at me last night, and there was a whole new you in there. I could see it in your eyes, the same look you had the first time I woke up and saw you there with a carving knife in your hand. I thought you were going to cut me open and—I don't know—fuck my liver or something. It was intense. And you stood there last night, and I honestly thought you were going to just reach out of the TV and tear me apart with your bare hands. And I thought 'that's it, he's fucking back. It's gonna be okay.' But I was wrong, wasn't I? You're not okay. It's going to take more than a concussion to fix you." She dipped her head and looked up at me with amused puppy eyes. "Not to worry." She smiled. "I'll get rid of her for you."

That was it. A wall of rage hit me like a truck, propelling me out of my seat and across the table in a desperate lunge for the gun. Erica's right hand got there first, her left sweeping up a crumb-covered plate and bringing it down hard enough across my knuckles to break it clean in two. I yelped as it tore open the skin; lost my balance and collapsed onto the table as I snatched away my fingers. Without hesitation, she slammed her fist down onto the toppled plastic Lyles bottle, unleashing a jet of syrup directly into my eyes. And then, as I slithered about helplessly on the polished oak, she threw her hand across my mouth and ground my head into the butter.

"Shhh," she hissed. "Car." She let go of my face and peered out through the window as the sound of crackling gravel drew near.

"I can't see," I protested.

"Oh, for Christ's sake." She took hold of my bleeding hand and hauled me off the table, letting me fall in a groaning heap on the floor. "Sorry," she whispered.

I staggered to my feet and thumped straight into the wall. "No. I mean I actually can't see, you mental b—"

"Look, I'm trying to give—" Her fingers found my wrist and she pressed a damp cloth into my hand. "There."

"You fucking *belong* in a cage," I said as I wiped the maple syrup from my eyes.

And then my day got even worse. Outside on the driveway was a dirty blue Ford. It had a rubber whip antenna, and its hubcaps were held on with cable ties.

CHAPTER
TWENTY-EIGHT

"Tell me you didn't call the police."

"I didn't call the police."

"Where did you hide the shotgun?"

"In the loft. What's going on? What do they want?"

"I don't know. For Christ's sake get rid of that thing."

"Oh, God." Erica whirled around, scanning the kitchen for somewhere to stash the revolver as I headed for the door. "Where?"

"Anywhere, just lose it." I stalled in the hall, furiously scrubbing my eyes with the cloth. "Hurry up!"

"Okay, it's gone."

"Oh, and I've framed you for murder, so you'd better bloody hide."

"You—"

I opened the front door as John Fairey was raising his fist, leaving him weakly punching the air. "Good morning, Detective Inspector." I smiled. "What an unexpected pleasure."

"It's all mine," he replied, taking a step back to look me up and down. "Are you, um...?" He furrowed his brow, took

in the trickling blood, the crack in my head, the syrup sliding down my face. "What in God's name happened to you?"

"Walked into a door."

He regarded me with undisguised contempt for a moment,
before shrugging his shoulders and chuckling to himself.
"Okay," he said, clearly savoring the moment. I let him have it.

"Thanks for your concern. Is there anything else I can help
you with, or did you just come by to see how I am?"

"Actually," he said, smiling, "I came by to have a little chat
with you. I hope this is a good time."

It quite obviously was not but, while his smile was innocuous enough, his tone suggested that I didn't have a choice.
"It's a bank holiday," I reminded him. "Shouldn't you be at
home pulling the legs off spiders or something?"

He laughed. "Well, that was what I said, right before I drew
the short straw." He relaxed then, took to an easy lean against
the porch post. "To be honest, I'm actually avoiding work by
being here. I didn't come to give you a hard time, it's just a chat.
Tie up some loose ends, give you my card, thank you for the tea,
that kind of thing." He shuffled himself comfortable, crossed his
big clown feet. "Milk and two sugars," he said, jacking a thumb
over his shoulder to where a beard in a shabby gray suit leaned
awkwardly against the car. "And the same for the constable."

"Cocky shit," I observed. "Go work on your tan for a minute. I need to clean my face."

———

To their credit, Fairey and his shadowy friend stayed put
while I tried and failed to work out where Erica had con-

cealed herself. Indeed, neither appeared to have moved at all by the time I returned with a clean shirt and their two teas.

Fairey clearly had little time for his colleague; he neither addressed the man as he passed him his tea, nor extended the courtesy of an introduction.

"Let's walk," he said simply, leading me away from the car and off toward the garden, throwing back as an afterthought a curt, "Wait with the car, Keith." The constable's hateful scowl connected only with the back of Fairey's head.

"Where's your mistress today?" I asked. "Is she pacing around a park somewhere with your lead in her hand? Asking passing joggers if they've seen you?"

Fairey, God bless him, graciously laughed. "Detective Sergeant Green," he replied, "has been having ideas above her station. She's been whisked off on some joint fucking taskforce or other. I think they're training her to be a sniffer dog or something."

"Good for her." I smiled. "It doesn't sound like you're bitter at all, either."

"I'll tell you what pisses me off," he said with a backward nod. "They sent *that* nonce to follow me around. He hasn't been out of uniform five fucking minutes. He just sits there in the car, staring out the window like he's on the Sunshine Bus. *And* they reckon he's a bit...you know."

"I don't—"

"Anyway, I'm not surprised she got the job. I'm white and male. She's half-Paki and a woman. They've got a quota to fill, right? Whatever, I don't want to talk about the uppity bitch. I didn't want the job, anyway. My hours are shitty enough as it is. You know what? I've worked every bank holiday for the last four years. It's the wife's birthday, and look where I am. All I get is 'Oh, you're never at home, and you've never got time for the baby, and you haven't even changed his bum yet, and he's gonna grow up not knowing who his dad is' and all that shit. Like he fucking cares. I'll be divorced by Christmas. Comes a point, you have to wonder whether it's all worth it."

"Well," I said, smirking, "if you ever need a shoulder to cry on…"

"Yeah, I'll bear it in mind." He sipped his tea, spilling more on his tie than he got in his mouth. "Bollocks," he mumbled. "She'll moan about that, as well."

The farther we wandered from the house, the more uneasy I felt. Fairey's efforts to ingratiate himself carried the distinct aroma of cheese—the kind one might apply to the sharp end of a mousetrap. I glanced back at Constable Keith; he was exactly where Fairey had left him, playing with his mobile, tea sitting ignored on the roof of the car. "So, come on," I said, "stop talking mindless, offensive shit and tell me why you're really here."

He finally lost the battle with his fixed false smile, and squinted up into the sun to disguise its rapid disintegration. "Ali Green's not stupid," he said.

"What do you mean?" I spluttered weakly.

"What I mean is, Mark Boon's lab results came back."

Whatever it was I was convinced I'd forgotten, it was about to bite me in the balls. My tender head churned over a thousand get-out clauses, but the only one to leap from my mouth was "Who?"

"Don't give me that crap. You know who I'm talking about, so let's not dance around it. There's no point in us insulting each other's intelligence." I wasn't convinced that I *could* insult his intelligence, but I let it pass. "She's ready to announce that they found Erica Shaw's DNA all over his flat. Sarah Abbott's, too. And Erica's fingerprints on the knife that cut him, which they seemingly can't quite establish didn't happen after he was dead, whatever that implies."

We'd strayed onto the rough ground out beyond the lawn and, given my agreement that dancing was an inappropriate diversion, I casually steered us toward the barn. Should the conversation take any more ominous a turn, a moment of shared privacy might prove invaluable. "What's this got to do with me?" I asked, in a pleasingly steady voice.

He flicked the last inch of tea from his mug; clearly a boy raised on strainers and leaves. "She's going to announce it tomorrow," he said, "but first she's coming out here to ask you what size boots you wear."

"I'll be happy to see her," I assured him, certain that bootprints were the least of my worries. "As we've discussed before, insinuations are one thing, but evidence is quite another."

"You're right." He nodded. "And she's got none."

"I know." I hoped. "And she doesn't know you're here, either, does she?"

"Of course she bloody doesn't."

"So why are you?"

Fairey took to a gentle, hand-in-pocket stroll, leading me out past the barn toward the edge of the woods. "Green's a thorn in my side as much as she is yours," he said. "She's had the knives out since the minute she set eyes on me, and she'll happily drag me through the mud if it means getting promoted over my head, the spiteful little cow. I don't know anyone who'd shed a tear if she fell off the edge of the Earth. Certainly not me. But hey, if your story holds up, then Boon's in the frame for everything she's suspected you of since the moment she met you. He's a convicted rapist and lady-batterer, so in everyone's mind he fits the profile. There's evidence that Erica's been in his flat at least once since she went missing, which more or less torpedoes any theory about you having abducted her, and if that's the case, then since she and Sarah disappeared together, you can't very well have taken her, either, can you? And I still can't prove you buried Kerry Fallow in a quarry, so I guess you could conceivably get away with that one, too."

"Farrow," I muttered.

"Yeah." He nodded. "You were right, of course. It wasn't her body we found."

"I didn't speculate on that." Nice try.

"No, fair play to you. You've done a pretty good job of covering your tracks." He smiled. "There's actually hardly any evidence at all that you could be the most prolific predator of women these three counties have ever seen."

Something in my throat began to twitch. I fought the urge to bury my mug in Fairey's skull as he stooped to collect something from the unkempt grass. "I'm almost disappointed," I said, my voice strained and wavering. "My life could have been so interesting."

He straightened up to examine his find—what looked like a small animal bone. "Oh, it will be." He nodded. He shot me a wry smile, one that reached his eyes this time. He considered me at length, rolling the bone idly between his fingers. "Listen…" He bent to fumble on the ground, came up with a second, larger bone. He hung his mug from his little finger, all the better to turn the two pieces over and around in his hands in a childlike effort to connect them. "I want to apologize for what happened between us the last time I was here. You know how to push my buttons, don't you, but that's no excuse for what I did, so...you know, thanks for not taking it any further."

"*That's* what I've been forgetting to do." I sighed.

"No, I appreciate it." He held up the two bones, which he'd finally managed to arrange into something resembling a joint. "What do you think this was?"

"Rabbit," I said, declining close inspection. "We get a lot of weasels here."

He nodded thoughtfully for a moment, admiring his reconstructive handiwork. "More likely stoats," he muttered. Finally, he issued a heavy sigh and cast the remnants back into the grass. "I'd like to bury the hatchet," he said, a familiar darkness about his face. "What I mean is, I'd like to keep our relationship light and breezy, because God knows we're going to be spending a lot more time together from now on."

Fist tightening around mug. "Let me guess. Caravan holiday?"

"Shut up and listen," he said. "Listen carefully. I know you know where Erica is, and I know you broke Boon's neck, and frankly he was a vile piece of shit, and I don't give any more fucks about him dead than I did alive, and he's Ali Green's problem anyway, and she can go suck a duck. But what I *do* care about is Kerry Farrow, because Kerry Farrow is still very much *my* problem, and it's a problem I'm going to solve if it's the last fucking thing I do. And I *know* you fucking did it, you son of a bitch, and God knows how many more, and I can't even begin to tell you how infinitesimally small the slip-up's going to be that's going to put you away for the rest of your fucking natural life, but believe me, when you make it, I'm going to be right here, just like this, as close as I am to you right now, because from here on in I'm going to be on you like the honey on your fucking face. I'm going to be the last thing you see when you close your eyes at night, and the first thing you see when you open them in the morning, and I'm going to ride your arse like a hen-night stripper until you're either in Belmarsh or you're dead from old age and misery. You get me?"

I told him I thought I'd caught the gist.

"I know you don't think very much of me," he said, perceptively, "but that's fine. I want you to underestimate me. You think you're going to get away with it forever, but trust me, any day now, you're going to run smack-bang out of luck."

"Thanks for popping by," I said.

He stared at me as though anticipating a punchline. Not getting one, he snorted through his nose and said, "I'm not fucking around here. You're on borrowed time."

"Likewise."

He nodded. Turned his smile to the ground. Took a deep breath and hummed the aggression out of his voice. "Good luck tomorrow," he said, slipping the mug from his finger and offering me his hand. "I'll see you on the other side."

I took the handshake, tolerated his effort to break my fingers. "I'm glad you're leaving," I replied. "I thought I was going to have to bury you alive."

He laughed, an almost covenly cackle. "Maybe I'll stick around, then," he said. "I'd love to see you try that."

"We'll save it for another time." I smiled. "Ride our luck a few days longer."

"Well, you know, I don't need luck, because the law's on my side."

"Maybe so," I conceded. "But the law's not here, is it? It's just you and me and the rabbits, and they don't like you, either, so if I'm the monster you say I am, then you'll need all the luck you can get just to make it back to your car. Won't you?"

I only hoped my face looked as unconcerned as his. "Nah." He shrugged. "Not your style. I'm wearing trousers."

Ouch. "I'm glad we had this talk," I concluded. "You're barking up completely the wrong tree, but I do admire your tenacity, so I wish you all the very best."

For one of us, however, the luck was to run out far sooner than expected, for as we turned to head back to the house, the source of my nagging discomfort became abundantly and unfortunately clear.

I'd forgotten to bury Samantha.

CHAPTER
TWENTY-NINE

Protestations of innocence, by their very nature, rely for their success on an element of reasonable doubt. In its absence, the customary citation of mitigating circumstances—I was drunk; I didn't see the sign; she told me she was eighteen—rarely acquits the red-handed perpetrator of even the most minor infraction. Inevitably, therefore, there comes a time in every man's life when, like it or not, he has little option but to address his own culpability.

Sammy had lost all of her sparkle. I'd stashed her in the barn eight nights ago, with the intention of returning to the grim task of her disposal once blinkered and numb from drink. Neither weather nor wildlife had been kind to her; the foxes, who had seemingly conspired en masse to drag her off to the woods, had given up halfway and simply stripped her from the toes up, to the extent that the long bones of her legs lay amid a mulchy black stain on the grass several feet from the rest of her. Thanks to the crows, her hair was patchy and matted, eyes absent from their sockets. Her blackened skin had shifted and torn as the tissue began to slide from her bones; it hung ragged over a crooked pelvis, trailing slippery, putrid flesh.

A haze of flies swirled around her, mingling with the army of beetles crawling inside to feast and spawn; the grass around her writhed with a million glistening maggots. Sammy neither looked nor smelled her best.

Fairey turned to me with an expression of wounded disbelief; teeth clenched, nostrils flared and whistling, eyes narrowed in hesitant accusation. He slowly and silently shook his head, clearly at a loss for adequate words.

It takes a strong and wise man to admit to his mistakes, to confess his sins and accept that the game is up. Face the music with dignity and humility. Stand tall and take the heat. "It's not what it looks like," I said.

He opened his mouth to speak then, but the only sound was a faint gurgle as, without warning, he unleashed a stream of thick orange vomit onto his shoes. His eyes bulged, and his chest heaved, and he doubled over, flattening the grass with the remains of his breakfast. He staggered back, a rope of glutinous bile swinging back and forth from his lip as he fumbled for his mobile phone.

For the sake of convenience, I let him hook it from his pocket before stepping in and planting my elbow in the hinge of his jaw. He toppled with a groan but clung tight to the mobile as he went down; I stepped on his throat and twisted his fingers but he was determined not to let go.

"Get off me," he croaked, squirming around underfoot.

"Give me the phone, then," I said.

"Fuck off, get off me."

"Give me the phone, and I will."

He gritted his teeth and thrashed his legs and squeezed his clammy fist shut, clawing at my leg with his free hand. "You're not fucking having it," he snarled.

Without the necessary balance to effectively crush his windpipe, I lifted my foot and shook it free of his grasping fingers before bringing it down hard in the center of his face. His nose cracked like a walnut and his upper lip split open, filling his mouth with blood. When he didn't let go of the phone, I did it again, snapping his front teeth off at the gum. He struggled and gagged, but still refused to loosen his grip. The third kick popped his cheekbone and the fourth shattered his jaw, at which point the phone finally jumped right out of his hand.

His disjointed face coated entirely in blood, he coughed a mouthful onto the grass along with his teeth and a chunk of lip. "Huck," he rasped through a tight-eyed grimace. "I'll huckin ha ya, ya hunt."

A swift kick to the temple shut him up.

———

Mindful of the need to contain the situation in some way I hadn't yet thought of, and sick to my stomach at having been caught unarmed, I slipped from behind the barn and headed for the drive, settling for a busy stride over an attention-grabbing sprint. Constable Keith was still waiting obediently by the car, prodding away at his touch screen. If Fairey stayed down, my unhurried pace and man-on-an-errand expression should give him no cause for concern.

His first glance was fleeting and casual, and I met it with

a weary, tight-lipped smile. His second, however, stopped my heart. It followed the first by a fraction of a second, riding on a violent snap of the constable's head, and carried that look of confused horror that was rapidly coming to symbolize my morning.

And then there was Erica, not so much hiding as staring out the kitchen window, hand raised to her brow to block out the sun. I was sure I didn't want to see what they were staring at, but I glanced behind me as I walked; sure enough, Fairey was up on his knees, clinging to the corner of the barn with one arm and weakly waving the other above his bloody, misshapen head. He quickly lost his balance, falling face-first into the weeds.

This was not the ideal scenario. Keith and I both knew I'd never make the hundred-yard dash faster than he could dial a phone number, but I was damned if I wasn't going to try. I broke into a run as he jabbed feebly at the screen, trying to back out of whatever application he was stuck in. Annoyingly, he didn't drop it. He didn't bend down to pick it up and crack his head on the car. He simply fumbled and swiped aimlessly for a split second before dragging his eyes away from me long enough to find his fingers.

Fortunately, that was the moment at which Erica caught up. Even at a gallop from sixty yards away, I could see the situation dawn across her face as she looked from the constable to me and back to the constable. Her jaw dropped, and her eyes bulged, and she mouthed the word *shit* as she scrambled for the door. And then, as she burst headlong from the house, she answered very concisely the question still forming in my mind—the one about where she'd hidden the gun.

"Stop!" she screamed, lifting her shirt and pulling the .38 from the back of her jeans. The detective spun around in horror as she strode toward him, cocking the pistol and leveling it directly at his face.

"Jesus!" he yelped, pressing his back to the car and throwing his hands up in front of him as though preparing to deflect her bullets. "Don't shoot! Think about it!"

I was at her side then, catching my breath and holding my hand out for the gun. "Erica…"

She tightened her grip, shot me a furious glare. "What the fuck's going on?" she snapped.

"Slight problem." I looked behind me to where Fairey was flailing about in the grass, presumably with no better idea than I had of where he was trying to crawl to. "Left a bit of, um…"

"We can resolve this," Keith stuttered. "Whatever's gone on—"

"Shut up." Erica's aim was rock-steady, her voice unwavering. "What do we do?" she said.

"*We* don't do anything." My hand renewed its request for the revolver. "*You* give me the gun and fetch me the keys to the van, and then you go back inside and stay there while I sort this mess out."

She thought for a moment, chewed her lip through a long, hard look at the constable. "Fine," she said. She relaxed her aim and handed me the gun, then went to the door and reached around for the hook on the inside wall. "I'll go and be the good little housewife, shall I? Clear the table, do the dishes, pull the garden fork out of the floor…" She tossed me my full set of keys—something else she clearly hadn't seen fit to hide.

"Whatever you're inclined to do," I said.

"Call me if you need any help."

"Naturally."

She gave Keith a respectful nod before turning her back and retreating into the house, closing the door behind her.

I was relieved by her compliance. As tough as she thought she was, and as much as I hadn't quite come up with a plan yet, I didn't want her to see what happened next.

———————

Due to my lingering headache and general nausea, it took me a full two hours to clean up. It took six bin bags, some imaginative folding and more than a little soil-turning, but by eleven o'clock I was loaded and ready to go.

I went straight to the bathroom to peel off my blood-soaked clothes and scrub my hands and face. In the bedroom, I discovered a wardrobe filled with skirts and dresses, lace-trimmed tops and bootleg jeans. She'd moved me into the spare room.

I found Erica downstairs, curled up on the sofa in front of a home makeover show. She tucked in her feet to make extra room, and I sat down beside her with a weary sigh.

"You can put my bedroom back how you found it, for a start," I said.

She tensed just a twitch; I sensed her pulse quicken and her breathing stiffen, but she had it under control in a moment and a deep breath and her chin tilted high with a roll of her neck. "Understood," she agreed. "Are you all done?"

I nodded. "Everything I can do here."

"I managed to get the fork out."

"Yes, thank you, I found it."

"The kitchen's spotless, apart from the floor. You've ruined two of the boards."

"Sorry," I said, although I wasn't sure why. It was my floor. "I've got some spare ones."

"If you tell me where they are, I'll have a crack at it."

"They need cutting. I'll do it tomorrow."

She raised an eyebrow and smirked to herself. "Well, you're the man," she muttered.

"I didn't mean it like that. And thank you for cleaning the kitchen."

"I vacuumed and dusted in here, too."

"I noticed," I lied. "Thank you."

"You're welcome."

We watched the rest of the program in silence; Erica with an expression of fascination and wonderment, me with a road map of the county swirling around in my head.

"I think we should do that in here," she mused as the credits rolled.

"Do what? I wasn't listening."

"Shutters," she said. "Over the windows, instead of curtains. Cup of tea?"

"Excellent idea," I agreed.

"What, the tea or the shut—"

"I'll make it while you go and put on something summery."

"Summery?"

"Light and airy."

Brow furrowed, eyes narrow. "Okay, obvious question, but why do I need to put on something summery to drink tea?"

"Because," I said, "when we've drunk it, we're going for a drive in the country."

CHAPTER
THIRTY

Not for the first time, I was in a heap of trouble.

The plan had at the time appeared foolproof, albeit tinged with paranoia. In an effort to distance myself from the fate of Detectives Fairey and Burke and their dirty blue Ford, I'd chosen to contain their disposal to a remote and privately owned location under the jurisdiction of my neighboring constabulary. If they burned well enough, if the local landowner took his time discovering the wreck and dragging it somewhere it might become a public nuisance, and, crucially, if my belief was correct that Fairey's visit was strictly off the record, it could be weeks before CID knew what had hit them. Job done.

I'd performed reasonably well up to this point; I'd accomplished the straightforward task of disabling the detectives' phones, and consequently triggering their last traceable signal, at a picnic stop fifteen miles in the opposite direction, close to the regional police headquarters, and I'd made the onward journey entirely without incident. I had one simple thing to do before I could go home and forget all about this ridiculous mess.

Thing was, though, I didn't want to do it. I didn't even want to look. I'd lifted the Ford's trunk a mere hand's width and been overcome by waves of nausea and panic; the former had failed to manifest, thank God, but the latter had rendered me a statue. And now, my mind was swamped with an irrational desire to undo what I'd already done; to drag my hindsight back in time and just talk to Fairey on the damn doorstep.

Erica, on the other hand, was a picture of tranquility. She stood beside the open door of the van, arms folded, drumming her fingers to a Rolling Stones cover on the radio and gazing vacantly into the dirt at her feet. She'd played her own part with the utmost efficiency; driven to the BP station on the bypass and filled up both the Transit and a small collection of jerry cans before following me out here to the arse-end of nowhere. She'd stuck to the B-roads, avoiding prying eyes and speed traps. She hadn't passed the same house twice or stopped to ask for directions, and she'd arrived mere moments after I had, despite what had to have been a lengthy pit stop. Her navigation and timekeeping, then, were exemplary. And therein lay the problem.

I'd been counting on a window of at least ten minutes to gather my thoughts, tidy one or two loose ends and mask the omission of a minor detail from her earlier briefing. And now, with the plan in tatters, it was surely only a matter of time before she noticed my inactivity and, in all probability, posed the two questions I was least prepared to answer: "Why are you staring at me?" and "How long does it take to set fire to a car?" She'd already brained me once over a minor lapse in concentration; thank God she was on the far side of the car and couldn't see what I was doing, because if she found out what was going on in my head right now, there was no telling what she might do.

Sure enough, as I stood there gawping at her, she straightened and shook her head clear, glanced over her shoulder toward the road before looking at me quizzically and mouthing the words *hurry up*.

She'd given me no choice. I gave the trunk a tug and let it swish up over my head to shed light on the root of my anxiety. Two at least semirespected officers of the law, bloody and bruised, folded double, bound and gagged with twine and rags but still, regrettably, very much alive.

———————

My rationalization had had something to do with the intricacies of forensic pathology as applied to a worst-case exhumation scenario; saw marks, spatter patterns, soil samples—I couldn't remember exactly, but I was confident that it made sense at the time.

Of course, it was also an out-and-out lie. My predicament had nothing to do with science; it was being driven by a twenty-year-old waitress with Elizabethan curls and a sailor's mouth. Whether out of concern for her peace of mind or, more selfishly perhaps, to avoid arousing her abhorrence, I'd striven to shield her from the ugly truth. She was under no illusions, I knew that, but the sound of gunshots and a bandsaw paints all too colorful a picture, and while there were still blanks for her mind to fill, she held the reins to her own distress. As such, I'd been happy to let her file those two quiet hours in the drawer marked *Left Unsaid*. I'd told her we were coming here to destroy the car, nothing more, and I'd considered it a harmless half-truth. Unfortunately, it had the bite of a fully grown lie.

I steeled myself. There was no other option, so I closed my mind to the muffled cries and writhing limbs and bulging eyes. I studied the bare underside of the parcel shelf, the heating elements in the glass, the shifting contours of my hand as I emptied two cans of petrol into the trunk. I implored myself to do the right thing, to at least knock these poor bastards unconscious, but I could feel Erica's eyes on me, a mere sideways step from an awkward revelation, and the best I could do as I slammed down the hatch was an unconvincing muttered apology.

I emptied the remaining fuel over the seats and in the footwells, and set the empty cans in the back of the van. I took the box of matches from Erica's outstretched hand and lined one up, ready to strike. "Stay back," I told her, struggling against a sudden cold sweat to keep my voice from cracking. And then things just got worse.

The match refused to ignite, each swipe at the box whittling down the head until all that remained was a grubby bent stick. I tossed it aside and slid out another, which snapped in half at the fifth strike. Somebody was trying to tell me something.

I took a deep breath and steadied my fingers, and the third match lit up first time. I glanced at Erica to ensure she was out of harm's way; looked back down to see the flame peter out in the breeze.

My head was pounding now, teeth clenched, hands trembling and slippery with sweat. My rising blood pressure made my fingers rigid and useless. I fumbled angrily with the matchbox until it escaped my grasp, spilling its contents onto the ground. It was all I could do not to scream.

I don't know why I let Erica pick it up. Something in her voice maybe, as she giggled and said, "Come here" or the familiar way she braced her hand against the small of my back as she swooped down to gather the matches. Whatever it was, it pulled the plug. The panic drained instantly, emptied my head and steadied my nerves and allowed me to watch her with pin-sharp clarity as she set light to the corner of the box.

"I can tell you never went to Brownies." She laughed, and with that she was away from me, scurrying toward the car.

"Erica—"

"Duck!" she yelled, amply drowning out my weak objection as the matchbox sailed out of her hand. She turned on her toes, sprinted back toward where I stood in all my slack-jawed ineffectuality beside the van, and as the first pillar of flame leaped from the Ford, she barreled into me, threw her arms around my neck and hauled herself onto my back, pressed her cheek against mine and whooped with childlike joy.

The fire took immediate hold. Ravenous, angry flames filled the car, exploding from the floor and the seats to curl across the ceiling, deforming and devouring, noisily sucking in air through the open window and exhaling a column of acrid smoke. Within seconds, its rasping breath became a furious roar, the flames whipped to a frenzy by falling globs of molten foam. Blackened glass buckled and shattered, a thousand vivid tongues lapping at the edges of the roof; paint blistered and consumed, plastic trim returned to oil. And finally, as a thin trail of smoke began to seep out below the tailgate, I decided enough was enough.

"We have to go," I muttered, shaking Erica from my back and turning her away from the blaze.

"But it's so cool," she protested, craning her neck for one last look.

I opened the driver's door for her, guided her to the step. "We haven't got time," I said. "You can drive. You know the way."

She affected a cartoonish pout as she climbed into the cab. "You ruin all my fun," she whimpered, and slammed the door behind her.

Despite the playful grin creeping across her face, I got the distinct and chilling impression that she wasn't joking.

○   ○   ○

The light on the answering machine was flashing. According to the display, I had two messages. I knew who they were from, and I was longing to hear her voice, but right now I was in no fit state to take it in, even without Erica standing over my shoulder.

"Aren't you going to listen to those? They might be important," she suggested as she filled the kettle.

"You know I'm not," I replied. My head was pounding again. "Jesus, I think I need a doctor."

She delved into the drawer below the toaster and pulled out a box of Nurofen; popped two into her palm and poured me a glass of water. "Open wide," she said. She slipped the pills into my mouth and then, after a moment's hesitation, gently trailed her fingertips down the side of my face. "I'm sorry I hurt you," she whispered.

I rode the wave of goose bumps, stunned and melted in equal measure and in neither case able to improve on a nod.

"We should start packing," she decided, sounding nothing like the idea had just occurred to her.

"For what?" although I already knew.

"They're going to come looking for the two policemen you just set fire to," she explained, slowly, each syllable clipped and clear as though she were reading *See Spot Run* to a toddler. "We can't very well stay here, can we?"

She was probably right. I don't know; it was all just noise in my head.

"I'm going to run a bath," she said. "I'm dirty and smoky. Swallow those, bring me a cup of tea and I'll do you something special for dinner. Deal?"

Try as I might, I couldn't say no.

———

The kettle boiled and cooled twice as I stood over it, my attention the subject of an intense battle between the flashing message light and the spider hanging outside the window.

I was stirred by a distant cry, a loaded enquiry as to whether I was still alive. Third time lucky, I poured the tea and carried it carefully to the top of the stairs where, despite my stealth, my presence was clearly felt.

Her voice floated on a trail of humidity from behind the

bathroom door. "I'm in here," she sang to an accompaniment of rippling water.

Uneasy, I nudged the door open with my toe, taking a step back to avoid anything that may have been aimed at my head. All that rose to greet me, though, was steam.

Erica was up to her neck in a sea of bubbles, eyes closed, resting her head with a contented smile. She didn't stir as I set the tea down on the side of the bath.

"I'll leave it there for you," I said, and turned toward the door, resisting a sudden urge to linger.

I'd barely taken a step when, with cat-like precision, she pounced. With one swift swipe, she hooked her fingers into the back of my leg, freezing my breath in my throat. Her arm aside, she hadn't moved a muscle. "Not so fast," she purred. "I need you to scrub my back."

CHAPTER
THIRTY-ONE

I woke at dawn to the sound of buckshot on tin. Rain, as it turned out, hammering the roof of the van where it protruded from the cover of the trees; a thunderous, dissonant roar made musical by the rhythmic drip-drip-drip from the leafy canopy above my head.

The heat of the night had been stifling, the air heavy and still and sticky to the touch. It had sapped in turn my strength and my resolve, so much so that the first stubborn root had put an end to the digging of Sammy's grave. I'd returned to my seat exhausted, my shirt soaked through. I'd told myself that I'd sit it out, wait for the cool air to roll in on the cusp of daylight. In truth, though, I'd simply dreaded going home, preferring just to be alone with my self-loathing.

Now I couldn't even bring myself to pitch Sammy into the undergrowth. I just sat there, trying to ignore the itch of ingrained dirt and dried sweat. Right arm tattooed with blood and soot. Left arm spotless to the elbow, infused with rose oil and chamomile. On the one hand, fiery death; on the other, aromatherapy. That a part of me wanted to laugh made me altogether rather queasy.

I needed a shower, and I needed my bed and so, as the morning light crept warily into the forest, I retreated with my spirit in tatters. I just hoped a good sleep would sort me out.

○ ○ ○

Nothing separates mind from body quite like waking up in a hurry. Your brain, hyperaware and strung out on urgency, races to make sense of time and place as it drags you to your feet. Your feet, however, are still half-asleep and can't quite decipher the garbled, panicked instructions being thrown at them. More often than not, you walk into a wall.

And so it was that I tripped over the pile of laundry beside my bed; yesterday's smoky clothes, this morning's damp bath towel, the heavy duvet thrashed aside to escape the heat.

It was not the hammering at the door that had woken me, but rather my sudden realization that it was actually happening. In my dream, it had been going on for some time; short bouts of increasing volume, punctuated by the distant, muffled sound of Rachel's voice. To my dismay, I'd been locked in a chest and unable to answer.

Now, though, free of such confinement, I rattled from table to wall to door, limbs left to their own devices while my head struggled with the where and when. I hadn't until now fully registered Erica's words to me—*you told her to swing by tomorrow...I'll get rid of her for you*—and I'd failed both to listen to Rachel's messages and to furnish the spare room with a clock. I had no way of knowing how long she'd been standing out in the rain.

It got worse when I finally made it onto the landing. Bedroom and bathroom doors wide-open. Erica's bed empty and neatly made.

I launched myself down the stairs. All momentum and no balance, and with both arms stuck fast in the balled-up sleeves of my dressing gown, I collided painfully with the coat stand in the hall. My efforts to disentangle myself brought it crashing down on top of me, leaving a strong impression of hand-crafted quality on my scrotum. Quite reasonably, I yelped.

That no one came running played tricks with my unease as I scrambled, naked, to my feet. Evidently, Erica and Rachel were not in the kitchen swapping illuminating home truths but, given Erica's statement of intent, the alternative was potentially far worse.

I tugged the robe free and punched out the sleeves; gingerly tied the belt as I limped to the door. And of course, there was no one there.

Nor, however, was there any question that someone had been. As quickly as hope struck me that my dream may have been just that, the truth announced itself quite undeniably in the shape of a Mazda MX-5.

———

The rain came down like a blanket, heavy and smothering, sucking in heat and forcing it into the ground. It pounded the driveway and the roof of the van, crackling and bouncing and flicking up flakes of gravel. I was soaked within seconds as I circled the little roadster, a thousand tiny shards of stone biting painfully at the soles of my feet.

Beacon-red and parked not fifteen feet from the door, the Mazda was conspicuous both in the unquestionable reality of its existence and in its failure to ignite in me the slightest flame of recognition. In itself, it offered no clue to its origin; its trunk was locked, its snug cockpit immaculately clean and bereft of foreign objects. I whirled around frantically, searching for some telltale movement or flash of color. There wasn't a soul in sight.

Clueless and leaden with dread, I stumbled back inside the house.

The kitchen was spotless but for the two splintered floorboards and a neat pile of freshly ironed clothes on the table. The answering machine was still flashing; I stabbed at it with a nervously clumsy finger, hitting everything but the playback button. I counted to ten and tried again.

"Hi, and congratulations! Courtesy of Top Flight Holidays, you've been specially selected—"

Fuck off.

"Hey, you! Just to let you know I'll be over in the morning, about ten. Ha ha. I've got such a surprise for you. It's so cute, you'll love it! I can't wait! Oh, and make sure it's sunny. Um…call me back if you're not there or something. But actually, don't not be there because I'm making a picnic, and I don't think I can eat it all by myself. Bye!"

My stomach flipped. Ten twenty-five; what's that in relation to *about ten*?

"End of messages."

I snatched up the handset, fighting the urge to throw it

across the kitchen. I dialed Rachel's number, waited for what felt like a generation to be connected.

"The number you are calling is not available. Please try ag—"

I sucked in air through clenched, bared teeth. Dialed her home number.

"The person you are calling is not availab—"

"Fuck!" I wrapped both hands around the phone, strangling and shaking and stabbing it down hard against the counter, imploring it against all reason to ring before I broke it into a thousand pieces. When it almost immediately did so, I was startled enough that it jumped from my grasp and skittered across the counter. I chased it, my furious hands succeeding only in batting it farther away until finally it clattered against the side of the fridge. I caught it more by luck than design. I needed to get a hold of myself.

"I'm here," I barked. "Where are you?"

A brief silence on the other end, and then, simply, "Oh." A female voice, shrouded in road roar. "Hi. It's, um… Are you okay?"

"Who is this?"

"I'm sorry. It's Ali Green. Look, if I've caught you at a bad time…"

Oh, Christ. I closed my eyes and forced a deep breath; it shuddered through my body, grating against every knot of tension. "No." I sighed. "Perfect timing. I'm having such a shitty day, you can't ruin it this time."

Her laugh sounded genuine enough. "Well," she said, "That wasn't my intention. I was hoping I might catch you, though."

"You don't say." I shrugged off my wet robe, grabbed the first pair of trousers from the pile.

"I'm on my way over. There are a few things we need to discuss. And," she added, "before you get upset, it's not all about you this time."

I moved to the window, scanned the fields and the tree line beyond. Nothing out there moved. I said, "I don't understand."

"No," she replied, "neither do I, and there's a strong chance the sky might fall down, but I've been over and over this in my head, and it's hugely irritating, but we might actually need each other's help. I'm about twenty minutes away. Okay?"

There was something about the barn. Too still, perhaps, or its shadows too dark. It stared back at me, doors flung open like outstretched arms, beckoning. "Actually, I was just about to go out," I said.

The humor fell out of her voice then. "You'll wait," she said. It was neither a guess nor a request.

She wasn't going to take no for an answer; it went without saying that a prolonged effort to put her off would serve only to raise suspicion and accelerate her arrival. I was already quite sure that this advance warning of hers was designed purely to double-bluff my fight-or-flight response; that she knew I'd be having this conversation with myself, and would expect me to expect that she expected me to run, in which case the thing to do would be to stay put, and so I'd naturally be inclined to do the opposite, but since I knew that she knew that, I'd have no choice but to stay. Whatever, there was no way on Earth I was going to risk her walking into a room with Erica and Rachel, so running was out of the question.

"Oh, yes, of course I will," I assured her, with a poor attempt at a misunderstood chuckle. "I'll be here. I just need to fix a leak out back, that's all, so if I'm not done by the time you get here, you can just make yourself at home, okay?" Did that sound cooperative or was I just making things worse?

"I've got a better idea." I was afraid of that. "How about I stop for a coffee and make it an hour?"

T-shirts. All T-shirts, nothing with sleeves. It's pissing down, for Christ's sake. "Better," I said. I knew she'd be here in ten minutes, drinking her coffee from a foam cup, in her car, at the end of my drive, but that was no problem as long as she stayed there. "Can you tell me what this is all ab…" Garage doors. Wide-open. Oh, sweet Jesus. My heart leaped into my mouth, gagging me. My temples throbbed, and my face burned.

Green hesitated for a moment, cleared her throat. "Are you…alone?" she asked.

Strange question. "Yes," I said.

"And you're sure you're okay?"

"Fine," I croaked, fighting my own churning head for control of my composure. "Sorry, I'm…getting dressed. Strangled myself."

"Right." She sounded unconvinced. "In that case, I'll get off the phone before you do yourself an injury. But to answer your question, we urgently need to discuss Erica Shaw."

And right on cue, Erica strolled out of the woods.

I pulled the drawers out two at a time, scooping out knives and corks and wooden spoons, letters and bills and bottles of aspirin. I clawed through cupboards, tipping over glasses and stacks of plates and littering the floor with dusters and boot polish and Oxy-Action Vanish. I looked in the freezer, the oven and the washing machine, the dryer and the breadbin and the dustbin. Not one of them contained a gun.

I took the stairs three at a time, tore open Erica's wardrobe. It was full of clothes still, but nothing else. I wrenched out her drawers onto the floor; bras and knickers and tights and socks. I threw aside her pillows and sheets and lifted up the mattress. I tipped the whole bed over and found nothing but dust underneath.

I popped the loft hatch and hauled myself up through the hole. Whatever the duplicitous bitch had said she'd hidden up here, there was no sign of it; the roofspace was empty but for the water tank, and the water tank held only water.

Desperate now, I bolted back to the kitchen and tipped out the contents of the knife block; grabbed for a carving knife as Erica flashed past the window. And as the rain grew louder and the hallway echoed with her footsteps, I slipped behind the door and held my breath.

CHAPTER
THIRTY-TWO

Erica met the breakfast table and doubled over, arms flailing, gasping as I ground her face into the oak.

"Where is she?" I snarled, forcing my feet between hers, my hand wound tightly into her dripping hair.

She bucked against me, kicked at my legs, screamed, "What the fuck—"

I jerked her head up and punched it back down onto the table, pressed my body into hers and the knife against her throat. "Tell me what you've done with her," I said, "or I'll take your fucking head off."

"Who?" she screeched, eyes wide, fists clenched, every muscle rigid and trembling. "What the fuck are you talking about? What have I done?"

"Rachel." I tightened my grip on the knife. "What have you done with Rachel?"

"What do you mean? I haven't even met her!"

"Where is she?" I roared.

She flinched; her face flushed and her eyes filled with tears. "I don't know what you mean."

I leaned in close enough to smell the damp forest in her hair; close enough to sink my teeth into her glistening neck. "You've got five seconds," I said. "What were you doing in the woods?"

She uncurled her left hand and pointed to the floor behind her; a small wicker basket lying in the midst of a broad smear of blood and skin. "Picking blackberries," she rasped.

"Blackberries..." I could see them now; hundreds of them, scattered and squashed to every edge and corner of the room. "You were picking blackberries," I muttered, my brain whimpering under the sudden weight of rational thought.

"I was going to make a crumble." I felt her relax beneath me as she sensed my deflation. Her hips slumped, and her arms fell to the table and she blew out a weary sigh. "You're hurting me," she said. "Get off."

I stood unthinkingly. The knife slipped from my fingers without instruction, clattering and dancing in front of her face. Her expression changed in an instant; her eyes darkened, her lips curled into a teasing smile. She stretched across the table with a luxurious moan, arched her back and pointed her toes and pushed herself hard up against me. "Fucking hell," she purred. "You know how to get a girl going, don't you?"

I backed away, incredulous, my sudden ineloquence adding to the swirling confusion in my head.

She rolled onto her back, kicking aside chairs and propping herself up on her elbows. "Forget about Rachel, I'm sure she'll turn up." Her stare sparked with undisguised menace.

"When she does," she said, "we can deal with her together."
She trailed her fingers over the soaked cotton clinging to her
breasts; laughed through pursed lips as she began unfastening
buttons. "In the meantime…"

———————

I hauled her by her arm back out into the rain. She stumbled and skated alongside me, working to pry open my fingers. "You know you'll never get me through the door," she
cackled.

"Oh, yes, I will," I assured her. "I'll break your arms if I
have to."

"Hey!" She punched me hard in the ribs. I tightened my
grip, dug my fingernails hard into her flesh. She just fought
harder.

"Make it easy," I warned her.

"Oh, come on." She laughed. "Asking me to stay in my
room would have been easy."

"If you're locked in, I don't have to trust you."

"Fucking—" She dug her heels in, skidded and spun and
toppled over, forcing me to drag her like a sack. She bucked
and thrashed, clawed at my hand, bit and hissed and spat. "Let
me fucking go," she snarled.

I should have listened. From inside the dark ruins of my
mind, my priorities had appeared simple and mutually detached, but the fog of panic had rendered me shortsighted.
Unable to see beyond the threat posed by an uncontained
Erica, I'd unwittingly relegated finding Rachel to a mere
notion in waiting. Any clear-thinking soul would have spot-

ted the yawning chasm in my logic, but it never entered my head that the border between these two distinct objectives might somehow blur when exposed to daylight. When the inevitable finally happened, therefore, I very nearly jumped out of my skin.

───────────

Rachel stood in the center of the garage beside the open cupboard door, arms folded tightly, thoughtfully tapping her thumbnail against her front teeth. She said nothing, just watched curiously as I dropped Erica flat on her back and gurgled in stunned horror.

I floundered and stuttered, rain pounding my head, wide, unblinking eyes darting between Rachel and Erica and the exposed stairwell. I could think of a number of words, but articulate none.

It was Erica who spoke first, as she pulled herself up by my trouser leg and stumbled to her feet. "Is that her?" she panted.

"Erica," I said, "go to your room."

"Oh, right—" she laughed "—*now* you get a clue."

"I mean it."

"No way," she said, huddling close beside me and slipping her arm around my waist. "I'm not going anywhere. I want to hear you try and talk your way out of this."

I peeled her off me and pushed her away. "Leave us," I snapped.

She came back like a giggling boomerang. "Hey, be nice," she teased. "You don't have to act all macho in front of her. And anyway, you said we were going to talk to her together."

"No," I spat, "I did not." I spun her around and pushed her again, harder this time, enough to send her tripping.

She threw me a poisonous glance over her shoulder, looked Rachel up and down with sneering contempt. "Sort it out," she said. "*I* mean it." And then she was gone, storming across the driveway, back toward the house.

I watched her until she ducked inside and slammed the door behind her. When she was out of sight, I just stared at the door, my relief at being alone with Rachel immediately overpowered by the undivided weight of her scrutiny. When I finally turned to face her, her expression was blank and impenetrable.

"I tried knocking," she said flatly. "I was getting wet. I thought I might find you in here."

"I…" closed my eyes. Covered my face. Rubbed my temples and willed myself to wake up sprawled across my bed, listening to the sound of fists on wood and wondering what the hell the time was. "I was asleep."

"Uh-huh. Rough night, was it?"

"You could say that."

"Want to tell me about it?"

"No." I stepped beneath the shelter of the garage door, swept the rain and sweat from my face. "You don't want to know."

"I don't want to know, or you don't want to tell me?"

That I had a breakdown trying to bury a corpse? "You don't want to know."

Something in her agreed; she simply nodded and said, "Your niece seems charming."

"She's…"

"Not *actually* your niece. No, I guessed that much. Who is she?"

"It's kind of complicated."

She arched her eyebrows and issued a humorless laugh, her gaze falling to the basement stairs. "You don't say," she muttered.

I didn't want to know if she'd been down there, but as hard as I tried to conjure some diversionary question or innocuous remark, my mouth was only willing to form two words: "Did you…?"

She answered with a nod; stood for an age in silent thought while my own brain raced through a thousand explanations, every one of them a hopeless blur. When she finally looked up into my eyes, her expression was one of wounded confusion. "You know," she said softly, "if it's a sex thing, we can talk about it. I can at least try and understand. I mean, it's not like you haven't had to put up with any of *my* weird shit…" She grimaced and bit her lip, snapped her eyes shut and mouthed the word *sorry*; shook her head clear and let out a deep sigh. "I won't share you," she said, "and I won't be lied to."

And there it was; a simple choice. A tailor-made lie, and a challenge not to use it. I could give her the unadulterated truth, watch her run to her car and vanish from my life. I could stand right here and wait for the search team to arrive; sit in shackles in the back of a patrol car while they rifled through the minutiae of my existence. I could watch Erica from the dock as she detailed my misdeeds. Live out the rest of my days in a cramped concrete cell, my only consolation the knowledge that for Rachel at least, the pain would be short-lived. Or I could accept her explanation, make all manner of declarations and promises; send Erica far, far away and wear my badge of deviance with pride. I could talk through my issues and watch in cleverly disguised self-loathing as day by day, month by month, Rachel struggled to adapt, to accept me, to convince me that a collar and leash made her feel anything but defiled. I could slowly but surely peel away her self-respect until all that remained was a broken, blackened heart.

In the end, it wasn't a choice at all. "That's not what it is," I said.

Her flinch told me she'd already explored the implications. She knew as well as I did that the alternative could only be worse.

"It's…" What? What could I possibly say? All I wanted was to fold her into my arms and tell her everything was going to be all right, as though such a prophecy might ever prove self-fulfilling beyond the realms of women's fiction. "I've got problems."

"I know," she said. "We both have, and we can fix them, but you need to help me understand."

"I don't know how."

"By talking to me. By telling me what this is all about. I came here expecting a nice romantic day out, albeit in the pissing rain, but no, I've found you dragging some poor girl around, about to throw her in a…a *dungeon* under your garage. For Christ's sake, do you realize how that looks? I mean, I'm sure there's a perfectly reasonable, sane explanation for it, but you really do need to tell me what it is because from where I'm standing it just looks really, really scary. Just…just please tell me it's not as bad as it looks."

"It's not as bad as…" God help me. We both knew it was. "Sometimes she's harder to control than I can manage."

"So…what?" She shrugged. "It's a discipline thing? She acts up and you throw her in the slammer, is that it?"

A lump rose in my throat and cracked my voice. "You have to understand," I pleaded, "this isn't who I am. Maybe it's a part of who I was, but that person…I don't even know who that person is anymore. It's all in the past. It's history."

"History? What, it was a phase you were going through? I mean, an ex-wife or…or getting caught shoplifting when you were twelve, *that's* history. This is a pretty fundamental problem, don't you think? It's not just something you grow out of. And I'll tell you what, it didn't look like history two minutes ago, either. It looked pretty fucking right-here-right-now."

"You saw her," I said. "You saw what she's like. You heard what she said. She's dangerous."

"Dangerous how?"

"She threatened you, Rachel. She wants you out of my life and the worst thing is, she doesn't even have any claim to me. She was a…an impulse, a stupid spur-of-the-moment mistake, and she's taken over my fucking life. She's obsessed. I didn't invite her here, she just moved in. I'm sleeping in the spare room because she's stolen my bed."

"Fuck—" She threw her arms in the air, stuttered and shook her head, pressed the heels of her hands into her eyes. "I'm sorry," she said, "I must have a really tiny brain or a shocking lack of life experience or something, because this is all going right over my head. Some stalker moves into your house without you noticing, and instead of doing what any sane person would do—you know, throwing her out, calling the police, changing the locks—you let her sleep in your bed and lock her in a cage when she's bad?"

Admittedly, it was a stretch, but for better or worse I stuck with it. "That's about the long and the short of it." I nodded. "I told you I had issues. What more do you want me to say? I'm losing my mind. I'm falling apart. I can't even think straight since I met you. I'm not eating properly. I spend hours just staring at the walls. I wake up and you're in my head. I think about you, and I get tied up in knots. I'm feeling all these things I've never felt before, and I don't understand a single one of them."

She strode toward me then, took me by both hands and tilted her face up close to mine and said, "I know. That's what happens, sweetie. That's what people do. You think I haven't been through all of that? It's every minute of every day, and it's weird and it's scary but you know what? I hold on to every single second of it because God knows it won't last forever and whatever the hell else is going on right now, it's the best thing that's ever happened to me. These things you're feeling…they're not the problem. Whatever's gone wrong, whatever you need help with, we can work through it and put it all behind us, but I need you to tell me the truth."

"No," I snapped. "No, you don't. You need me to tell you what you want to hear, and I'm trying, Rachel, I really am, but you already know the truth, don't you? The truth is I hurt people. It's what I do. It's *all* I do. It's all I've ever done. I'm not…*normal.* Whatever it is you've got in your head that you don't want to admit to yourself because it's too damn grim to think it could ever happen to you, *that's* the truth."

She was silent for a moment, studying in turn my trembling hands and my burning face. Finally, she said, "Are you going to hurt *me*?"

I cracked. My chest shuddered, and my eyes spilled over and the pressure exploded from me in a great heaving sob. "No," I croaked. "Of course not."

Her lip quivered, and her shoulders heaved, and she threw her hand to stifle a gasp as her own eyes filled with tears. "She needs help," she whispered.

"I know."

"She needs getting out of here. Today. Right now."

"I want that."

"Oh, God, what have you done to her?" Her legs were shaking, her breathing sharp and heavy. She backed away from me and almost buckled; stared at me sorrowfully, the sparkle falling from her eyes as the truth fully settled over her.

"I can't do this on my own," I said.

"I know," she replied, although she clearly didn't know, not yet, because she flinched and screwed her eyes shut and steeled her jaw and took a deep, long, shuddering breath and thought so hard I could almost hear it, and my heart didn't beat again until finally she nodded and opened her eyes and said, advisedly this time, "I know. You don't have to. We'll take care of it. She's okay. I'll…help you take care of her and then you can tell me all about it, just tell me everything I need to know, and we can figure out what comes next." And then she reached for my hand and pulled me close to her, folded her arms around me and said, "Everything's going to be all right." And for a few brief seconds, I almost believed it was true.

CHAPTER
THIRTY-THREE

Life, of course, rarely resembles a fairy tale. Popular fiction would have us believe that every cloud has a silver lining, every story a happily-ever-after. Gallant princes on white chargers routinely overcome the powers of evil for the love of enchanting, blue-eyed princesses in distress. Ordinary men beat extraordinary odds to save the world and get the girl, their victory marked by a crescendo of violins and a slick one-liner. And then she tells him he needn't have bothered because he had her at "Hello," and there isn't a dry eye in the house.

Out here in the real world, though, clouds only exist to make rain, and only catastrophe makes the news.

It was the distant echo of an engine that foiled my happy ending, just as Erica put an end to her own.

———

I heard the sound as Rachel calmly closed the stairway door and took me by the hand to lead me from the garage.

It rattled through the trees, barely audible above the roar of the rain on the driveway and the white noise of anxiety in my head. On any other day, my evaluation of its significance would have been immediate and instinctive. Today, though, it bypassed my subconscious and arrived in my frontal lobe as a curiosity, demanding analysis: its distance from the house and direction of travel, the cause and effect of an uninvited guest. A hundred yards along the winding driveway, or a mile and a half away, speeding across the heath? In the forest in a downpour, it's impossible to tell. Indeed, the only question I failed to ask was whether I already knew the answer.

The answer, though, was unimportant, because it was the question that engaged my senses, occupied my conscious thoughts and pulled my gaze back over my shoulder. Such was the extent of my distraction that as the sound grew louder and my efforts to pinpoint it greater, I barely heard Rachel speak. I didn't even notice when she stopped dead in her tracks and tightened her grip on my hand. It wasn't until I blindly passed her by, and she pulled me up short at the end of her reach, and I caught the look of incredulous horror on her face that it occurred to me there might be a problem. By the time I turned around, it was already too late to avoid it.

——————

I knew what was about to happen even before Erica. I'd seen the look on her face too many times, a look that preceded impulsive, unthinking violence. The hateful fury in her eyes was borne out by her purposeful stride, the tension in her wrist, the tight coil of her index finger as she raised my

snubnosed .38 and aimed it at Rachel's chest. I knew without
question that she was going to fire.

"You fucking spineless bastard!" she screamed, squeezing
the trigger as I whirled around and threw myself in front of
Rachel. The gun roared once, twice…a powerful thump and
searing heat in my upper right arm, and then shards of splintering pain as a third shot clipped my shoulder. Rachel drew
herself in, ducked her head behind her arms and huddled,
gasping, close to my chest as Erica's fourth bullet whistled
past my ear.

I screamed, clamping my eyes shut and gritting my teeth
against the pain, throwing my hands behind my head and
waiting for the final, decisive shot. For a split second, I even
wondered whether I'd hear it.

I didn't. What I heard was the tortured clatter and whine
of a stressed turbodiesel and the rasping scrabble of locked-up
tires. I heard Erica squeal as she skated to a stumbling halt.
I heard doors thrown open, the crackle of a two-way radio
and Ali Green's voice shouting, "Erica! Put it down! Put it
down now!"

I held my breath, searched the silence behind me for any
sign of intent. Heard only rain.

"Erica, put the gun down. Put it down and talk to me,
okay? Look…I'm unarmed."

I looked. Twenty yards away, a white Ford Focus, Green
crouched behind the open driver's door, peering through the
glass with her hands to the sky.

I could feel Erica behind me, hear her breathing now as it
grew ragged with panic. And then, a reprieve; the slap of the
gun against soaked denim as she dropped her aim.

"That's it. All the way down, sweetheart. Drop it on the ground and back away."

A metallic clatter as Erica released the gun; a sob and a graunching thud as she fell to her knees.

Green stood, mouthed the word *Quick* as she gestured to me to send Rachel across the driveway. "Good girl, Erica," she shouted. "Just stay where you are."

I gripped Rachel's shoulders and tried to ease her away from me. "Go," I told her. "Run. Get behind the car."

I couldn't move her; she clung to my shirt, her body rigid and trembling. "I don't think I can," she gasped.

"Yes, you can. I'll be right behind you."

She looked up at me, eyes wide with an almost apologetic fear. The rain mingled with the blood splashed across her face, a dozen vivid streams trickling over her pale cheeks and running down her neck, darkening her collar and soaking into the front of her jacket, collecting in a widening pool at her feet where it met the staccato drip from my arm. It flowed over and among the stones, jumped and danced with the raindrops; a thousand dark rivers, their pale extremities straying ever farther until the ground beneath us swam scarlet. And as the puddle grew, so, too, did the notion that this was too much blood, that it was somehow greater than the sum of my wounds.

The pain was intense, but it wasn't overpowering; I could feel the tension in every nerve, every muscle in my body, and I knew I hadn't overlooked some gaping hole or severed artery. And yet this insight offered no relief from the bitter dread churning in the pit of my stomach, because the blood was still flowing, and Rachel's face had turned a ghostly white, and she was shaking her head and saying "I can't" as she clutched at my arms for support. And as hard as I tried to convince myself otherwise, the front of her jacket grew darker by the second, a heavy, glistening stain spreading from a tear in the fabric at the center of her chest.

My pain was instantly forgotten, displaced by this morbid realization. I hooked my arms under hers, struggled for balance as her knees tried to buckle. An urgent "No" was all I could force from my mouth.

She held my stare as her breathing slowed, and her grip on my arms weakened and then, as the strength left her body, her legs folded beneath her, and she slumped between my arms to the crimson driveway, pulling me to my knees as she fell. I made some reflexive move to press my hand over the hole in her jacket but the blood was spreading from beneath her faster than it surged out over my fingers, and I knew I was powerless to stop it.

So, it seemed, did she. She tried to speak, but her efforts, like mine, were in vain; her words gave way to a faint gasp, carried out on a fine mist of blood. Instead, she simply took my hand and, with the slightest trace of a smile, eased it from her chest. In that moment, a single second stretched seemingly to eternity; she had no need for words. I read in the last defiant sparkle of her eyes everything she wanted me to know: sorrow and loss, anticipation and hope, fear, longing and love. And then, as suddenly and as finally as I came to understand all of these things, the light on them flickered out. Rachel's gaze and her fingers slipped from my own, and her body settled to the ground.

I closed my eyes, and my mind fell silent. When I opened

them, the spinning had stopped. There was no spiraling panic, no train of reason careening out of control. In that moment, I was completely alone.

Green broke the silence with a cry of "Shit!" as she bolted from the car. My ears flooded with sound: the crackle of the rain, the pounding of footsteps, a muffled male voice barking instructions into a radio. Distant sirens. The slamming of a car door. And above them all, the breathless whimper of a broken soul.

I craned my neck to see Erica rocking on her haunches, her chest heaving, her face contorted with horror. As I looked into her swollen, red eyes, she shook her head *no* and let out a tortured wail; grabbed handfuls of her hair and pulled her face down to hide behind her knees.

Green was with Rachel in a heartbeat, bumping and elbowing me and muttering "Come on, come on, come on," as she worked to revive her.

"She's gone," I said.

She ignored me, her hands making a sickening squelch as she pumped Rachel's chest. "Keep pressure on that arm," she said. "The ambulance is on its way." She raised her voice. "Erica, honey, listen to me."

Erica glanced up from her lap, her fetal form shuddering uncontrollably. The gun lay on the ground behind her, well within her reach.

"I want you to do me a favor and lie down on your front for me, okay?"

Erica looked at me as if seeking my approval, though she surely knew that while there were still bullets in the gun and breath in my body, I wouldn't allow her to be taken in for a debrief and a plea bargain. And if shock denied her the initiative, I was damn sure I could outpace Green in a twenty-foot lunge, with or without both arms.

As quickly as I plotted my trajectory, though, the matter was out of my hands. The voice from the car had become a shadowy figure at the corner of my eye, darting across the driveway while Erica's eyes were lowered. He skirted the far end of the Transit, silently rolling his footsteps as he approached her from behind. He clutched a telescopic baton in his right hand, his left flung out to the side as though clinging for balance to an invisible rail. His face was bunched in concentration, his clean-shaven chin twitching as he chewed the inside of his lip. A mouse wouldn't have heard him coming.

Erica, though, had no need to hear him; despite her hysteria, she reacted instantly to my shifting stare. She spun around to face him and was on her feet before he could blink, the gun dancing about in her outstretched hand. "Get the fuck back!" she screamed. The detective's eyes bulged, and he skipped backward with a startled howl. "Get on the floor!"

"Oh, God…" Green clambered to her feet and stepped around me, planting a protective hand on the top of my head. "Erica!" she yelled. "Don't be stupid! Put it down!"

"Get on your fucking knees," Erica growled, the revolver inches from the man's face.

"Kevin, do as she says."

He dropped to his knees in front of her, staring wide-eyed into the barrel. "Please don't," he stuttered, dropping his baton.

"Erica, just calm down." Green took a step toward her, body open, palms upturned. "He's not going to hurt you, and you're not going to hurt him. Just point the gun away from him, okay? He won't make a move. Right, Kevin?"

Kevin nodded, his eyes pleading. "Right," he whispered. "You're all right."

"This is the only chance you'll get, Erica. Can you hear those sirens?" They were audibly closer. Monsoon or no, some sounds just don't lie. "There's an armed response coming. Men with guns. Do you understand?"

Almost doubled over, frantically gulping down lungfuls of air, she moved behind Kevin and pressed the revolver against the back of his head. "You're not taking me away," she sobbed.

"They'll shoot you. If you don't drop the gun, they'll shoot you dead." Green was rock-steady as she took a final step toward the weapon. "I mean it," she said. "You need to give it to me now."

Erica shook her head, and the gun with it. Her aim swayed every which way and for a brief moment, I thought she might buckle. She looked in turn at Green, at Kevin and at the revolver in her hand, and her panic began to subside. She relaxed her grip and slowly lowered her arm.

Green reached out to her. "There's a good girl," she said. "Just lay it on the ground and come here to me. Everything's going to be okay."

She almost did it; would have, had she not looked to me first for some kind of validation. She found none; what she got as I raised my left hand was a clear instruction. I folded my fingers to the shape of a pistol, pressed the barrel to my temple and with one shot erased the doubt from her mind.

I was a fool to expect her to obey. That she'd burned her bridges would be unquestionable even to the most ruined mind, but the survival instinct is engineered to withstand the power of suggestion. "I'm sorry," she cried, drawing back the gun and whipping it down hard on the top of Kevin's head, and as he crumpled to the ground with his hands clamped over his gushing scalp, she leveled it at Green's face and screamed, "You're not putting me back in a cage!"

With nowhere to go, Green simply turned away her head and closed her eyes, and I did the same as Erica squeezed the trigger.

CHAPTER
THIRTY-FOUR

It should have been an easy reprieve; a five-minute window of opportunity before the cavalry arrived. Five minutes to satisfy my lust for Erica's blood and ensure that only the uninformed and the unsuspecting knew my name. Four fallen. One survivor. A deranged murderess, slain by her own hand. A clean slate for the price of a hole in my arm and a couple of dead coppers. Convenient? Without a doubt.

The mind, though, is a curious thing. A simple "No" was all it said; the whispered answer to a question I didn't hear myself ask.

Ali Green had looked me in the eye and had cared whether I lived or died. She'd been prepared to step unquestioningly between me and a loaded gun. And I was willing to sacrifice her for the sake of my own convenience? Like hell I was.

My throw was scattershot, the handful of blood-soaked gravel exploding in the air and most of it missing Erica's face, but it was enough to make her recoil. She clenched her fist and the hammer fell, the shot answered not by a fountain of blood and brain and skull but by the sharp crack of splintered garage roof tiles.

Green reacted instantly, snatching for the revolver with her left hand and driving the heel of her right into Erica's nose, knocking her clean off her feet. She followed her down, kneeling hard on her chest and pinning her to the drive by her throat. "Let it go!" she barked, screwing her thumb into the base of Erica's wrist and then squealing in pain as, in return, Erica sunk her five free talons into the detective's face. Green released her stranglehold to pull the claws from her flesh, and then she was in trouble; with all of her weight on one hand, it only took a buck of Erica's hips to throw her off balance.

Erica pitched her assailant sideways, kicking her leg up against Green's head and slamming her to the ground. "Get off me," she screeched, her wrist still held firm, the gun pointing aimlessly up at the sky as Green rolled onto her back and doubled her grip, elbows locked, fists clenched, knuckles white.

I found my feet, staggered upright as Erica raised herself to her knees and drilled her fingers into Green's armpit, throwing her weight against her arms, growling dementedly as they began to tremble and bend. "Let me fucking go," she cried.

I was behind her then. Her breath caught in her throat as I curled around her, enveloping her body. I felt her skin draw tight as I pressed my cheek to hers, hot and slick and smooth but for the faint trace of Kerry's scar. "No more," I said, and I pulled with the last of my strength.

Erica sucked in a startled gasp as I dragged her clear of Green. She threw her hand to my face, held it tight against her own as I staggered back against the side of the van. She stumbled free as I released her; watched in shock as my legs gave way and I spiraled to my knees. She shook her head and cried, "No!" and tried in vain to catch me.

"It's over," I rasped, grimacing against the pain. "Forget about her. You've got one shot left. Don't waste it." I could hear Green's protests, feel her horrified stare boring into me as she lay motionless in the gravel, but I was way beyond concern for her approval. I'd made my choice; fate had one last shot at my atonement, its sole bearer the last woman standing.

She looked down at the gun, opened the hand that held it and gazed childlike and bewildered through her tears as though seeing it for the first time. And as righteous as I longed to feel in my vengeance, and as hard as my hands ached to tear a tunnel through her flesh and wrench the stolen life from inside her, my face flushed with shame, and my stomach turned sour at the thought of any more blood shed on my account. This, all of this, was down to me; Erica's finger was on the trigger, but I couldn't pretend I hadn't put the gun in her hand. Deny as I might, I wanted only to see her go free, whatever the consequences to me. I didn't want to watch her die, and she knew it.

I didn't have to tell her to go; she saw it in my eyes, in the sadness with which they flickered toward the door of the van. Her nod of understanding was barely perceptible, but it speared the tension from my body, tipping me back onto my heels. "Sorry." She sniffed, taking a shuddering breath and wiping the tears from her eyes. "I'm going now," she said, turning the gun back to Green. "I won't miss you again. If you try to stop me, I'll shoot you in the face." Then she pulled open the door and tossed in the gun and said, "Just like I did your mate."

My heart stopped. Erica looked down at me, conspiracy drawing her lips into a sad half smile. "Bye," she breathed. And then she was in the van and turning the key and crashing the gearbox and gunning the engine and gone.

"What the fuck did you just do?" Green scrambled to me on her hands and knees, panting, her face scratched and bleeding. "God, your arm…"

I held it out to her; my hand was coated crimson, my fingertips dripping blood at a bothersome rate. "It's all right, I've got another one," I said, but neither of us found it funny.

"Don't try to stand," she said, clambering to her feet and heading for her car.

I wanted to defy her, to get up and run screaming to the woods, to bury myself in the dirt and bleed quietly to death; anything not to face the catastrophe I'd brought about. But there was no chance. The driveway was spinning, and I didn't know which way was backward. I had little of anything left in me.

I sat and watched the van bounce across the field, growing smaller and smaller until it finally melted into the trees. There are no logging trails or farm tracks out there; Erica would soon be on foot, and she was out of shape in every way. She was running blind, the territory alien to her. There'd be dogs here soon, and marksmen; trained hunters and killers, and none of them willing to take a chance with a cornered animal. I closed my eyes and prayed for her to find her way.

"Ambulance is going to be twenty minutes." Green knelt down beside me, rummaging in a medikit she'd retrieved from the car. "Hold still," she said. "Try to relax it for me." She pulled a pinch of shirtsleeve free of my arm and pierced it with a pair of scissors; tilted her head from side to side and rolled her jaw, obviously in some discomfort as she peeled the fabric away from the wound.

"You okay?" I groaned, my voice suddenly weak.

"Yeah. Bit deaf, but I'll live." She wound a length of gauze around my arm, pulled it tight enough that it made me flinch, pinned it in place and tossed the bag in the general direction of Kevin, whom I could hear lazily vomiting behind me. Then, as she regarded her work with a curious mixture of pride and consternation, plucking a stray thread and fussily straightening the edges, she cleared her throat and quietly said, "Thanks to you."

CHAPTER
THIRTY-FIVE

A Volvo full of guns took off across the driveway in a shower of wet shrapnel, thunking onto the field with an animal snarl-hiss-bark.

I knelt, startled, before the empty vessel that had carried Rachel so unerringly from one wretched fate to the next as Green huddled beside me, wide umbrella propped awkwardly between her knees, and took my hand to hold it in her lap. "Come on," she said. "We need to get you inside."

I pulled away; couldn't breathe; didn't know what to do. Was I supposed to kiss Rachel goodbye where she fell, ice-cold in the driving rain? Or save it for the chapel, leaning into a pine box to caress a hard, shiny layer of sealing wax? The question was absurd, inconceivable. Goodbye: the one constant in my life, rendered alien, impossible.

"I can't leave her," I said.

Green crooked the umbrella and took my elbow in a firm grip and simply stood up. She was tiny but strong, enough to lift me off my haunches at least, and her instruction was firm and compelling. "It's not safe out here," she said. "I need to get you inside and get some fluid in you and keep you warm until we get the all-clear. Rachel's fine, she won't be on her own for many minutes." She gave me a hefty tug, a little closer to the hole in my arm this time. "Let's go," she demanded. "Come on."

I glanced around at the Volvo, already offloading its cargo of black-clad gunmen at the edge of the wood. I swallowed the sick in my throat and looked into Rachel's eyes—nothing behind them, no one there—and then finally I resigned myself to quietly accept a comforting hand from an officer of the law, a hand she slid across my back and rested on my shoulder, pulling me gently from the scene of a crime of which I was considered not the perpetrator but a pitiful, helpless victim.

Green steered me away from Rachel and the garage and the groggy-looking Kevin now sheltering inside, one hand clutching a compress to his scalp and the other bravely giving her the thumbs-up. She guided me in through the front door and pointed me toward the sitting room; shook her umbrella out behind her and propped it under the porch. "Go and sit down," she said. "Get that wet shirt off. I'll find you a towel and make some tea."

I did as I was told. I sat on the sofa, shirtless, dazed and all but oblivious to the pain in my arm, but keenly aware of a greater agony deep inside some other part of me, a real, physical pain that buzzed my ears and blurred my eyes whenever I tried to think of anything but the way Rachel looked at me.

I could hear Green in the kitchen, on the phone, voice raised to compete with the boiling kettle, but I didn't care enough to hear what she said, even long after the kettle had boiled and she was shouting over sirens and engines and the sudden, rattling buzz of the helicopter that passed low over the house and bounced the dishes off the draining board.

When she finally returned with tea, though, and slipped my mug into my hand and draped a bath towel across my shoulders and sat down beside me on the sofa and flicked on the TV presumably for a bit of comforting background noise and sympathetically cleared her throat, she fixed me with a look that made damn sure I had her attention. "I'm going to want to know what happened yesterday," she began.

I wasn't ready for this, but I couldn't think of the words to tell her so. My brain was frozen in entirely the wrong moment. "What do you mean?" I whispered.

"You know what I mean. John Fairey was here, and nobody's heard from him since."

I shook my head. "I wasn't here yesterday. I don't know what to tell you."

"Yes, you do," she said. "I'm hoping he's got himself locked in a pub somewhere, but…" She dropped her gaze to my reddening field dressing. She didn't need to finish her sentence.

"I only know what Erica just said," I assured her. "I was with Rach—" The words caught in my throat, the obscenity of Rachel's unanswerable complicity far from lost on me.

I locked my eyes onto Green's, mind spinning pitifully. Was it too late? Had she heard it? Could I delete those last few words—change the names to protect the innocent? And then what? Dare I deploy Annie again? I was sure she'd step up, and certain she'd never ask what I'd done. Like Rachel, she'd seen me for what I was, more or less, and she'd taken a step toward me, not away. Annie far-from-average, my only friend in the world. The only person ever to *give* me their door key.

"Listen," I muttered. My voice sounded thin, defeated. "If Erica was out here, then she could have been up to anything. I don't even lock the door half the time."

Green nodded slowly, considering my blatant and somewhat amateurish signposting.

"Look," I said, "I'm a mess. My head's all over the place. Can we do this later?"

"Sure." She studied my face, scouring my features quite openly for the slightest twitch, the merest glance in any direction she didn't like. "Although hopefully we won't have to. Because like you said, most of my questions can only be answered by Erica. Isn't that right?"

I nodded, but, "You know you'll never take her alive, don't you?"

"Oh, yes," she said. "She's not going back in a cage, is she?" My neck bristled at the words, my tired brain hunting for an answer. "What do you think she meant by that?"

"I dread to think," I said. "Maybe when you find out where she's been all this time…"

"Yeah, about that—" she began, but her phone interrupted. She fished it from her pocket, checked the display and silenced it.

I glanced through the window at the horde of vehicles now spreading across the driveway; the dog van and the gunships, the patrol cars and the big green Ford with the whip antenna and the cable-tied wheel trims. A string of fluorescent yellow coats stretched out over the field, scouring the path of Erica's flight to the forest and the river and the road beyond.

I looked to the hunters melting into the tree line, and the helicopter hovering in the murky middle distance; the medics hoisting equipment packs from the back of a Jeep and the uniforms bustling around Rachel's prone body.

Green saw me looking, and whatever she found on my face changed her in an instant. The warmth drained from her, and her eyes turned to steel, and she said, "I'd expect you to want us to find her, under the circumstances. But you don't, do you? You'd rather she shot herself, or we did it for her. That's why you sent her away with a gun with one bullet in it—so she wouldn't be around to contradict whatever yarn you're going to try and spin to convince everyone that none of this is your fault. Which it is, isn't it? Because I know you know where she's been, and whatever else has gone on and whatever crackpot theories anyone might have, I *fucking* warned you that you were playing with fire." Her phone rang again, and she prodded it with a grimace and barked, "Eli, I'll call you back," and threw it on the coffee table and said, "Oh, for Christ's sake," because my head had fallen onto my knees, and my eyes had overflowed and frankly I'd just about given up. She softened again then, or at least put her compassionate face back on. "Come on," she cooed, shuffling closer to me and setting her stroking hand back to work across the towel stuck to my clammy back. "You're right, we'll talk about all of this later. I'm sorry, I can be insensitive sometimes." She smiled thinly and patted my ungrazed shoulder and craned to peer out the window and said, "The ambulance is here. Don't tell them I did that bandage unless they say it's good."

I feebly agreed, and then, as her phone began to vibrate and dance around the table, she sighed and ran out of things to say, and so we just sat and stared at the television while we waited for the paramedics.

There wasn't much on. Just some show about that nice fellow Diaz, standing in a cage with his phone pressed to his ear, waiting for someone to answer.

It was a strange feeling. I'd only ever feared one thing in my life, and for the past few weeks the very real prospect of my game being up had made me a wet-eyed, clumsy disaster. But when I saw the hairs stand up on the back of Green's neck, all of that scurried away. The instrument of my undoing was right there beside me on the sofa, close enough to bite—close enough to put my hands together and just snap her clean in half—but the only thought in my head was *Oh, well, that's that, then.*

She was silent for a long moment, watching her colleague bounce his phone off the rubber floor in frustration. Then, finally, she turned again to look at me, her brow lined with perplexity, lips pursed in hurried calculation.

She opened her mouth, and took a breath to speak.

I closed my eyes.

★ ★ ★ ★ ★

ACKNOWLEDGMENTS

I'd like you to think this book is all my own work, but the truth is, writing is rarely a solitary endeavor. You wouldn't be reading *Normal* if it weren't for:

The patience and understanding of my wife, Tracie, who allowed me the time, space, and peace and quiet I needed to sit and write it.

The dedication and repeated forgiveness of my long-suffering partner-in-crime and both the angel and the devil on my shoulder, Jamie Mason, for more reasons than I can begin to list. It's been a ride, hasn't it?

The Terminator-like tenacity of my agent, Amy Moore-Benson, who absolutely would not stop until she'd found a home for it. You're a wizard, Amy.

The hard work, skill and impeccable taste of my editor, Emily Ohanjanians, who, along with Tara Parsons and the whole amazing team at MIRA Books, believed enough to take a chance on me.

And more years than I'd care to count filled with support,

encouragement and the answers to all those random niggling questions that pop up in the small, dark hours of the morning from Carole Oldroyd and Sara Carlson, who've stuck with me on this journey through thick and thin from the very beginning, and from other terrific folks who've joined in along the way, like Hayley Webster, Beth Duke, Kim Michele Richardson, Claire Bryans, Caroline Mole, Jessica Macdonald and, as I've just been informed by my mother, my mother.

Finally, and most important, thanks to you for taking the time to read this far. If it weren't for you, there would be no books at all.

A CONVERSATION WITH
GRAEME CAMERON

What inspired you to write Normal?

It was a radio interview with an FBI profiler that inspired me to write a novel about a serial killer, but I never really felt I had anything new to say on what's a very well-explored subject. In the end it happened entirely by accident; frustrated with a story I couldn't seem to get my teeth into, I came home from a walk in the forest one day and sat down with a clean sheet and no plan except to blow away some cobwebs by writing something lurid and unprintable for my own amusement. And as is the wont of things, one led to another.

How did it feel to get inside the mind of a killer?

It's an author's job to shine a torch into every dark corner of human nature. We're all made from the same basic components, so I think if, as a writer, you're uncomfortable exploring how those pieces fall within minds that are unlike your own, then you're in the wrong job.

You never name your main character or really describe him in any physical detail. Tell us about your thinking behind that.

I grew up watching films like *Jaws* and *Alien*, in which part of the monster's power was that you couldn't see it. Your imagination filled in the blanks with its own worst-case scenario, which was inevitably far scarier than the hokey rubber puppet they wheeled out in the third act.

With *Normal*, I wanted to invite you, the reader, to similarly fill those blanks with a monster that's exactly that: normal and familiar and individual to you. Everyman. Because that's who this killer is: he's someone you served a coffee this morning, or who sat behind you on the train, or brushed up against you in the supermarket while you were choosing a flavor of ice cream. He wouldn't be able to hide in plain sight like that if I told you what he looked like!

Is there a character in the story that you identify with? Or a favorite character among the varied cast?

All of them! Unfortunately (for my chances of dropping them back there), I didn't find the cast in a dark alley behind the bus station. Each character is a product of my imagination, so naturally they all share a little something of me, be it a simple memory or a catastrophic personality flaw. However, I'd say the one I'd most want to set about drinkin' with is Annie. I like her dry sense of humor, and she has a say-yes, crack-on attitude that I'd love to explore further.

What kind of research, if any, went into writing Normal?

I learned to make a delicious stew. Don't print that.

What was the most challenging part of writing this book? What was the most enjoyable?

Making a serial killer sympathetic enough to keep you reading was both of those things. The most challenging by far for obvious reasons, but also the most enjoyable because (for me at least) the only way really to achieve that is through humor, and by playfully exploring the boundaries of what is acceptable to laugh at.

Normal *is the first full-length novel you've published, but you've been writing for quite some time. How is this book different from anything else you've written?*

I finished it! I've been writing stories since I could hold a pencil, but I'm all beginnings and ends. The patience to craft a middle bloomed late in me.

Actually, *Normal* is technically my second novel. Shortly after leaving school I wrote an action-packed thriller about an ex-cop private detective with a tragic past, an awkward family secret and a long-suffering ex-wife who took him back in the end. It was as good as it sounds and all known copies are buried under concrete in a landfill in New Mexico.

Is the anti-hero a theme that particularly interests you, and does it feature in your other writing?

Yes. I find a wrong'un altogether more relatable.

Can you describe your writing process? Do you tend to outline first or dive right in and figure out the details as you go along?

I gave *Normal* a rough outline once I was well into the story, but writing a novel is a long process and during that time

I'm out in the world living my life and learning new things, having new experiences and new ideas, which inevitably are brought to bear on my writing. At the same time, I'm becoming more intimately familiar with the ways my characters work and think, and inevitably that makes them less inclined to stick to a tight plan I cooked up for them six months ago. So it's a very fluid process; I set out knowing where I want to go, but the route is often plagued with diversions!

Can you tell us anything about what you're working on right now?

I may or may not have given you a clue already.

CAMERON